After the Dance

IAIN CRICHTON SMITH was born in Glasgow in 1928 and raised by his widowed mother on the Isle of Lewis before going to Aberdeen to attend university. As a sensitive and complex poet in both English and Gaelic, he published more than twenty-five books of verse, from *The Long River* in 1955 to *A Country for Old Men*, posthumously published in 2000. In his 1986 collection, *A Life*, the poet looked back over his time in Lewis and Aberdeen, recalling a spell of National Service in the fifties, and then his years as an English teacher, working first in Clydebank and Dumbarton and then at Oban High School, where he taught until his retirement in 1977. Shortly afterwards he married, and lived contentedly with his wife, Donalda, in Taynuilt until his death in 1998.

As well as a number of plays and stories in Gaelic, Iain Crichton Smith published several novels, including *Consider the Lilies* (1968), *In the Middle of the Wood* (1987) and *An Honourable Death* (1992). In total, he produced ten collections of stories, including *The Hermit and Other Stories* (1977) and *Thoughts of Murdo* (1993).

Alan Warner grew up in Connel, near Oban. He is the author of seven novels including *Morvern Callar* (1995), winner of a Somerset Maugham Award, which was later adapted as a feature film; *These Demented Lands* (1997), winner of the Encore Award; *The Sopranos* (1998), winner of the Saltire Society Scottish Book of the Year Award; and more recently *The Stars in the Bright Sky* (2010) which was long-listed for the Man Booker Prize, and *The Deadman's Pedal* (2013).

He lives in Scotland, mostly.

After the Dance

Selected Stories of
Iain Crichton Smith

Edited with an introduction by
ALAN WARNER

Polygon

This edition first published
in paperback in Great Britain in 2017 by
Polygon, an imprint of Birlinn Ltd
West Newington House
10 Newington Road
Edinburgh EH9 1QS
www.polygonbooks.co.uk

ISBN: 978 1 84697 403 8

British Library Cataloguing-in-Publication Data

A catalogue record for this book is available on request
from the British Library

Typeset by Antony Gray
Printed and bound by Clays Ltd, St Ives plc

Contents

Introduction

In the nineteen-eighties, Iain Crichton Smith and I both lived near Oban. One day I saw him approaching me up the town's main street. It was a small town where everyone more or less knew everyone else and since we had met before, I hailed him. If memory serves, over his shoulder, Iain was carrying a black binliner of his washing for the laundrette – not the image we would always associate with the figure of 'famous poet' yet, familiar from his great alter-ego, Murdo, who you will read about in these stories. Iain and I chatted away about what books we were then reading, but we were soon interrupted by an elegantly arranged lady of senior years who looked askance at his binliner but nevertheless said, 'Oh, Mr Crichton Smith. Just who I was so hoping I would run into! We were wondering if you are going to say yes to speaking a few words and maybe reading some of your wee poems at the opening of our tea afternoon and sale of work?'

I found my lurking, teenage presence immediately unwelcome to this good lady, so I made my excuses and despite the slight look of desperation on Iain's face, I abandoned him to the price of fame in Oban.

Some days later I ran into Iain again, 'down the town' or, 'up the street' – depending where you had started out from. I soon asked, 'Well. Are you going to say a few words at yon one's tea evening?'

Iain raised his eyebrows towards his pleasingly bald head, 'Och, I had to say yes to her. She was ever so insistent a personality. A very insistent personality indeed. The kind of person you end up saying goodbye to through your own letter box.'

I remember laughing out aloud at this comment and I still laugh today – over thirty long years later. It's the kind of warmly wry human observation you would expect both from the man himself and from the author of these short stories which show such a wise understanding of people, but also an outsider's amazement, fascination and sometimes horror with us all.

In many ways, I believe Iain was always an outsider – perhaps writers must be? Many of these stories like, 'A Day in the Life of . . . ' and 'The Exiles', feature lonely, isolated individuals at odds with the society and the values around them.

Iain was born in 1928 and he grew up in the shieling of a very small village on the Isle of Lewis. Fatherless, he was raised by his mother in some poverty, along with his two brothers. Gaelic, not English was Iain's first language. Very many of the stories here, like 'The Telegram', 'Mother and Son', 'In the Silence', and 'The Painter', evoke this rural background and his fascination with the taut dynamics of close-knit communities. Many stories, like 'Home', and 'An American Sky', also show an ambiguous attitude towards concepts of hearth and home – or to the illusion of community. 'The Wedding' is an interesting weighing up of cultural difference and change. Yet 'The Long Happy Life of Murdina the Maid' is a gloriously scandalous satire of Gaelic culture and rural small–mindedness which would still outrage devotees of the strict religious creeds on Lewis. Many of the iconoclastic Murdo stories also tease at the shibboleths of the larger Scottish Gaelic world.

In the nineteen-sixties, Iain had become known as a very fine poet, mostly through poems written in his second language, though he also wrote many important ones in Gaelic. In 1968 his first and most famous novel in English, *Consider the Lilies*, had been published. It enjoys – at least in the Highlands – the status of a classic, exploring the cruel historical realities of the Clearances from the point of view of a vulnerable, stubborn but admirable old woman. As a Gael, educated at Aberdeen University during the years of the second world war, Iain was formed between these two changing cultures, neither of which he was ever able to fully embrace; that is of a Gaelic, rural world in a small, religious, traditional community and that of an English-speaking, modern intellectual in a technologising society. While he cared passionately about Gaelic culture and language, he did not sentimentalise that culture. He was never prepared to pretend the islands were some sort of Eden which could be contrasted to the turmoil and horrors of the twentieth century. As a high school English teacher who taught war poetry, we can see in these stories his fascination with the two world wars, which took so many young men from the islands.

I have included several of his hilarious Murdo stories as I believe they are among the finest things he ever wrote. With the creation of Murdo, Iain was able to reconcile in fiction, the serious intellectual side of his character – which loved ideas and modern literature – with his natural and huge sense of humour. This results in a disarming salvo of send-up, scorning any lofty attitudes. Murdo emerges as one of the most unpredictable and certainly one of the most welcome characters in recent Scottish writing. Murdo should have his own Facebook page!

Like all interesting writers, Iain made joy, and wonder and fascination for us out of his own inner turmoil. I hope you enjoy all these stories as much as I did re-reading them.

ALAN WARNER
Edinburgh. July 2013

Murdo Leaves the Bank

'I want to see you in my office,' said Mr Maxwell the bank manager, to Murdo. When Murdo entered, Mr Maxwell, with his hands clasped behind his back, was gazing out at the yachts in the bay. He turned round and said, 'Imphm.'

Then he continued, 'Murdo, you are not happy here. I can see that.

'The fact is, your behaviour has been odd. Leaving aside the question of the mask, and the toy gun, there have been other peculiarities. First of all, as I have often told you, your clothes are not suitable. Your kilt is not the attire most suitable for a bank. There have been complaints from other sources as well. Mrs Carruthers objected to your long tirade on the evils of capitalism and the idle rich. Major Shaw said you delivered to him a lecture on Marxism and what you were pleased to call the dialectic.

'Some of your other activities have been odd as well. Why for instance did you put up a notice saying, THIS IS A BANK WHEREON THE WILD THYME BLOWS? And why, when I entrusted you with buying a watch for Mr Gray's retirement did you buy an alarm clock?

'Why did you say to Mrs Harper that it was time the two of you escaped to South America with, I quote, "the takings": and show her what purported to be two air tickets in the name of Olivera? You told her, and I quote, "I'll be the driver while you bring the money out to me. I have arranged everything, even to the matter of disguises."

'You also said, and I quote, "The mild breezes of the Pacific will smoothe away our sin."

'No wonder Mrs Harper left the bank and joined the staff of Woolworths. Other oddnesses of yours can be catalogued, as

for instance the advertisement you designed saying, THIS IS
THE BANK THAT LIKES TO SAY 'PERHAPS'.

'I have therefore decided, Murdo, that banking is not your
forte, and that we have come to the parting of the ways: and
this I may say has been confirmed by Head Office. I understand, however, that you are writing a book, and that you have
always intended to be an author. We cannot, however, have
such odd behaviour in an institution such as this. Imphm.

'Also, you phoned Mrs Carruthers to tell her that her invest-
ments were in imminent danger because of a war in Ecuador
but that you were quite willing to fly out for a fortnight to act
as her agent. When she asked you who you were, you said,
"Mr Maxwell, and his ilk."

'You also suggested that an eye should be kept on Mr Gray
as, in your opinion, he was going blind, but he was too proud
to tell the bank owing to his sense of loyalty and to his fear
that he might lose his job, as he was supporting three grandchildren. Such a man deserved more than money, you said, he
required respect, even veneration.

'You have in fact been a disruptive influence on this office,
with your various-coloured suits, your balloons, and your
random bursting into song.

'Have you anything to say for yourself?'

'It is true,' said Murdo, after a long pause, 'that I have been
writing a book, which I shall continue after I have suffered
your brutal action of dismissal. It will be about the work of a
clerk in a bank, and how he fought for Blake's grain of sand
against watches and umbrellas. Banks, in my opinion, should
be havens of joy and pulsing realities. That is why I have
introduced fictions, balloons, masks, toy guns, and songs.

'You yourself, if I may say so, have become to my sorrow
little better than an automaton. I do not advert to your sex life,
and to your obsession with yachts, but I do advert to the
gravestone of your countenance, to your strangled "Imphm",
and to your waistcoat. Was this, I ask myself, what you always
wanted to be, when you were playing as a young child at sand
castles? Is this the denouement of your open, childish, innocent

face? Why is there no tragedy in your life, no comedy, no, even melodrama? You have hidden behind a mound of silver, behind a black dog and a Nissan Micra. Regard yourself, are you the result of your own dreams? What would Dostoevsky think of you, or Nietzsche? Are the stars meaningless to you, the common joys and sorrows? You may pretend otherwise, Mr Maxwell, but you have lost the simple clownish heart of the child. Nor indeed does Mrs Maxwell have it as far as my observations go. I leave you with this prophecy. There will come a day when the vault will fail and the banknote subside. The horses of hilarity will leap over the counter and the leopards of dishevelment will change their spots. The waves will pour over the cravat and the bank that I have labelled 'Perhaps' will be swallowed by the indubitable sands of fatuity. What price your dog then, your debits, and your accounts? What price your percentages in the new avalanche of persiflage? In the day when the giant will overturn the House of the Seven Birches what will you do except crumble to the dust? Nor shall there be special offers in those days, and the brochures will be silent. Additions and subtraction will fail, and divisions will not be feeling so good. Computers will collapse, and customers will cast off their chains. Cravats will cease and crevasses will no longer be concealed.'

In a stunned silence, he rose and said, 'That is my last word to you, Mr Maxwell, and may God protect you in his infinite mercy.'

He pulled the door behind him and walked in a dignified manner to the street, in his impeccable red kilt and hat with the red feather in it.

Mr Heine

It was ten o'clock at night and Mr Bingham was talking to the mirror. He said 'Ladies and gentlemen,' and then stopped, clearing his throat, before beginning again, 'Headmaster and colleagues, it is now forty years since I first entered the teaching profession. – Will that do as a start, dear?'

'It will do well as a start, dear,' said his wife Lorna.

'Do you think I should perhaps put in a few jokes,' said her husband anxiously. 'When Mr Currie retired, his speech was well received because he had a number of jokes in it. My speech will be delivered in one of the rooms of the Domestic Science Department where they will have tea and scones prepared. It will be after class hours.'

'A few jokes would be acceptable,' said his wife, 'but I think that the general tone should be serious.'

Mr Bingham squared his shoulders, preparing to address the mirror again, but at that moment the doorbell rang.

'Who can that be at this time of night?' he said irritably.

'I don't know, dear. Shall I answer it?'

'If you would, dear.'

His wife carefully laid down her knitting and went to the door. Mr Bingham heard a murmur of voices and after a while his wife came back into the living-room with a man of perhaps forty-five or so who had a pale rather haunted face, but who seemed eager and enthusiastic and slightly jaunty.

'You won't know me,' he said to Mr Bingham. 'My name is Heine. I am in advertising. I compose little jingles such as the following:

> When your dog is feeling depressed
> Give him Dalton's. It's the best.

I used to be in your class in 1944-5. I heard you were retiring so I came along to offer you my felicitations.'

'Oh?' said Mr Bingham turning away from the mirror regretfully.

'Isn't that nice of Mr Heine?' said his wife.

'Won't you sit down?' she said and Mr Heine sat down, carefully pulling up his trouser legs so that he wouldn't crease them.

'My landlady of course has seen you about the town,' he said to Mr Bingham. 'For a long time she thought you were a farmer. It shows one how frail fame is. I think it is because of your red healthy face. I told her you had been my English teacher for a year. Now I am in advertising. One of my best rhymes is:

> Dalton's Dogfood makes your collie
> Obedient and rather jolly.

You taught me Tennyson and Pope. I remember both rather well.'

'The fact,' said Mr Bingham, 'that I don't remember you says nothing against you personally. Thousands of pupils have passed through my hands. Some of them come to speak to me now and again. Isn't that right, dear?'

'Yes,' said Mrs Bingham, 'that happens quite regularly.'

'Perhaps you could make a cup of coffee, dear,' said Mr Bingham and when his wife rose and went into the kitchen, Mr Heine leaned forward eagerly.

'I remember that you had a son,' he said. 'Where is he now?'

'He is in educational administration,' said Mr Bingham proudly. 'He has done well.'

'When I was in your class,' said Mr Heine, 'I was eleven or twelve years old. There was a group of boys who used to make fun of me. I don't know whether I have told you but I am a Jew. One of the boys was called Colin. He was taller than me, and fair-haired.'

'You are not trying to insinuate that it was my son,' said Mr Bingham angrily. 'His name was Colin but he would never do such a thing. He would never use physical violence against anyone.'

'Well,' said Mr Heine affably. 'It was a long time ago, and in any case

> The past is past and for the present
> It may be equally unpleasant.

Colin was the ringleader, and he had blue eyes. In those days I had a lisp which sometimes returns in moments of nervousness. Ah, there is Mrs Bingham with the coffee. Thank you, madam.'

'Mr Heine says that when he was in school he used to be terrorised by a boy called Colin who was fair-haired,' said Mr Bingham to his wife.

'It is true,' said Mr Heine, 'but as I have said it was a long time ago and best forgotten about. I was small and defenceless and I wore glasses. I think, Mrs Bingham, that you yourself taught in the school in those days.'

'Sugar?' said Mrs Bingham. 'Yes. As it was during the war years and most of the men were away I taught Latin. My husband was deferred.'

'*Amo, amas, amat*,' said Mr Heine. 'I remember I was in your class as well.

'I was not a memorable child,' he added, stirring his coffee reflectively, 'so you probably won't remember me either. But I do remember the strong rhymes of Pope which have greatly influenced me. And so, Mr Bingham, when I heard you were retiring I came along as quickly as my legs would carry me, without tarrying. I am sure that you chose the right profession. I myself have chosen the right profession. You, sir, though you did not know it at the time placed me in that profession.'

Mr Bingham glanced proudly at his wife.

'I remember the particular incident very well,' said Mr Heine. 'You must remember that I was a lonely little boy and not good at games.

> Keeping wicket was not cricket.
> Bat and ball were not for me suitable at all.

And then again I was being set upon by older boys and given a drubbing every morning in the boiler room before classes commenced. The boiler room was very hot. I had a little talent in those days, not much certainly, but a small poetic talent. I wrote verses which in the general course of things I kept secret. Thus it happened one afternoon that I brought them along to show you, Mr Bingham. I don't know whether you will remember the little incident, sir.'

'No,' said Mr Bingham, 'I can't say that I do.'

'I admired you, sir, as a man who was very enthusiastic about poetry, especially Tennyson. That is why I showed you my poems. I remember that afternoon well. It was raining heavily and the room was indeed so gloomy that you asked one of the boys to switch on the lights. You said, "Let's have some light on the subject, Hughes." I can remember Hughes quite clearly, as indeed I can remember your quips and jokes. In any case Hughes switched on the lights and it was a grey day, not in May but in December, an ember of the done sun in the sky. You read one of my poems. As I say, I can't remember it now but it was not in rhyme. "Now I will show you the difference between good poetry and bad poetry," you said, comparing my little effort with Tennyson's work, which was mostly in rhyme. When I left the room I was surrounded by a pack of boys led by blue-eyed fair-haired Colin. The moral of this story is that I went into advertising and therefore into rhyme. It was a revelation to me.

> A revelation straight from God
> That I should rhyme as I was taught.

So you can see, sir, that you are responsible for the career in which I have flourished.'

'I don't believe it, sir,' said Mr Bingham furiously.

'Don't believe what, sir?'

'That that ever happened. I can't remember it.'

'It was Mrs Gross my landlady who saw the relevant passage about you in the paper. I must go immediately, I told her. You thought he was a farmer but I knew differently. That man does not know the influence he has had on his scholars. That is why I came,' he said simply.

'Tell me, sir,' he added, 'is your son married now?'

'Colin?'

'The same, sir.'

'Yes, he's married. Why do you wish to know?'

'For no reason, sir. Ah, I see a photograph on the mantelpiece. In colour. It is a photograph of the bridegroom and the bride.

> How should we not hail the blooming bride
> With her good husband at her side?

What is more calculated to stabilise a man than marriage? Alas I never married myself. I think I never had the confidence for such a beautiful institution. May I ask the name of the fortunate lady?'

'Her name is Norah,' said Mrs Bingham sharply. 'Norah Mason.'

'Well, well,' said Mr Heine enthusiastically. 'Norah, eh? We all remember Norah, don't we? She was a lady of free charm and great beauty. But I must not go on. All those unseemly pranks of childhood which we should consign to the dustbins of the past. Norah Mason, eh?' and he smiled brightly. 'I am so happy that your son has married Norah.'

'Look here,' said Mr Bingham, raising his voice.

'I hope that my felicitations, congratulations, will be in order for them too, I sincerely hope so, sir. Tell me, did your son Colin have a scar on his brow which he received as a result of having been hit on the head by a cricket ball?'

'And what if he had?' said Mr Bingham.

'Merely the sign of recognition, sir, as in the Greek tragedies. My breath in these days came in short pants, sir, and I was near-sighted. I deserved all that I got. And now sir, forgetful of all that, let me say that my real purpose in coming here was to give you a small monetary gift which would come particularly from myself and not from the generality. My salary is a very comfortable one. I thought of something in the region of . . . Oh look at the time. It is nearly half-past eleven at night.

> At eleven o'clock at night
> The shades come out and then they fight.

I was, as I say, thinking of something in the order of . . . '

'Get out, sir,' said Mr Bingham angrily. 'Get out, sir, with your insinuations. I do not wish to hear any more.'

'I beg your pardon,' said Mr Heine in a wounded voice.

'I said "Get out, sir." It is nearly midnight. Get out.'

Mr Heine rose to his feet. 'If that is the way you feel, sir. I only wished to bring my felicitations.'

'We do not want your felicitations,' said Mrs Bingham. 'We have enough of them from others.'

'Then I wish you both goodnight and you particularly, Mr Bingham as you leave the profession you have adorned for so long.'

'Get out, sir,' Mr Bingham shouted, the veins standing out on his forehead.

Mr Heine walked slowly to the door, seemed to wish to stop and say something else, but then changed his mind and the two left in the room heard the door being shut.

'I think we should both go to bed, dear,' said Mr Bingham, panting heavily.

'Of course, dear,' said his wife. She locked the door and said, 'Will you put the lights out or shall I?'

'You may put them out, dear,' said Mr Bingham. When the lights had been switched off they stood for a while in the darkness, listening to the little noises of the night from which Mr Heine had so abruptly and outrageously come.

'I can't remember him. I don't believe he was in the school at all,' said Mrs Bingham decisively.

'You are right, dear,' said Mr Bingham who could make out the outline of his wife in the half-darkness. 'You are quite right, dear.'

'I have a good memory and I should know,' said Mrs Bingham as they lay side by side in the bed. Mr Bingham heard the cry of the owl, throatily soft, and turned over and was soon fast asleep. His wife listened to his snoring, staring sightlessly at the objects and furniture of the bedroom which she had gathered with such persistence and passion over the years.

The Play

When he started teaching first Mark Mason was very enthusiastic, thinking that he could bring to the pupils gifts of the poetry of Wordsworth, Shakespeare and Keats. But it wasn't going to be like that, at least not with Class 3g. 3g was a class of girls who, before the raising of the school-leaving age, were to leave at the end of their fifteenth year. Mark brought them 'relevant' poems and novels including *Timothy Winters* and *Jane Eyre* but quickly discovered that they had a fixed antipathy to the written word. It was not that they were undisciplined – that is to say they were not actively mischievous – but they were thrawn: he felt that there was a solid wall between himself and them and that no matter how hard he sold them *Jane Eyre*, by reading chapters of it aloud, and comparing for instance the food in the school refectory that Jane Eyre had to eat with that which they themselves got in their school canteen, they were not interested. Indeed one day when he was walking down one of the aisles between two rows of desks he asked one of the girls, whose name was Lorna and who was pasty-faced and blond, what was the last book she had read, and she replied,

'Please, sir, I never read any books.'

This answer amazed him for he could not conceive of a world where one never read any books and he was the more determined to introduce them to the activity which had given himself so much pleasure. But the more enthusiastic he became, the more eloquent his words, the more they withdrew into themselves till finally he had to admit that he was completely failing with the class. As he was very conscientious this troubled him, and not even his success with the academic classes compensated for his obvious lack of success with this particular class. He believed in any event that failure with the non-academic classes constituted failure as a teacher. He tried to do creative writing with them first by bringing in reproductions of paintings by Magritte which were intended to awaken in their minds a glimmer of the unexpectedness and strangeness of ordinary things, but they would simply look at them and point out to him their lack of resemblance to reality. He was in despair. His failure began to obsess him so much that he discussed the problem with the Head of Department who happened to be teaching Rasselas to the Sixth Form at the time with what success Mark could not gauge.

'I suggest you make them do the work,' said his Head of Department. 'There comes a point where if you do not impose your personality they will take advantage of you.'

But somehow or another Mark could not impose his personality on them: they had a habit for instance of forcing him to deviate from the text he was studying with them by mentioning something that had appeared in the newspaper.

'Sir,' they would say, 'did you see in the papers that there were two babies born from two wombs in the one woman.' Mark would flush angrily and say, 'I don't see what this has to do with our work,' but before he knew where he was he was in the middle of an animated discussion which was proceeding all around him about the anatomical significance of this piece of news. The fact was that he did not know how to deal with them: if they had been boys he might have threatened them with the last sanction of the belt, or at least frightened them in some way. But girls were different, one couldn't belt girls, and certainly he couldn't frighten this particular lot. They all wanted to be hairdressers: and one wanted to be an engineer having read in a paper that this was now a possible job for girls. He couldn't find it in his heart to tell her that it was highly unlikely that she could do this without Highers. They fantasised a great deal about jobs and chose ones which were well beyond their scope. It seemed to him that his years in Training College hadn't prepared him for this varied apathy and animated gossip. Sometimes one or two of them were absent and when he asked where they were was told that they were baby sitting. He dreaded the periods he had to try and teach them in, for as the year passed and autumn darkened into winter he knew that he had not taught them anything and he could not bear it.

He talked to other teachers about them, and the history man shrugged his shoulders and said that he gave them pictures to look at, for instance one showing women at the munitions during the First World War. It became clear to him that their other teachers had written them off since they would be leaving at the end of the session, anyway, and as long as they were quiet they were allowed to talk and now and again glance at the books with which they had been provided.

But Mark, whose first year this was, felt weighed down by his failure and would not admit to it. There must be something he could do with them, the failure was his fault and not theirs. Like a missionary he had come to them bearing gifts, but they refused them, turning away from them with total lack of interest. Keats, Shakespeare, even the ballads, shrivelled in front of his eyes. It was, curiously enough, Mr Morrison who gave him his most helpful advice. Mr Morrison spent most of his time making sure that his register was immaculate, first writing in the Os in pencil and then rubbing them out and re-writing them in ink. Mark had been told that during the Second World War while Hitler was advancing into France, Africa and Russia he had been insisting that his register was faultlessly kept and the names written in carefully. Morrison understood the importance of this though no one else did.

'What you have to do with them,' said Morrison, looking at Mark through his round glasses which were like the twin barrels of a gun, 'is to find out what they want to do.'

'But,' said Mark in astonishment, 'that would be abdicating responsibility.'

'That's right,' said Morrison equably.

'If that were carried to its conclusion,' said Mark, but before he could finish the sentence Morrison said,

'In teaching nothing ought to be carried to its logical conclusion.'

'I see,' said Mark, who didn't. But at least Morrison had introduced a new idea into his mind which was at the time entirely empty.

'I see,' he said again. But he was not yet ready to go as far as Morrison had implied that he should. The following day however he asked the class for the words of 'Paper Roses', one of the few pop songs that he had ever heard of. For the first time he saw a glimmer of interest in their eyes, for the first time they were actually using pens. In a short while they had given him the words from memory. Then he took out a book of Burns' poems and copied on to the board the verses of 'My Love is Like a Red Red Rose'. He asked them to compare the two poems but found that the wall of apathy had descended again and that it was as impenetrable as before. Not completely daunted, he asked them if they would bring in a record of 'Paper Roses', and himself found one of 'My Love is Like a Red Red Rose', with Kenneth McKellar singing it. He played both songs, one after the other, on his own record player. They were happy listening to 'Paper Roses' but showed no interest in the other song. The discussion he had planned petered out, except that the following day a small girl with black hair and a pale face brought in a huge pile of records which she requested that he play and which he adamantly refused to do. It occurred to him that the girls simply did not have the ability to handle discussion, that in all cases where discussion was initiated it degenerated rapidly into gossip or vituperation or argument, that the concept of reason was alien to them, that in fact the long line of philosophers beginning with Plato was irrelevant to them. For a long time they brought in records now that they knew he had a record player but he refused to play any of them. Hadn't he gone far enough by playing 'Paper Roses'? No, he was damned if he would go the whole hog and surrender completely. And yet, he sensed that somewhere in this area of their interest was what he wanted, that from here he might find the lever which would move their world.

He noticed that their leader was a girl called Tracy, a fairly tall pleasant-looking girl to whom they all seemed to turn for response or rejection. Nor was this girl stupid: nor were any of them stupid. He knew that he must hang on to that, he must not believe that they were stupid. When they did come into the room it was as if they were searching for substance, a food which he could not provide. He began to study Tracy more and more as if she might perhaps give him the solution to his problem, but she did not appear interested enough to do so. Now and again she would hum the words of a song while engaged in combing another girl's hair, an activity which would satisfy them for hours, and indeed some of the girls had said to him, 'Tracy has a good voice, sir. She can sing any pop song you like.' And Tracy had regarded him with the sublime self-confidence of one who indeed could do this. But what use would that be to him? More and more he felt himself, as it were, sliding into their world when what he had wanted was to drag them out of the darkness into his world. That was how he himself had been taught and that was how it should be. And the weeks passed and he had taught them nothing. Their jotters were blank apart from the words of pop songs and certain secret drawings of their own. Yet they were human beings, they were not stupid. That there was no such thing as stupidity was the faith by which he lived. In many ways they were quicker than he was, they found out more swiftly than he did the dates of examinations and holidays. They were quite reconciled to the fact that they would not be able to pass any examinations. They would say,

'We're the stupid ones, sir.' And yet he would not allow them that easy option, the fault was not with them, it was with him. He had seen some of them serving in shops, in restaurants, and they were neatly dressed, good with money and polite. Indeed they seemed to like him, and that made matters worse for he felt that he did not deserve their liking. They are not fed, he quoted to himself from *Lycidas*, as he watched them at the checkout desks of supermarkets flashing a smile at him, placing the messages in bags much more expertly than he would have done. And indeed he felt that a question was being asked of him but not at all pressingly. At night he would read Shakespeare and think, There are some

people to whom all this is closed. There are some who will
never shiver as they read the lines

> Absent thee from felicity awhile
> and in this harsh world draw thy breath in pain
> to tell my story.

If he had read those lines to them they would have thought
that it was Hamlet saying farewell to a girl called Felicity, he
thought wryly. He smiled for the first time in weeks. Am I
taking this too seriously, he asked himself. They are not taking
it seriously. Shakespeare is not necessary for hairdressing. As
they endlessly combed each other's hair he thought of the
ballad of Sir Patrick Spens and the line

> wi gowd kaims in their hair.

These girls were entirely sensuous, words were closed to
them. They would look after babies with tenderness but they
were not interested in the alien world of language.

Or was he being a male chauvinist pig? No, he had tried
everything he could think of and he had still failed. The fact
was that language, the written word, was their enemy, McLuhan
was right after all. The day of the record player and television
had transformed the secure academic world in which he had
been brought up. And yet he did not wish to surrender, to get
on with correction while they sat talking quietly to each other,
and dreamed of the jobs which were in fact shut against them.
School was simply irrelevant to them, they did not even
protest, they withdrew from it gently and without fuss. They
had looked at education and turned away from it. It was their
indifferent gentleness that bothered him more than anything.
But they also had the maturity to distinguish between himself
and education, which was a large thing to do. They recognised
that he had a job to do, that he wasn't at all unlikeable and
was in fact a prisoner like themselves. But they were already
perming some woman's hair in a luxurious shop.

The more he pondered, the more he realised that they were
the key to his failure or success in education. If he failed with

them then he had failed totally, a permanent mark would be left on his psyche. In some way it was necessary for him to change, but the point was, could he change to the extent that was demanded of him, and in what direction and with what purpose should he change? School for himself had been a discipline and an order but to them this discipline and order had become meaningless.

The words on the blackboard were ghostly and distant as if they belonged to another age, another universe. He recalled what Morrison had said, 'You must find out what they want to do', but they themselves did not know what they wanted to do, it was for him to tell them that, and till he told them that they would remain indifferent and apathetic. Sometimes he sensed that they themselves were growing tired of their lives, that they wished to prove themselves but didn't know how to set about it. They were like lost children, irrelevantly stored in desks, and they only lighted up like street lamps in the evening or when they were working in the shops. He felt that they were the living dead, and he would have given anything to see their eyes become illuminated, become interested, for if he could find the magic formula he knew that they would become enthusiastic, they were *not* stupid. But how to find the magic key which would release the sleeping beauties from their sleep? He had no idea what it was and felt that in the end if he ever discovered it he would stumble over it and not be led to it by reflection or logic. And that was exactly what happened.

One morning he happened to be late coming into the room and there was Tracy swanning about in front of the class, as if she were wearing a gown, and saying some words to them he guessed in imitation of himself, while at the same time uncannily reproducing his mannerisms, leaning for instance despairingly across his desk, his chin on his hand while at the same time glaring helplessly at the class. It was like seeing himself slightly distorted in water, slightly comic, frustrated and yet angrily determined. When he opened the door there was a quick scurry and the class had arranged themselves, presenting blank dull faces as before. He pretended he had seen nothing, but knew now what he had to do. The solution

had come to him as a gift from heaven, from the gods themselves, and the class sensed a new confidence and purposefulness
in his voice.

'Tracy,' he said, 'and Lorna.' He paused. 'And Helen. I want
you to come out here.'

They came out to the floor looking at him uneasily. O my
wooden O, he said to himself, my draughty echo help me now.

'Listen,' he said, 'I've been thinking. It's quite clear to me
that you don't want to do any writing, so we won't do any
writing. But I'll tell you what we're going to do instead. We're
going to act.'

A ripple of noise ran through the class, like the wind on an
autumn day, and he saw their faces brightening. The shades of
Shakespeare and Sophocles forgive me for what I am to do, he
prayed.

'We are going,' he said, 'to do a serial and it's going to be
called "The Rise of a Pop Star".' It was as if animation had
returned to their blank dull faces, he could see life sparkling in
their eyes, he could see interest in the way they turned to look
at each other, he could hear it in the stir of movement that
enlivened the room.

'Tracy,' he said, 'you will be the pop star. You are coming
home from school to your parents' house. I'm afraid,' he
added, 'that as in the reverse of the days of Shakespeare the
men's parts will have be to be acted by the girls. Tracy,
you have decided to leave home. Your parents of course dis-
approve. But you want to be a pop star, you have always
wanted to be one. They think that that is a ridiculous idea.
Lorna, you will be the mother, and Helen, you will be the
father.'

He was astonished by the manner in which Tracy took over,
by the ingenuity with which she and the other two created the
first scene in front of his eyes. The scene grew and became
meaningful, all their frustrated enthusiasm was poured into it.

First of all without any prompting Tracy got her school bag
and rushed into the house while Lorna, the mother, pretended
to be ironing on a desk that was quickly dragged out into the
middle of the floor, and Helen the father read the paper, which

was his own Manchester Guardian snatched from the top of his desk.

'Well, that's it over,' said Tracy, the future pop star.

'And what are you thinking of doing with yourself now?' said the mother, pausing from her ironing.

'I'm going to be a pop star,' said Tracy.

'What's that you said?' – her father, laying down the paper.

'That's what I want to do,' said Tracy, 'other people have done it.'

'What nonsense,' said the father. 'I thought you were going in for hairdressing.'

'I've changed my mind,' said Tracy.

'You won't stay in this house if you're going to be a pop star,' said the father. 'I'll tell you that for free.'

'I don't care whether I do or not,' said Tracy.

'And how are you going to be a pop star?' said her mother.

'I'll go to London,' said Tracy.

'London. And where are you going to get your fare from?' said the father, mockingly, picking up the paper again.

Mark could see that Tracy was thinking this over: it was a real objection. Where was her fare going to come from? She paused, her mind grappling with the problem.

'I'll sell my records,' she said at last.

Her father burst out laughing. 'You're the first one who starts out as a pop star by selling all your records.' And then in a sudden rage in which Mark could hear echoes of reality he shouted,

'All right then. Bloody well go then.'

Helen glanced at Mark, but his expression remained benevolent and unchanged.

Tracy, turning at the door, said, 'Well then, I'm going. And I'm taking the records with me.' She suddenly seemed very thin and pale and scrawny.

'Go on then,' said her father.

'That's what I'm doing. I'm going.' Her mother glanced from daughter to father and then back again but said nothing.

'I'm going then,' said Tracy, pretending to go to another room and then taking the phantom records in her arms. The father's face was fixed and determined and then Tracy looked at the two of them for the last time and left the room. The father and mother were left alone.

'She'll come back soon enough,' said the father but the mother still remained silent. Now and again the father would look at a phantom clock on a phantom mantelpiece but still Tracy did not return. The father pretended to go and lock a door and then said to his wife,

'I think we'd better go to bed.'

And then Lorna and Helen went back to their seats while Mark thought, this was exactly how dramas began in their bareness and naivety, through which at the same time an innocent genuine feeling coursed or peered as between ragged curtains.

When the bell rang after the first scene was over he found himself thinking about Tracy wandering the streets of London, as if she were a real waif sheltering in transient doss-houses or under bridges dripping with rain. The girls became real to him in their rôles whereas they had not been real before, nor even individualistic behind their wall of apathy. That day in the staff-room he heard about Tracy's saga and was proud and non-committal.

The next day the story continued. Tracy paced up and down the bare boards of the classroom, now and again stopping to look at ghostly billboards, advertisements. The girls had clearly been considering the next development during the interval they had been away from him, and had decided on the direction of the plot. The next scene was in fact an Attempted Seduction Scene.

Tracy was sitting disconsolately at a desk which he presumed was a table in what he presumed was a café.

'Hello, Mark,' she said to the man who came over to sit beside her. At this point Tracy glanced wickedly at the real Mark. The Mark in the play was the dark-haired girl who had asked for the records and whose name was Annie.

'Hello,' said Annie. And then, 'I could get you a spot, you know.'

'What do you mean?'

'There's a night club where they have a singer and she's sick. I could get you to take her place.' He put his hands on hers and she quickly withdrew her own.

'I mean it,' he said. 'If you come to my place I can introduce you to the man who owns the night club.'

Tracy searched his face with forlorn longing.

Was this another lie like the many she had experienced before? Should she, shouldn't she? She looked tired, her shoulders were slumped.

Finally she rose from the table and said, 'All right then.' Together they walked about the room in search of his luxurious flat.

They found it. Willing hands dragged another desk out and set the two desks at a slight distance from each other.

The Mark of the play went over to the window-sill on which there was a large bottle which had once contained ink but was now empty. He poured wine into two phantom glasses and brought them over.

'Where is this man then?' said Tracy.

'He won't be long,' said Mark.

Tracy accepted the drink and Annie drank as well.

After a while Annie tried to put her hand around Tracy's waist. Mark the teacher glanced at the class: he thought that at this turn of events they would be convulsed with raucous laughter. But in fact they were staring enraptured at the two, enthralled by their performance. It occurred to him that he would never be as unselfconscious as Annie and Tracy in a million years. Such a shorn abject thing, such dialogue borrowed from television, and yet it was early drama that what he was seeing reminded him of. He had a quick vision of a flag gracing the roof of the 'theatre', as if the school now belonged to the early age of Elizabethanism. His poor wooden O was in fact echoing with real emotions and real situations, borrowed from the pages of subterraneous pop magazines.

Tracy stood up. 'I am not that kind of girl,' she said.

'What kind of girl?'

'That kind of girl.'

But Annie was insistent. 'You'll not get anything if you don't play along with me,' she said, and Mark could have sworn that there was an American tone to her voice.

'Well, I'm not playing along with you,' said Tracy. She swayed a little on her feet, almost falling against the blackboard. 'I'm bloody well not playing along with you,' she said. 'And that's final.' With a shock of recognition Mark heard her father's voice behind her own as one might see behind a similar painting the first original strokes.

And then she collapsed on the floor and Annie was bending over her.

'I didn't mean it,' she was saying. 'I really didn't mean it. I'm sorry.'

But Tracy lay there motionless and pale. She was like the Lady of Shalott in her boat. The girls in the class were staring at her. Look what they have done to me, Tracy was implying. Will they not be sorry now? There was a profound silence in the room and Mark was aware of the power of drama, even here in this bare classroom with the green peeling walls, the window-pole in the corner like a disused spear. There was nothing here but the hopeless emotion of the young.

Annie raised Tracy to her feet and sat her down in a chair.

'It's true,' he said, 'it's true that I know this man.' He went over to the wall and pretended to dial on a phantom phone. And at that moment Tracy turned to the class and winked at them. It was a bold outrageous thing to do, thought Mark, it was as if she was saying, That faint was of course a trick, a feint, that is the sort of thing people like us have to do in order to survive: he thought he was tricking me but all the time I was tricking him. I am alive, fighting, I know exactly what I am doing. All of us are in conspiracy against this Mark. So much, thought Mark, was conveyed by that wink, so much that was essentially dramatic. It was pure instinct of genius.

The stage Mark turned away from the phone and said, 'He says he wants to see you. He'll give you an audition. His usual girl's sick. She's got . . . ' Annie paused and tried to say 'laryngitis', but it came out as not quite right, and it was as if the word poked through the drama like a real error, and Mark thought of the Miracle plays in which ordinary people played

Christ and Noah and Abraham with such unconscious style, as if there was no oddity in Abraham being a joiner or a miller.

'Look, I'll call you,' said the stage Mark and the bell rang and the finale was postponed. In the noise and chatter in which desks and chairs were replaced Mark was again aware of the movement of life, and he was happy. Absurdly he began to see them as if for the first time, their faces real and interested, and recognised the paradox that only in the drama had he begun to know them, as if only behind such a protection, a screen, were they willing to reveal themselves. And he began to wonder whether he himself had broken through the persona of the teacher and begun to 'act' in the real world. Their faces were more individual, sad or happy, private, extrovert, determined, yet vulnerable. It seemed to him that he had failed to see what Shakespeare was really about, he had taken the wrong road to find him.

'A babble of green fields,' he thought with a smile. So that was what it meant, that Wooden O, that resonator of the transient, of the real, beyond all the marble of their books, the white In Memoriams which they could not read.

How extraordinarily curious it all was.

The final part of the play was to take place on the following day.

'Please sir,' said Lorna to him, as he was about to leave.

'What is it?'

But she couldn't put into words what she wanted to say. And it took him a long time to decipher from her broken language what it was she wanted. She and the other actresses wanted an audience. Of course, why had he not thought of that before? How could he not have realised that an audience was essential? And he promised her that he would find one.

By the next day he had found an audience which was composed of a 3A class which Miss Stewart next door was taking. She grumbled a little about the Interpretation they were missing but eventually agreed. Additional seats were taken into Mark's room from her room and Miss Stewart sat at the back, her spectacles glittering.

Tracy pretended to knock on a door which was in fact the

blackboard and then a voice invited her in. The manager of the night club pointed to a chair which stood on the 'stage'.

'What do you want?'

'I want to sing, sir.'

'I see. Many girls want to sing. I get girls in here every day. They all want to sing.'

Mark heard titters of laughter from some of the boys in 3A and fixed a ferocious glare on them. They settled down again.

'But I know I can sing, sir,' said Tracy. 'I know I can.'

'They all say that too.' His voice suddenly rose, 'They all bloody well say that.'

Mark saw Miss Stewart sitting straight up in her seat and then glancing at him disapprovingly. Shades of Pygmalion, he thought to himself, smiling. You would expect it from Shaw, inside inverted commas.

'Give it to them, sock it to them,' he pleaded silently. The virginal Miss Stewart looked sternly on.

'Only five minutes then,' said the night club manager, glancing at his watch. Actually there was no watch on his hand at all. 'What song do you want to sing?'

Mark saw Lorna pushing a desk out to the floor and sitting in it. This was to be the piano, then. The absence of props bothered him and he wondered whether imagination had first begun among the poor, since they had such few material possessions. Lorna waited, her hands poised above the desk. He heard more sniggerings from the boys and this time he looked so angry that he saw one of them turning a dirty white.

The hands hovered above the desk. Then Tracy began to sing. She chose the song 'Heartache'.

> My heart, dear, is aching;
> I'm feeling so blue.
> Don't give me more heartaches,
> I'm pleading with you.

It seemed to him that at that moment, as she stood there pale and thin, she was putting all her experience and desires into her song. It was a moment he thought such as it is given to few to experience. She was in fact auditioning before a phantom audience, she and the heroine of the play were the same, she was searching for recognition on the streets of London, in a school. She stood up in her vulnerability, in her purity, on a bare stage where there was no furniture of any value, of any price: on just such a stage had actors and actresses acted many years before, before the full flood of Shakespearean drama. Behind her on the blackboard were written notes about the Tragic Hero, a concept which he had been discussing with the Sixth Year.

'The hero has a weakness and the plot of the play attacks this specific weakness.'

'We feel a sense of waste.'

'And yet triumph.'

Tracy's voice, youthful and yearning and vulnerable, soared to the cracked ceiling. It was as if her frustrations were released in the song.

> Don't give me more heartaches,
> I'm pleading with you.

The voice soared on and then after a long silence the bell rang.

The boys from 3A began to chatter and he thought, 'You don't even try. You wouldn't have the nerve to sing like that, to be so naked.' But another voice said to him, 'You're wrong. They're the same. It is we who have made them different.' But were they in fact the same, those who had been reduced to the nakedness, and those others who were the protected ones. He stood there trembling as if visited by a revelation which was only broken when Miss Stewart said,

'Not quite Old Vic standard.' And then she was gone with her own superior brood. You stupid bitch, he muttered under his breath, you Observer-Magazine-reading bitch who never liked anything in your life till some critic made it respectable, who wouldn't recognise a good line of poetry or prose till sanctified by the voice of London, who would never have arrived at Shakespeare on your own till you were given the crutches.

And he knew as he watched her walking, so seemingly self-sufficient, in her black gown across the hall that she was as he had been and would be no longer. He had taken a journey with his class, a pilgrimage across the wooden boards, the poor abject furnitureless room which was like their vision of life, and from that journey he and they had learned in spite of everything. In spite of everything, he shouted in his mind, we have put a flag out there and it is there even during the plague, even if Miss Stewart visits it. It is there in spite of Miss Stewart, in spite of her shelter and her glasses, in spite of her very vulnerable armour, in spite of her, in spite of everything.

The Telegram

The two women – one fat and one thin – sat at the window of the thin woman's house drinking tea and looking down the road which ran through the village. They were like two birds, one a fat domestic bird perhaps, the other more aquiline, more gaunt, or, to be precise, more like a buzzard.

It was wartime and though the village appeared quiet, much had gone on in it. Reverberations from a war fought far away had reached it: many of its young men had been killed, or rather drowned, since nearly all of them had joined the navy, and their ships had sunk in seas which they had never seen except on maps which hung on the walls of the local school which they all had at one time or another unwillingly attended. One had been drowned on a destroyer after a leave during which he had told his family that he would never come back again. (Or at least that was the rumour in the village which was still, as it had always been, a superstitious place.) Another had been drowned during the pursuit of the *Bismarck*.

What the war had to do with them the people of the village did not know. It came on them as a strange plague, taking their sons away and then killing them, meaninglessly, randomly. They watched the road often for the telegrams.

The telegrams were brought to the houses by the local elder who, clad in black, would walk along the road and then stop at the house to which the telegram was directed. People began to think of the telegram as a strange missile pointed at them from abroad. They did not know what to associate it with, certainly not with God, but it was a weapon of some kind, it picked a door and entered it, and left desolation just like any other weapon.

The two women who watched the street were different, not

only physically but socially. For the thin woman's son was a sub-lieutenant in the Navy while the fat woman's son was only an ordinary seaman. The fat woman's son had to salute the thin woman's son. One got more pay than the other, and wore better uniform. One had been at university and had therefore become an officer, the other had left school at the age of fourteen.

When they looked out the window they could see cows wandering lazily about, but little other movement. The fat woman's cow used to eat the thin woman's washing and she was looking out for it but she couldn't see it. The thin woman was not popular in the village. She was an incomer from another village and had only been in this one for thirty years or so. The fat woman had lived in the village all her days; she was a native. Also the thin woman was ambitious: she had sent her son to university though she only had a widow's pension of ten shillings a week.

As they watched they could see at the far end of the street the tall man in black clothes carrying in his hand a piece of yellow paper. This was a bare village with little colour and therefore the yellow was both strange and unnatural.

The fat woman said: 'It's Macleod again.'

'I wonder where he's going today.'

They were both frightened for he could be coming to their house. And so they watched him and as they watched him they spoke feverishly as if by speaking continually and watching his every move they would be able to keep from themselves whatever plague he was bringing. The thin woman said:

'Don't worry, Sarah, it won't be for you. Donald only left home last week.'

'You don't know,' said the fat woman, 'you don't know.'

And then she added without thinking, 'It's different for the officers.'

'Why is it different for the officers?' said the thin woman in an even voice without taking her eyes from the black figure.

'Well, I just thought they're better off,' said the fat woman in a confused tone, 'they get better food and they get better conditions.'

'They're still on the ship,' said the thin woman who was thinking that the fat woman was very stupid. But then most of them were: they were large, fat and lazy. Most of them could have better afforded to send their sons and daughters to university but they didn't want to be thought of as snobbish.

'They are that,' said the fat woman. 'But your son is educated,' she added irrelevantly. Of course her son didn't salute the thin woman's son if they were both home on leave at the same time. It had happened once they had been. But naturally there was the uneasiness.

'I made sacrifices to have my son educated,' said the thin woman. 'I lived on a pension of ten shillings a week. I was in nobody's debt. More tea?'

'No thank you,' said the fat woman. 'He's passed Bessie's house. That means it can't be Roddy. He's safe.'

For a terrible moment she realised that she had hoped that the elder would have turned in at Bessie's house. Not that she had anything against either Bessie or Roddy. But still one thought of one's own family first.

The thin woman continued remorselessly as if she were pecking away at something she had pecked at for many years. 'The teacher told me to send Iain to University. He came to see me. I had no thought of sending him before he came. "Send your son to university," he said to me. "He's got a good head on him." And I'll tell you, Sarah, I had to save every penny. Ten shillings isn't much. When did you see me with good clothes in the church?'

'That's true,' said the fat woman absently. 'We have to make sacrifices.' It was difficult to know what she was thinking of – the whale meat or the saccharines? Or the lack of clothes? Her mind was vague and diffused except when she was thinking about herself.

The thin woman continued: 'Many's the night I used to sit here in this room and knit clothes for him when he was young. I even knitted trousers for him. And for all I know he may marry an English girl and where will I be? He might go and work in England. He was staying in a house there at Christmas. He met a girl at a dance and he found out later that her father was a mayor. I'm sure she smokes and drinks. And he might not give me anything after all I've done for him.'

'Donald spends all his money,' said the fat woman. 'He never sends me anything. When he comes home on leave he's never in the house. But I don't mind. He was always like that. Meeting strange people and buying them drinks. It's his nature and he can't go against his nature. He's passed the Smiths. That means Tommy's all right.'

There were only another three houses before he would reach her own, and then the last one was the one where she was sitting.

'I think I'll take a cup of tea,' she said. And then, 'I'm sorry about the cow.' But no matter how you tried you never could like the thin woman. She was always putting on airs. Mayor indeed. Sending her son to university. Why did she want to be better than anyone else? Saving and scrimping all the time. And everybody said that her son wasn't as clever as all that. He had failed some of his exams too. Her own Donald was just as clever and could have gone to university but he was too fond of fishing and being out with the boys.

As she drank her tea her heart was beating and she was frightened and she didn't know what to talk about and yet she wanted to talk. She liked talking, after all what else was there to do? But the thin woman didn't gossip much. You couldn't feel at ease with her, you had the idea all the time that she was thinking about something else.

The thin woman came and sat down beside her.

'Did you hear,' said the fat woman, 'that Malcolm Mackay was up on a drunken charge? He smashed his car, so they say. It was in the black-out.'

'I didn't hear that,' said the thin woman.

'It was coming home last night with the meat. He had it in the van and he smashed it at the burn. But they say he's all right. I don't know how they kept him out of the war. They said it was his heart but there was nothing wrong with his heart. Everyone knows it was influence. What's wrong with his heart if he can drink and smash a car?'

The thin woman drank her tea very delicately. She used to

be away on service a long time before she was married and she
had a dainty way of doing things. She sipped her tea, her little
finger elegantly curled in an irritating way.

'Why do you keep your finger like that?' said the fat woman
suddenly.

'Like what?'

The fat woman demonstrated.

'Oh, it was the way I saw the guests drinking tea in the
hotels when I was on service. They always drank like that.'

'He's passed the Stewarts,' said the fat woman. Two houses to
go. They looked at each other wildly. It must be one of them.
Surely. They could see the elder quite clearly now, walking
very stiff, very upright, wearing his black hat. He walked in a
stately dignified manner, eyes straight ahead of him.

'He's proud of what he's doing,' said the fat woman suddenly.
'You'd think he was proud of it. Knowing before anyone else.
And he himself was never in the war.'

'Yes,' said the thin woman, 'it gives him a position.' They
watched him. They both knew him well. He was a stiff, quiet
man who kept himself to himself, more than ever now. He
didn't mix with people and he always carried the Bible into the
pulpit for the minister.

'They say his wife had one of her fits again,' said the fat
woman viciously. He had passed the Murrays. The next house
was her own. She sat perfectly still. Oh, pray God it wasn't
hers. And yet it must be hers. Surely it must be hers. She had
dreamt of this happening, her son drowning in the Atlantic
ocean, her own child whom she had reared, whom she had
seen going to play football in his green jersey and white shorts,
whom she had seen running home from school. She could see
him drowning but she couldn't make out the name of the ship.
She had never seen a really big ship and what she imagined
was more like the mailboat than a cruiser. Her son couldn't
drown out there for no reason that she could understand. God
couldn't do that to people. It was impossible. God was kinder
than that. God helped you in your sore trouble. She began to
mutter a prayer over and over. She said it quickly like the
Catholics, O God save my son O God save my son O God

save my son. She was ashamed of prattling in that way as if she was counting beads but she couldn't stop herself, and on top of that she would soon cry. She knew it and she didn't want to cry in front of that woman, that foreigner. It would be weakness. She felt the arm of the thin woman around her shoulders, the thin arm, and it was like first love, it was like the time Murdo had taken her hand in his when they were coming home from the dance, such an innocent gesture, such a spontaneous gesture. So unexpected, so strange, so much a gift. She was crying and she couldn't look . . .

'He has passed your house,' said the thin woman in a distant firm voice, and she looked up. He was walking along and he had indeed passed her house. She wanted to stand up and dance all round the kitchen, all fifteen stone of her, and shout and cry and sing a song but then she stopped. She couldn't do that. How could she do that when it must be the thin woman's son? There was no other house. The thin woman was looking out at the elder, her lips pressed closely together, white and bloodless. Where had she learnt that self-control? She wasn't crying or shaking. She was looking out at something she had always dreaded but she wasn't going to cry or surrender or give herself away to anyone.

And at that moment the fat woman saw. She saw the years of discipline, she remembered how thin and unfed and pale the thin woman had always looked, how sometimes she had had to borrow money, even a shilling to buy food. She saw what it must have been like to be a widow bringing up a son in a village not her own. She saw it so clearly that she was astounded. It was as if she had an extra vision, as if the air itself brought the past with all its details nearer. The number of times the thin woman had been ill and people had said that she was weak and useless. She looked down at the thin woman's arm. It was so shrivelled, and dry.

And the elder walked on. A few yards now till he reached the plank. But the thin woman hadn't cried. She was steady and still, her lips still compressed, sitting upright in her chair. And, miracle of miracles, the elder passed the plank and walked straight on.

They looked at each other. What did it all mean? Where was the elder going, clutching his telegram in his hand, walking like a man in a daze? There were no other houses so where was he going? They drank their tea in silence, turning away from each other. The fat woman said, 'I must be going.' They parted for the moment without speaking. The thin woman still sat at the window looking out. Once or twice the fat woman made as if to turn back as if she had something to say, some message to pass on, but she didn't. She walked away.

It wasn't till later that night that they discovered what had happened. The elder had a telegram directed to himself, to tell him of the drowning of his own son. He should never have seen it just like that, but there had been a mistake at the post office, owing to the fact that there were two boys in the village with the same name. His walk through the village was a somnambulistic wandering. He didn't want to go home and tell his wife what had happened. He was walking along not knowing where he was going when later he was stopped half way to the next village. Perhaps he was going in search of his son. Altogether he had walked six miles. The telegram was crushed in his fingers and so sweaty that they could hardly make out the writing.

Murdo's Xmas Letter

Dear Friends,

Another Christmas has come again, and I am sending you a report of my activities during the year. It doesn't seem so long ago since last Christmas was here, but as we all know it is twelve months ago – no more and no less.

My main project in the early part of the year was to encourage Scottish writing, by running a competition for short stories. I asked for, a sum of ten pounds to be enclosed with each story: this was to cover administrative costs, coffee, stamps, and whisky, etc. The prizes which I presented in March were ten pounds for the best story, one pound for the next story and 10p for third best. I hope to do something similar for Scottish Writing next year. I shall advise entrants that a maximum of 200 words is entirely reasonable, as it seems to me that one of the faults of Scottish Writing is that it is too long, and with shorter short stories I shall be able to apply better my critical techniques. Far more emphasis should be placed on the single word, which is the hallmark of the truly great writer. What I look for first is good typing, then originality.

Another project in which I was involved gave me great satisfaction. I have noticed in the past that the standards of In Memoriams in the local paper is very low, and it seems to me that with a little practice they could be improved. I therefore started a workshop for that purpose. I told my class that epitaphs have concentrated mainly on names and dates, without referring in depth to the individual nature of the dead person. I told them that the best writing of the twentieth century is above all truthful. Thus if the dead person was highly sexed, perverted, or a habitual thief, this should be stated. As a result of our final workshop (the cost for the whole course was £50 to each member) I shall put together a small anthology of the best In Memoriams.

Here are two examples:
"May James Campbell's randy bones rest in peace."
and
"May John MacDonald be able to find his way to his own grave."
The classic, I think, was
"Let her RIP."
I may say that the sales of the local newspaper have soared since these epitaphs were inserted and I had a congratulatory message from the editor.

Old clothes is another area of my research, the idea for which I got from the local Oxfam. I have started a campaign by which I hope to convince people that old clothes are better than new ones. The logic of my argument goes like this. Community, I say, is the basis of our life here in the island, and what would be more communal than to wear clothes which in the past have been worn by someone else. In this way we inherit history, sweat, stains and genealogy. Old clothes are like a time machine: they give an insight into the past that cannot be gained in any other way. Look, I say, at these rags which better men and women than you have worn. They did not know where their next meal was coming from. Indeed they did not know where their last meal had come from. Do you not wish to have thoughts like them, pure healthy thoughts, and not impure unhealthy thoughts such as people who wear new clothes have?

Such people, I say, existed on bread and sour milk. Many of my hearers, and I don't blame them for this, have been so moved by my rhetoric that they have stripped off their new clothes on the spot and have taken old clothes of a similar size. This, I say, is what Christianity was really about. Did Christ shop at Harrods? Such a statement has only to be made for the absurdity of it to be revealed. Nor in fact has anyone found an answer to my logic and I do not think anyone will.

So you see, my friends, that I have not been idle.

I have also decided during the course of this year to change the subject of my novel. It was originally to be about a bank clerk, but I have noticed on television a resurgence of the detective story. Thus I have created a private eye called Sam Spaid who walks, as I write, the mean streets of Portree. He wears a bowler hat, and when he is in his office listens to tapes of Free Church sermons. He doesn't drink or smoke and his only vice is sniffing. In his first case he opened his door to find a stunning Free Church woman there. He immediately knew that she spelt trouble. The elastic which she kept round her Bible had been stolen. This investigation, which of course ended in success, took Sam Spaid to a cache of black elastic in Inverness. Sam Spaid's fee, which never varies, is £20 per day plus expenses! He will never be rich but he will be an interesting moral phenomenon. His next case will involve the serial murders of Free Church ministers by a crazed sniper who was made to spend his early years in the Sunday School.

I hope you are not bored at hearing about my projects at great length but at this season of the year such ramblings may be forgiven, as Christmas carols are.

My final project has to do with a taxi service that I run for drunks at the New Year. For this purpose I have a number of advertisements run off, which read, "Drink as much as you like. Murdo will run you home." In small print it reads, "Ditches, lavatories, cemeteries, scoured for those who have INDULGED too much." The taxi is of course my own car and I am happy for it to be used for such a Christian purpose. In the course of this work I have become very humble, as I have been beaten up and vomited on many times. Hence I have developed a servile stance which has served me well. I call my customers "Sir" or "My Lord" and am especially friendly to large people, and to those whose jackets are flecked with a mixture of lager and sickness. It seems to me reasonable that I should charge extra for taking people to their doors or to their lavatories or even to their bedrooms. I wear protective clothing and sometimes a gas-mask. I charge also for burns from cigarettes on the seat of my car. I consider what I am doing to be a Christian duty which money in itself cannot pay. I could tell you of some little contretemps I have had, as for example a drug-crazed addict from Shawbost who attacked me with a graip, but I shall refrain. Nor will I mention that time I took one of my customers to the wrong bedroom. This arose from the fact that there are many Norman MacLeods on the island.

As you can see therefore I have had a busy and eventful year. Blessings on you wherever you are and may we exchange literature such as this often in the future.

Yours as ever

Murdo.

Home

The black polished car drew up outside the brown tenement and he rested for a moment, his hands still on the wheel. He was a big man with a weatherbeaten red-veined face and a strong jaw. On one finger of his right hand was a square red ring. He looked both competent and hard.

After a while he got out, gazing round him and up at the sky with a hungry look as if he were scanning the veldt. His wife in furs got out more slowly. Her face had a haggard brownness like that of a desiccated gipsy and seemed to be held together, like a lacy bag, by the wrinkles.

He glanced up at the tenement with the cheerful animation of one who had left it, and yet with a certain curiosity.

'Lock the car, dear,' said his wife.

He stared at her for a moment in surprise and then said as if he had been listening to a witticism, 'But they don't steal things here.'

She smiled disdainfully.

They walked into the close whose walls were brown above and a dirty blue below, pitted with scars. Somebody had written in chalk the words Ya Bass. It looked for a moment African, and he stared at it as if it had recalled some memory. On the other side of the road the flat-faced shops looked back at them blankly.

He pointed upwards to a window.

'Mind the Jamiesons?' he said.

She remembered them but took no pleasure in the memory. The Jamiesons had lived above them and were, of course, Protestant. Not that at that level you could distinguish Catholic from Protestant except that the former went to chapel and the latter didn't. The O'Rahilly's house – for instance – had been full of wee ornaments, and once she had seen a complete ornamental house showing, outside it, like Europeans outside a verandah, Christ and the twelve disciples, the whole thing painted a distasteful green.

She remembered Jamieson all right. Every Friday night he would dress up in his best blue suit, neat as a ray or razor, and would wave to his wife who was following his progress to the road from an open window, her scarf tight round her head. He would go off to the pub and pick a fight with a Catholic, or more likely three Catholics. At midnight he would come home covered with blood, his face bruised a fine Protestant blue, his clothes dirty and brown. He would walk like a victorious gladiator up the stair and then start a fight with his wife, uprooting chairs and wardrobes till the silence of exhaustion settled over the flats at about one in the morning. The next day his wife would descend the stair, her eyes black and blue, and say that she had stumbled at the sink. Her repertoire of invention was endless.

'I remember,' she said.

The town had changed a lot since they had left it, that much was clear. Now the old tenements were being knocked down and the people shuttled out to huge featureless estates where the windows revealed the blue sky of TV. There were hardly any picture houses left: they had been converted into bingo halls. Instead of small shops supermarkets were springing up, flexing their huge muscles. The lover's lane had disappeared. The park seemed to have lost its atmosphere of pastoral carelessness and was being decorated for the visitors with literate slogans in flowers.

'It's thirty-five years since we left,' said her husband.

And the wallet bulged from his breast pocket, a wife, two children, and a good job in administration.

He moved about restlessly. He wanted to tell someone how well he had done but how could he do that? All the people he had known were gone elsewhere, many of them presumably dead and completely forgotten.

'Do you mind old Hannah?' he said.

She had been a fat old woman who sat day after day at the

window leaning out of it talking to the passers-by. A fat woman with arthritis. He wondered vaguely what had happened to her.

'I wonder if the coal-house is still here. Come on.'

He took his wife by the hand and they walked down the close to the back. The coal-houses were incredibly still there, all padlocked and all beside each other, all with discoloured doors.

She kept her fur coat as far away from them as she could.

'Do you mind the day I went to the factor?' he said. The factor had been a small, buttoned-up, black-suited lawyer. In those days of poverty he himself had been frightened to visit him in his wee office with the dim glass door. He imagined what he would do to that factor now.

He had gone there after coming home from the office, and the wee lawyer in the undertaker's suit had said to him over his shoulder,

'What do you want?'

'I want to report the rain coming through the roof.'

'How much do you pay Jackson?'

'Fifteen shillings a week.'

'And what do you expect for fifteen shillings a week?' said the factor, as if even giving words away were an agony of the spirit. In a corner of the office an umbrella dripped what seemed to be black rain.

'I was hoping that the house would be dry anyway.'

'I'll send someone round tomorrow,' and the factor had bent down to study a ledger with a rusty red cover.

'You said that a week ago.'

'And I'm saying it again. I'm a busy man. I've got a lot to do.' At that moment he had been filled with a terrible reckless anger and was about to raise his fist when the factor looked up. His mouth opened slightly showing one gold tooth in the middle of the bottom row of teeth, and he said carefully, 'Next week.'

So he had walked out past the dispirited receptionist in the glass cage – the one with the limp and the ageing mother – and then home.

Thinking back on it now, he thought: I was treated like a black. That's what it amounted to. By God, like a black.

He wished that that factor was alive now so that he could show him his bank balance. The wee nyaff. The Scottish words rose unbidden to his mouth like bile.

For a moment he did in fact see himself as a black, cringing in that rotting office, suffering the contempt, hearing the black rain dripping behind him from the furled umbrella.

But then a black would buy a bicycle and forget all about his humiliation. Blacks weren't like us.

As he turned away from the coal-house door he saw the washing hanging from the ropes on the green.

'Ye widna like to be daeing that noo,' he told his wife jocularly.

'What would the Bruces say if they saw you running about in this dirty place like a schoolboy?' she said coldly.

'Whit dae ye mean?'

'Simply what I said. There was no need to come here at all. Or do you want to take a photograph and show it to them? "The Place Where I Was Born".'

'I wasna born here. I just lived here for five years.'

'What would they think of you, I wonder.'

'I don't give a damn about the Bruces,' he burst out, the veins on his forehead swelling. 'What's he but a doctor anyway? I'm not ashamed of it. And, by God, why should you be ashamed of it? You weren't brought up in a fine house either. You worked in a factory till I picked you up at that dance.'

She turned away.

'Do you mind that night?' he asked contritely. 'You were standing by the wall and I went up to you and I said, "Could I have the honour?" And when we were coming home we walked down lovers' lane, where they had all the seats and the statues.'

'And you made a clown of yourself,' she said unforgivingly.

'Yes, didn't I just?' remembering how he had climbed the statue in the moonlight to show off. From the top of it he could see the Clyde, the ships and the cranes.

'And remember the flicks?' he said. 'We used tae get in wi

jam jars. And do you mind the man who used to come down the passage at the interval spraying us with disinfectant?'

The interior of the cinema came back to him in a warm flood: the children in the front rows keeping up a continual barrage of noise, the ushers hushing them, the smoke, the warmth, the pies slapping against faces, the carved cherubs in the flaking roof blowing their trumpets.

'You'd like that, wouldn't you?' she said. 'Remember it was me who drove you to the top.'

'Whit dae ye mean?' – like a bull wounded in the arena.

'You were lazy, that was what was wrong with you. You'd go out ferreting when you were here. You liked being with the boys.'

'Nothing wrong with that. What's wrong wi that?'

'What do you want? That they should all wave flags? That all the dirty boys and girls should line the street with banners five miles high? They don't give a damn about you, you know that. They're all dead and rotting and we should be back in Africa where we belong.'

He heard the voices round him. It was New Year's Eve and they were all dancing in a restaurant which had a fountain in the middle, and in the basin hundreds of pennies.

'Knees up, Mother Brown,' Jamieson was shouting to Hannah.

'You used to dance, too,' he said, 'on New Year's Night.'

'I saw old Manson dying in that room,' he said, pointing at a window. The floor and the ceiling and the walls seemed to have drops of perspiration and Manson had a brown flannel cloth wrapped round his neck. He couldn't breathe. And he heard the mice scuttering behind the walls.

She turned on him. 'What are you bringing that up for? Why don't you forget it? Do you enjoy thinking about these things?'

'Shut up,' he shouted, 'you didn't even have proper table manners when I met you.'

She stalked out to the car and he stayed where he was. To hell with her. She couldn't drive anyway.

He just wondered if anyone they had known still remained.

He climbed the stair quietly till he came to the door of their old flat. No gaslight there now. On the door was written the name 'Rafferty', and as he leaned down against the letter box he heard the blast of a radio playing a pop song.

He went down again quietly.

He thought of their own two rooms there once, the living room with the table, the huge Victorian wardrobe (which was too big for the bedroom) and the huge Victorian dresser.

As he looked out of the close he saw that his car was surrounded by a pack of children, his wife, sheltered behind glass, staring ahead of her, an empress surrounded by prairie dogs.

He rushed out. 'Hey,' he said, 'don't scratch my car.'

'Whit is it?' a hard voice shouted from above.

He looked up. 'Nothing,' he said, 'I was just telling them not to scratch my car.'

'Why have you goat it there onyway?'

The woman was thin and stringy and wore a cheap bracelet round her throat. A bit like Mrs Jamieson but less self-effacing.

'I was just paying a visit,' he said. 'I used to live here.'

'They're no dacing onything to your caur,' said the voice which was like a saw that would cut through steel forever.

'It's an expensive car,' he said, watching his wife who was sitting in it like a graven image, lips firmly pressed together. Another window opened. 'Hey, you there! I'm on night shift. Let's get a bit of sleep. Right?'

A pair of hairy hands slammed the window down again. Two tall youngsters chewing gum approached.

'Hey, mister, whit are you on about?' They stared at him, legs crossed, delicate narrow toes.

'Nice bus,' said the one with the long curving moustache. 'Nice bus, eh Charley?'

They moved forward in concert, a ballet.

'Look,' he began, 'I was just visiting.' Then he stopped. Should he tell them that he was a rich man who had made good? It might not be advisable. One of them absently kicked one of the front tyres and then suddenly said to his wife, 'Peek a boo'. She showed no sign that she had seen him. They reminded him of some Africans he had seen, insolent young toughs, town-bred.

'All right, boys,' he said in an ingratiating voice. 'We're going anyway. We've seen all we want.'

'Did you hear that, Micky? He's seen all he wants to see. Would you say that was an insult?' Micky gazed benevolently at him through a lot of hair.

'Depends. What have you seen, daddy?'

'I used to live here,' he said jovially. 'In the old days. The best years of my life.' The words rang hollow between them.

'Hear that?' said Micky. 'Hear him. He's left us. Daddy's left us.'

He came up close and said quietly, 'Get out of here, daddy, before we cut you up, and take your camera and your bus with you. And your bag too. Right?'

The one with the curving moustache spat and said quietly, 'Tourist.'

He got into the car beside his still unsmiling wife who was still staring straight ahead of her. The car gathered speed and made its way down the main street. In the mirror he could see the brown tenement diminishing. The thin stringy woman was still at the window looking out, screaming at the children.

The shops along both sides of the street were all changed.

There used to be a road down to the river and the lavatories but he couldn't see anything there now. Later on he passed a new yellow petrol-station, behind a miniature park with a blue bench on it.

'Mind we used to take the bus out past here?' he said, looking towards the woods on their right, where all the secret shades were, and the squirrels leaped.

The sky was darkening and the light seemed concentrated ahead of them in steely rays.

Suddenly he said, 'I wish to God we were home.'

She smiled for the first time. But he was still thinking of the scarred tenement and of what he should have said to these youths. Punks. He should have said, 'This is my home too. More than yours. You're just passing through.'

Punks with Edwardian moustaches. By God, if they were in

Africa they would be sorted out. A word in the ear of the Chief Inspector over a cigar and that would be it. By God, they knew how to deal with punks where he came from.

He thought of razor-suited Jamieson setting out on a Friday night in his lone battle with the Catholics. Where was he now? Used to be a boiler-man or something. By God, he would have sorted them out. And his wife used to clean the cinema steps on those big draughty winter days.

'So you admit you were wrong,' said his wife.

He drove on, accelerating past a smaller car and blaring his horn savagely. There was no space in this bloody country. Everybody crowded together like rats.

'Here, look at that,' he said, 'that didn't use to be there.' It was a big building, probably a hospital.

'Remember we used to come down here on the bus,' he said.

'That didn't use to be there.'

He drove into the small town and got out of the car to stretch. The yellow lights rayed the road and the cafés had red globes above them. He could hardly recognise the place.

'We'd better find a hotel,' he said. His wife's face brightened.

They stopped at the Admiral and were back home when the boy in the blue uniform with the yellow edgings took their rich brown leather cases. People could be seen drinking in the bar which faced directly on to the street. They were standing about with globes of whisky in their hands. He recognised who they were. They had red faces and red necks, and they stood there decisively as if they belonged there. Their wives wore cool gowns and looked haggard and dissipated.

His own wife put her hand in his as they got out of the car. Now she was smiling and trailing her fur coat. She walked with a certain exaggerated delicacy. It looked as if it might be a good evening after all. He could tell the boys about his sentimental journey, it would make a good talking point, they would get some laughs from it. No, on second thoughts perhaps not. He'd say something about Scotland anyway, and not forget to make sure that they got to know how well he had done.

The two of them walked in. 'Waiter,' he said loudly, 'two

whiskies with ice.' Some of them looked at him, then turned away again. That waiter should have his hair cut. After a few whiskies they would gravitate into the neighbourhood of the others, those men who ran Scotland, the backbone of the nation. People like himself. By God, less than him. He had had the guts to travel.

Outside it was quite dark. Difficult to get used to this climate.

His wife was smiling as if she expected someone to photograph her.

Now she was home. In a place much like Africa, the bar of a first class hotel.

He took out a cigar to show who he was, and began to cut it.

In the lights pouring out from the hotel he could see his car bulging like a black wave.

He placed his hand over his wife's and said, 'Well, dear, it's been a tiring day.'

With a piercing stab of pain he recalled Africa, the drinkers on the verandah, the sky large and open and protective, the place where one knew where one was, among Europeans like oneself.

To have found one's true home was important after all. He sniffed his whisky, swirling it around in the goblet, golden and clear and thin and burningly pure.

The Red Door

When Murdo woke up after Hallowe'en and went out into the
cold air to see whether anything was stirring in the world
around him, he discovered that his door which had formerly
been painted green was now painted red. He stared at it for a
long time, scratching his head slowly as if at first he didn't
believe that it was his own door. In fact he went into the
house again and had a look at his frugally prepared breakfast –
porridge, scones and tea – and even studied the damp patch on
the wall before he convinced himself that it was his own house.

Now Murdo was a bachelor who had never brought himself
to propose marriage to anyone. He lived by himself, prepared
his own food, darned his own socks, washed his own clothes
and cultivated his own small piece of ground. He was liked
by everybody since he didn't offend anyone by gossiping
and maintained a long silence unless he had something of
importance to say.

The previous night children had knocked on his door and
sung songs to him. He had given them apples, oranges, and
nuts which he had bought specially from a shop. He had gazed
in amazement at the mask of senility on one face, at the mask
of a wildcat on another and at the mask of a spaceman on the
face of a little boy whom he could swear he knew.

Having made sure that he was in his own house again he
went out and studied the door for a second time. When he
touched the red paint he found that it was quite dry. He had
no feeling of anger at all, only puzzlement. After all, no one in
his experience had had a red door in the village before. Green
doors, yellow doors, and even blue doors, but never a red
door. It certainly singled him out. The door was as red as the
winter sun he saw in the sky.

Murdo had never in his life done anything unusual. Indeed because he was a bachelor he felt it necessary that he should be as like the other villagers as possible. He read the *Daily Record* as they did, after dinner he slept by the fire as they did, he would converse with his neighbour while hammering a post into the ground. He would even play draughts with one of them sometimes.

Nevertheless there were times when he felt that there was more to life than that. He would feel this especially on summer nights when the harvest moon was in the sky – the moon that ripened the barley – and the earth was painted with an un-earthly glow and the sea was like a strange volume which none could read except by means of the imagination.

At times too he would find it difficult to get up in the morning but would lie in a pleasant half dream looking up at the ceiling. He would say to himself, 'After all, I have nothing to get up for really. I could if I liked stay in bed all day and all night and none would notice the difference. I used to do this when I was a child. Why can't I do it now?'

For he had been a very serious child who found it difficult to talk to children even of his own age. Only once had he shown enthusiasm and that was when in a school playground he had seen in the sky an aeroplane and had lisped excitedly, 'Thee, an aeroplane', a rather ambiguous not to say almost unintelligible exclamation which had been repeated as a sign of his foolishness. He had never taken part in the school sports because he was rather clumsy: and his accomplishments in mathematics were meagre. When he became an adolescent he had taken a job as cook on board a fishing boat but had lost the job because he had put sugar instead of salt into the soup thus causing much diarrhoea.

Most of the time – while his father and mother dreamed their way towards death – he spent working on the land in a dull concentrated manner. In summer and autumn he would be seen with a scythe in the fields, the sunlight sparkling from the blade while he himself, squat and dull, swung it remorselessly. There had in fact been one romance in his life. He had made overtures – if such tentative motions might even be called that – to a spinster in the village who lived with her grossly religious mother in the house opposite him and who was very stout. However he had ceased to visit her when once she had provided him with cocoa and salt herring for his supper, a diet so ferocious that even he could not look forward to its repetition with tranquillity.

There was another spinster in the village who wrote poetry and who lived by herself and he had certain feelings too tenuous to be called love towards her. Her name was Mary and she had inherited from her mother a large number of books in brown leather covers. She dressed in red clothes and was seen pottering vaguely about during the day and sometimes during the night as well. But she was more good looking than the first though she neglected herself in the service of books and poetry and was considered slightly odd by the villagers. Murdo thought that anybody who read a lot of books and wrote poetry must be very clever.

As he stared at the door he felt strange flutterings within him. First of all the door had been painted very lovingly so that it shone with a deep inward shine such as one might find in pictures. And indeed it looked like a picture against the rest of the house which wasn't at all modern but on the contrary was old and intertwined with all sorts of rusty pipes like snakes.

He went back from the door and looked at it from a distance as people in art galleries have to do when studying an oil painting. The more he regarded it the more he liked it. It certainly stood out against the drab landscape as if it were a work of art. On the other hand the more he looked at it the more it seemed to express something in himself which had been deeply buried for years. After a while there was something boring about green and as for blue it wouldn't have suited the door at all. Blue would have been too blatant in a cold way. And anyway the sky was already blue.

But mixed with his satisfaction he felt what could only be described as puzzlement, a slight deviation from the normal as if his head were spinning and he were going round in circles. What would the neighbours say about it, he wondered. Never in the history of the village had there been a red door before.

For that matter he couldn't remember seeing even a blue door himself, though he had heard of the existence of one.

The morning was breaking all over the village as he looked. Blue smoke was ascending from chimneys, a cock was crowing, belligerent and heraldic, its red claws sunk into the earth, its metallic breast oriental and strange. There was a dew all about him and lying on the fences ahead of him. He recognised that the village would wake to a new morning, for the red door would gather attention to itself.

And he thought to himself, 'I have always sought to hide among other people. I agree to whatever anybody tells me to do. If they think I should go to church, I go to church. If they want me to cut peats for them, I do. I have never,' he thought with wonder, 'been myself.' He looked down at his grey fisherman's jersey and his wellingtons and he thought, 'I have always worn these things because everybody else does. I have never had the courage to wear what I wanted to wear, for example a coloured waistcoat and a coloured jacket.'

The red door stood out against the whiteness of the frost and the glimmerings of snow. It seemed to be saying something to him, to be asking him a question. Perhaps it was pleading with him not to destroy it. Perhaps it was saying, 'I don't want to be green. There must be a place somewhere for me as myself. I wish to be red. What is wrong with red anyway?' The door seemed to him to have its own courage.

Wine of course was red and so was blood. He drank none of the former and only saw the latter when he cut himself while repairing a fence or working with wood when a nail would prick his finger.

But really was he happy? That was the question. When he considered it carefully he knew that he wasn't. He didn't like eating alone, he didn't like sitting in the house alone, he didn't like having none who belonged to him, to whom he could tell his secret thoughts, for example that such and such was a mean devil and that that other one was an ungrateful rat.

He had to keep a perpetually smiling face to the world, that was his trouble. But the red door didn't do that. It was foreign and confident. It seemed to be saying what it was, not what it thought others expected it to say. On the other hand, he didn't like wellingtons and a fisherman's jersey. He hated them in fact: they had no elegance.

Now Mary had elegance. Though she was a bit odd, she had elegance. It was true that the villagers didn't understand her but that was because she read many books, her father having been a teacher. And on the other hand she made no concessions to anybody. She seemed to be saying, 'You can take me or leave me.' She never gossiped. She was proud and distant. She had a world of her own. She paid for everything on the nail. She was quite well off. But her world was her own, depending on none.

She was very fond of children and used to make up masks for them at Hallowe'en. As well as this she would walk by herself at night, which argued that she was romantic. And it was said that she had sudden bursts of rage which too might be the sign of a spirit without servility. One couldn't marry a clod.

Murdo stared at the door and as he looked at it he seemed to be drawn inside it into its deep caves with all sorts of veins and passages. It was like a magic door out of the village but at the same time it pulsed with a deep red light which made it appear alive. It was all very odd and very puzzling, to think that a red door could make such a difference to house and moors and streams.

Solid and heavy he stood in front of it in his wellingtons, scratching his head. But the red door was not a mirror and he couldn't see himself in it. Rather he was sucked into it as if it were a place of heat and colour and reality. But it was different and it was his.

It was true that the villagers when they woke would see it and perhaps make fun of it, and would advise him to repaint it. They might not even want him in the village if he insisted on having a red door. Still they could all have red doors if they wanted to. Or they could hunt him out of the village.

Hunt him out of the village? He paused for a moment, stunned by the thought. It had never occurred to him that he could leave the village, especially at his age, forty-six. But then other people had left the village and some had prospered though it was true that many had failed. As for himself, he could work hard, he had always done so. And perhaps he had never really belonged to the village. Perhaps his belonging had been like the Hallowe'en mask. If he were a true villager would he like the door so much? Other villagers would have been angry if their door had been painted red in the night, their anger reflected in the red door, but he didn't feel at all angry, in fact he felt admiration that someone should actually have thought of this, should actually have seen the possibility of a red door, in a green and black landscape.

He felt a certain childlikeness stirring within him as if he were on Christmas day stealing barefooted over the cold red linoleum to the stocking hanging at the chimney, to see if Santa Claus had come in the night while he slept.

Having studied the door for a while and having had a long look round the village which was rousing itself to a new day, repetitive as all the previous ones, he turned into the house. He ate his breakfast and thinking carefully and joyously and having washed the dishes he set off to see Mary though in fact it was still early.

His wellingtons creaked among the sparkling frost. Its virginal new diamonds glittered around him, millions of them. Before he knocked on her door he looked at his own door from a distance. It shone bravely against the frost and the drab patches without frost or snow. There was pride and spirit about it. It had emerged out of the old and the habitual, brightly and vulnerably. It said, 'Please let me live my own life.' He knocked on the door.

The Button

One day the old man and the old woman stopped talking to each other. They sat for a lot of the time in the same room but they didn't speak. She would make the breakfast and the dinner and the tea and lay them at regular times on the table and they would both sit and eat but they remained silent. Neither would pass anything to the other, but each would stretch across to get the salt or the pepper or whatever was required. At night they would go to bed and turn their backs on each other and go to sleep.

And yet in their early days they had been lovers. They had married young and gone through life together as other couples had done. They had a house of their own and in those days they would discuss what furniture they should buy for it. They would go out and visit and talk to other people. They had a garden where flowers grew every summer and withered every autumn. They were the same age, grew up together and no one was surprised when they married, as they seemed destined for each other. They had children and he worked at his work and came home every night. They sometimes joked and sometimes quarrelled and sometimes they took life very seriously.

Then one day in their old age ceased to speak to each other. It was as if they had no longer anything to say to each other, as if they had run out of thoughts, and so their minds became secretive and inward. They each had dreams of what they might have done differently but they concealed these dreams from each other. He would sometimes read the newspaper and she would sew and they wouldn't speak. And in a strange way they felt comfortable with each other, their silence was not bristling and hostile, it was a silence of emptiness. It was as if they were waiting for the grave into which they would be lowered. Nothing particular had happened to cause this, they hadn't had a major quarrel. They were like clocks which had run down.

When someone came to visit them, which was rare, they spoke to the visitor but wouldn't speak directly to each other. The visitors noticed this and stayed away in order not to embarrass them. They didn't know what to make of it all since they themselves couldn't imagine a world without speech. Who could imagine it?

It was a most peculiar situation and yet after a while it became natural to the two of them. They would brush past each other on their way to a room and ignore each other as if each were a wardrobe or a chair or a table. They had in fact become like pieces of walking breathing furniture. And they did not feel this as an emptiness or a tragedy. The world had long become opaque to them. It had gone past the stage of significance or even of being a game. It simply was and they simply were. Perhaps after all they were closer to being plants. They almost ceased being aware of each other. And in a sense they gained a kind of freedom from this silence, though it was not a fruitful or creative silence. It was a silence of surrender. Speech had made them tired and they simply ceased being tired. This silence would have gone on for a long time except for a strange trivial accident, if accident it was. The old man always wore a jacket with three buttons on it. It was a grey jacket and he had worn it for thirty years. It was frayed in places and it had been repaired here and there. One day the old woman noticed that one of the buttons was hanging by a thread. For some reason this disturbed her and she wished to sew the button on again. The trouble was however that her husband wore the woollen jacket to bed as it was winter time and he never took it off. He even left his shirt on and sometimes his tie. Every day and every night she would see this button which was a black one hanging by the single thread and it became an obsession with her. She was afraid that the button would fall off and she would never be able to find it again. She would follow him about looking down at the floor or at the ground to make sure that it hadn't fallen. She almost spoke to him in order to point out the danger to the button. But in fact he seemed completely unconscious that the button was about to fall off. He had always been like that, not caring what condition his clothes were in. Often in the past she had to tell him to wear a fresh suit when he went out visiting. For he really genuinely didn't care how he was dressed. The button, black and round, became an obsession. She could see it in her dreams. It expanded and filled her consciousness. And sublimely ignorant of her thoughts he went about, not caring what happened to the button. She grew angry and simmered quietly. Why on earth couldn't he pay attention to important things like that? If he had only two buttons instead of three he would look untidy and people would think that she wasn't looking after him. But even that was not what bothered her. What really bothered her like a toothache was the lack of symmetry. It was the lowest of the three buttons and he would look silly walking about with the lower part of his jacket spread wide. The black button became as large as a globe. It became a whole earth, round and fatal and trivial. It hung from a single thread and at any moment the thread might snap. The button would fall to the ground and she would never see it again. There would never again be found a button exactly like that one. Also, her sight wasn't very good and if the button fell she would probably never find it again. Sometimes she had the greatest difficulty in not stretching forward and seizing hold of the button and tearing it off so that she could keep it and sew it on later in the summer months when he might shed the jacket. In the morning she would look for the button in case it had fallen off in the bed at night. And sublimely indifferent to what was happening to him, her husband would continue in his sloppiness, making the silence untidy and incomplete. What could one say about him except that he was insensitive, that he did not understand her feelings, that no matter how hard she looked at the button he didn't seem to notice, that he didn't appreciate the importance of the button in the universe but carried on reading his newspaper? Of what importance was the newspaper in comparison with the button? It was like an aching tooth whose pain could not be relieved. The world went by as an accident without speech but the button belonged to the past, it had a position in space, it demanded this position in space, it agonised and throbbed in this position. It was more important to her than anything in the whole world. She watched it as she might watch a sick child, she thought about it sleeplessly all night as her husband slept, or turned so extravagantly and thoughtlessly in his bed. She hung on the button as on the speech of a lover. No, it was no good, it would drive her mad.

One morning when she saw that the thread was about to snap she said to him, breaking the silence, 'I think that button needs to be sewn again or you'll lose it.'

He looked at her in surprise and then, like her, returned from the world of silence with regret and sorrow as if he had come home from a holiday in the unknown. After that they talked to each other as before. The button was sewn close to his woollen jacket. She no longer even noticed it, it had become part of the world of things. But they never again went back to their world of silence. They had come home again.

Murdo's Application for a Bursary

Dear Sir,

I wish to apply for a bursary from you in order that I may complete my book **Down the Mean Streets of Portree**. This is a detective story in which the private eye is a member of the Free Church. His name is Sam Spaid, and he is a convinced Presbyterian. I do not see why the Catholics should have Father Brown and we Protestants nobody. I have written a few pages, which I enclose. These are only a first draft and I hope to complicate the cases further by introducing the idea of Predestination and the Elect, etc. This first case is called 'The Mess of Pottage'.

I notice from your letter that you require a referee to substantiate my application. As you will understand, I live here in a very isolated situation, and referees who are competent to judge my work are thin on the ground. I thought at first of the headmaster and the minister, but the headmaster for various complicated reasons does not speak to me, and the minister would not approve of my novel. I have, however, a neighbour who is a simple crofter and whose name is Malcolm Campbell. He is an honest man, owner of a few acres of land, and he is quite willing to be my referee. Please excuse his writing as he is not one of these people who will put his signature to anything. He has a view of life which is unsophisticated and true. Thus though he does not understand the finer minutiae of my work, he knows me well enough to appreciate that I would not put in false claims. He is a regular reader of the Bible and Robert Burns and some selected parts of Spurgeon, and what better literary background could one have? Also he wishes me to get the grant as I owe him a trifling sum for certain repairs he made to my draughty house some time ago. I have tidied up this application a little as he left school at 15 years of age. It is good, as you will appreciate, to have such staunch friends in adversity.

I see also that you require a note of income. Last year I made £200 altogether. Most of this was the income from a Short Story Competition which I ran, in order to encourage Scottish Writing. The rest was in the form of a workshop on "In Memoriams" which was not as lucrative as I expected.

I have other projects as well. One of my stories requires that Sam Spaid go to Peru in order to capture a criminal who has been trying to undercut the Bible market. I hope to apply for a Travel Grant for that, as of course I would need to study the laws, the social mores, etc, for authentic detail. There is a scene where Sam Spaid confronts a Peruvian god which will require considerable research. I am at the moment trying to find out how much bed and breakfast costs in Lima. Another project of mine involves a visit by Sam Spaid to Israel. This has to do with a secret weapon a crazed member of the Free Church congregation is importing in stages from a fanatical Jewish sect. I will, however, keep in touch with you about this.

There is one other project I am working on as well. In past years some of the islanders when working with The Hudson Bay Company, married and brought home Cree women. Now, the psychology of these women when confronted by our island ways has not been sufficiently investigated. Was the Cree woman frightened, puzzled, enthralled? Did her thoughts return to tepees, pipes of peace, tomahawks, memories of buffalo, etc? There is much research to be done on this; indeed none at all has been done.

It is not enough to say that perhaps only two such women appeared on the island. Two is quite enough for my financial purposes, and if numbers were to be the final arbiter what would we say of the victory of the heavily outnumbered Athenians at Marathon. And furthermore on such a premise our ideas of democracy would be in dire jeopardy, as a moment's thought is enough to show. How indeed are the thoughts, griefs, joys, etc, of one Cree woman any less important than our own? She too had her ambitions, melancholy, and elations. She too had her fears and her hopes. As she saw the sun rise in the morning over the Muirneag, memories of her home on the plain must have returned to her, of her aged chieftain father, various mothers, and so on. And she must also have thought of the young brave from whom her religious husband tore her, to take her to a strange and barbarous island where a minority language was spoken. As you can see, therefore, I have many projects on hand.

I also note that you require a track record of publication. The reason why I have published nothing is very clear. First of all, I am a perfectionist and secondly I am not greatly impressed by the magazines I see on bookstalls. Their stories and poems seem to me to lack a central plan such as I myself have, though I have not put it on paper yet. This vision glimmers before me day and night, and I try in vain to grasp it. It seems to me that these inferior writers have grasped their ideas and put them on paper too soon. Decades, generations, centuries, are not enough for me to grasp this vision. And indeed only my need for financial security – for bread, payment of council tax, payment of new carpet – forces me to frame it in a narrow compass now. It is for visions such as these that you should be paying, intangible, magnificent visions which indeed may come to nothing, but which on the other hand may result in unexpected masterpieces. I often feel that you are lacking in faith, if I may venture a criticism, and that you snatch at the inferior manuscript when you should be supporting the visionary and as yet unwritten text.

However, that is by the bye, and I hope I have not offended you in any way. Beggars such as I cannot be choosers, and great, though as yet unidentified success, leaves a salt taste on the tongue. A pair of trousers, a slice of bread, may be lost by true and sincere criticism. Furthermore, there are many talents born to blush unseen and waste their sweetness on the desert air. It might be that had your organisation existed in the eighteenth century, Robert Burns might have applied for a bursary and lived to a hale old age, where he would have written companions to such deathless poems as "To a Mouse". And John Keats might have done the same as well. And Shelley, if he had not been drowned.

If you will bear with me for a moment I will share with you my vision of what an Arts Council should be. Instead of asking for samples and incomes, it should be a source of largesse. It should be the DHSS of the aspiring writer till such time as he can get into print. For he may – and this is where the act of faith comes in – write a masterpiece. Could an early Arts Council have foreseen Paradise Lost or The Divine Comedy? Did even Homer see the Iliad in advance? The logic is irrefutable. The Arts Council should give a bursary to all applicants in case a potential Catullus is neglected.

I return to democracy again. Even one Lucretius or Sir Thomas Wyatt would be a justification of such a policy. Therefore, I appeal to you in the name of such a vision, open your purses: give, give, give, even to those who cannot provide samples, but who have exciting visions of the future. For it may be that by asking for samples you are toadying to the opportunist and the materialist. Is it not in fact in his interests to provide such samples? Are there not inducements for him to do so? But what of the awkward unspeaking one, who is possessed by a vision that he cannot put on paper. What of him? Is he to be ignored in favour of the smooth con-man? Those great inarticulate ones of whom the Statue of Liberty speaks, are they not to be brought to your arms? – I think they are.

I say, think of these things, and I hope also that this letter is not too long, and that what I have said may be taken on board. I know that inflation eats into your budget and I know also that the going rate for a bursary at the moment is £5,000.

Yours in anticipation,,
Murdo Macrae

The Mess of Pottage

Sam Spaid was reading the second chapter of Deuteronomy when there was a timid knock at the door.

'Come in,' he shouted, closing his Bible reluctantly.

A small woman, wearing a black hat, black coat, and shoes from Macdonald and Sons, Portree, entered. She stood with her hands folded, her gaze fixed on the floor, away from the great detective. He recognised her at once: she was Annie Macleod who sat three rows behind him in the church every Sunday.

'You look ill,' he said, 'would you like a cup of water? I don't keep coffee.'

'No thank you,' she said.

'Is there anything wrong?' he said, drawing out for her the chair he kept for clients, for he knew at once that she was a client.

How can she afford me, he thought, but put the thought away from him at once.

Suddenly she said, 'It's my husband Donnie. He's run away.'

Donnie, he thought, that sinful atheist. Aloud, he said, 'Run away?'

'I know he has. He left a note saying, "I've had enough".'

Sam took the note, but not before he had equipped himself with a pair of black woollen gloves, also from Macdonald and Sons, Portree.

'You are sure this is his handwriting?'

'Yes I am sure. You will notice his spelling of "enuff".'

'I see,' said Sam. 'I can tell little from this note except that it is from the edge of a newspaper, and that it is clearly the work of a disturbed man. What is this?' and he lent forward, scenting a clue. 'A spot of red.'

'It might be blood,' said Annie timidly. 'He might have cut himself shaving.'

'Not while he wrote the note,' said Sam contemptuously. 'No, this spot is something more sinister than that. However, you may continue.'

His eyes took in the woman's worn coat. No, there would not be much money to be made from this case.

'After all I have done for him.' said Annie, taking out a small white handkerchief and dabbing her eyes. 'It was I who introduced him to the blessing of the Gospel. I used to read a chapter of the Bible to him every night. I talked to him about his sinful life. Whenever he was backsliding I prayed for his soul.'

'And?' said Sam keenly.

'Recently I noticed a change in him. When I read to him he would stare into space or click his teeth. Sometimes he would mutter to himself. He spent a lot of time in his room. I think he had a woman in there.'

'What makes you think that?'

'Perfume, powder, things like that.'

'Who could this woman be? Did he go out much?'

'He didn't go out at all. I also found a pile of magazines under his bed. Unspeakable. Naked men and women . . . ' She paused for a moment.

'You did not bring them with you?' said Sam.

'No, I did not think you . . . '

'They would have been evidence,' said Sam curtly. Why did he have to tell these people everything? Why, since the Clearances, could they not think for themselves? He felt his toothache beginning again. He wanted to hit this woman. Why don't you fight? he wanted to shout at her.

'Did you bring a photograph?' he asked.

'No, I thought you knew . . . '

'I do, I do, but a photograph would have been useful. People change, you know.'

'But you only saw him last week.'

'Did I? Maybe I did. But I wasn't observing. Observation is everything.' Again he felt a twinge of hatred for this woman who was sitting so docilely in front of him.

'How long have you been married?' he asked irrelevantly.

'Thirty years. I met him when I was coming out of the Claymore Hotel. He was in fact drunk and shouting at the people who were passing. From that moment I decided to save him. I was thirty-five, and all my suitors had left me because I was too religious.'

'So you are in fact older than him.'

'By ten years. But that was not a barrier at first,' and she smiled.

Enough of this, you contemptible woman, Sam thought bitterly. He himself had been married once, but his wife had left him when he had become a detective. Her figure with its black costume, and shoes from Macdonald and Sons, Portree, haunted him still. He pushed the thought away from him.

'I charge £20 a day plus expenses,' he said sharply.

'£20 a day. But how could I . . . Donnie was on the dole and I have my pension.'

'Do you want him back or don't you?' said Sam in a frenzy of rage, though his voice was outwardly calm. He felt a twinge of his arthritis starting. Out of the window he could see people making their way to the Coop next door as if nothing was happening. This is my domain, he meditated, this is the mean street down which I must go. This is where I must come to, after my childhood. He pondered the delights of predestination.

'I will find the money somehow,' said Annie pathetically.

'Good,' said Sam. 'Now you may go.' As she left he had the most intense desire to throw at her the paperweight that was lying on the desk. Highlanders! Would they never learn to give correct efficient evidence? Would they always accept their fate? Why would they not fight for their identity? For their language?

He adjusted his bowler hat and suit from Macdonald and Sons, as he stared into the sinful mirror in front of him. He threw a last look at the photograph of the Rev. John Macdonald which sat on the wall, and made his way down to the pier, where the ferry was waiting.

'Any news?' said Norman MacMillan, who had a pile of tickets in his hand.

'Only the good news of the Gospel,' said Sam curtly. 'I would like to ask you, when did you see Donnie Macleod last?'

'Donnie Macleod,' said Norman a few times.

(You slow thinking spud, thought Sam savagely, are you some kind of inanimate cabbage? He wanted to kick Norman MacMillan in the shin.)

The wheel of Norman's mind ground to a halt. 'Yes,' he said. 'Funnily enough I saw him yesterday. He was on the ferry.'

'Was he carrying a case?' asked Sam.

There was another long silence in which Sam visualised a torture machine of the most marvellous complexity.

'He was, and I thought it funny at the time.'

(Why did you think it funny at the time? He was on a ferry, wasn't he?)

'Did he look worried?'

'Worried? Worried? Worried? No, he didn't look worried. He said a strange thing to me though. A very strange thing. You must know that I do not know Donnie well. He hasn't left the house for years. His father, as you remember, was that Angus Macleod who went suddenly mad and jumped over the side of the ferry . . . '

(These oral stories, thought Sam savagely. This tradition they pride themselves on – how can a detective exist in such an environment. His eye rested on a bollard and he wished he could heave it out of the stone and hammer Norman's bald head with it.)

' . . . not of course that many people speak about it now. But anyway he was standing just about where you are, or perhaps a little to the left, and he said, "A change is good for a man", just as I was taking his ticket and he was making his way to the ferry. And he looked odd.'

'Odd. What do you mean by odd?'

'What do I mean by odd? I mean odd. His eyes were flashing. That's the only way I can describe it. Flashing.'

(You retarded idiot, thought Sam. That's the only way you can describe it. Of course it is. You were never well-known for your discriminate style.)

'And then,' Norman said, leaning forward and speaking in a whisper, 'his very words were, "A change is good for a man." ' Norman withdrew his head so quickly that he nearly butted Sam in the face, while at the same time his left eye winked rapidly at the great detective.

'He looked devilish,' said Norman, 'and another thing. He came very close to me.'

'Did he do that before?'

'Not as close as that, not as close as that.'

'I see,' said Sam, who did not see at all. What had this to do with anything? (You winking parrot, he thought fiercely.)

'How much will my ticket be?' he asked.

'Same as always,' said Norman, and laughed uproariously. 'Same as always.'

Sam threw a gaze of hatred after him as he made his way to the nonsmoking saloon where he sat very upright and watched a child making faces at him.

Devilish, he thought. Devilish. So Donnie was on the ferry after all. He hadn't been killed by Annie, of whom Sam was suspicious from the very beginning because her hair was shorter than the church of St. Paul strictly allowed.

When the ferry docked he strode over to the bus and sat in the back seat. He closed his eyes, feeling suddenly that his blood pressure was rising. He made a mental note that he must take more exercise. His contempt for the easy-going Highland way of life was beginning, he knew, to affect his health.

When he opened his eyes he was horrified to see straight ahead of him above the driver's head a screen on which there was a picture of a man and a woman in a naked embrace. For a moment he was worried that this was the content of his sinful mind, but when he looked about him he saw that the passengers were following the film with interest.

Without thinking, he strode down the aisle and said to the driver, 'I want you to turn that filth off at once.'

The driver, manoeuvring equably between a foreign car and a truck, said, 'I can't do that sir. The passengers are watching it.'

'And I am not a passenger, then?'

The driver considered this, chewing gum all the while – he was in fact quite young, and he wore a uniform and a pair of boots from Macdonald and Sons – and then said, 'I suppose you are, in a manner of speaking.'

'What do you mean, in a manner of speaking?' said Sam loudly. He wanted to kill this young man, he wanted to wrench his bones apart, he wanted to spatter his blood all over the bus.

While he was standing there, a large man with a red face touched him lightly on the shoulder, 'Had you not better sit down, Papa? The rest of us can't see the screen.'

Sam turned round abruptly. He should really kick this man in the groin, but on the other hand reasoning might be better.

'This is pornographic filth,' he said. 'This man should be ashamed of showing it.'

'We like pornographic filth,' said the large man simply. 'Don't we?' and he turned to the other passengers. There was a chorus of 'yes'.

'You tell that bowler-hatted nyaff to sit down,' said a woman with red hair, who was sitting in one of the middle seats.

'You tell him to sit down or you will kick his balls in,' said a fat woman with a fat chin, who was sitting in the front seat.

'You sit there, Papa,' he said, 'We don't want to put you out.'

I will report that driver, thought Sam, in incoherent rage. I will report him and hope that he will be dismissed from his job and turned out on to the street of whatever town he lives in. I wish to see him starving and indigent, begging for food, subservient, humble, asking for mercy as the whip lashes his back.

He maintained a resentful silence till the bus pulled into the bus station at Inverness, imagining only the large man's flesh dripping from his bones in hell. He then got off the bus in the same silence, making a note, however, of its number. He should have slugged that bus driver, and that large man. He felt a familiar contempt: his toothache throbbed, his arthritis hurt, his blood pressure was rising, and now he felt a pain just above his heart.

When he was biting into the pie which he had bought at the café at the bus station, he belched. Thank God it wasn't his heart, it was indigestion. He looked around him savagely. The usual crowd of nonentities, fodder of the Clearances, remnants of the '45. He felt such unutterable contempt that he almost vomited on the spot. The good ones had gone to America and now he was left with illogical dross, who winked their eyes and seemed to have a secretive tradition which they would only tell after eons of time had elapsed. 'You should do something about your salt,' he said to the proprietor as he left, and felt the deep satisfaction which his parting shot had given.

The question however still remained. Had Donnie stayed in Inverness, or had he gone further afield? He felt a sudden pain in his kidneys and went into the lavatory at the side of the café. After he had finished he looked around him for a towel but there was none available.

'You use that machine over there,' said a young man with a grin.

Sam pushed the button on the machine but finding that no towel came out of it he left in the worst of humours.

What else could he do but parade the streets of Inverness.

If it hadn't been for that film he could have questioned the bus driver about Donnie Macleod. But he could not ask a pervert for information and in any case he would have lied to him. I have to assume that he is still in Inverness, he thought, there is nothing else that I can do. I have to rely on the intuition of the great detective. I feel in my bones that he is still here.

In comparison with Portree, Inverness was a metropolis. He counted ten churches before giving up: the Woolworths too was larger. Feeling tired, he sat down on a bench for a while. He took a blue tablet from his pocket and swallowed it; it should keep his thrombosis at bay.

A man who appeared to be a beggar came and asked him for money for a cup of tea.

'No, thank you,' said Sam. The beggar looked at him for a moment and then scuttled away.

Sam gazed straight ahead of him at what appeared to be a

cinema, and whose lights flashed intermittently. A moment's thought however told him that it was not a cinema. It was in fact some kind of a club as he deduced from the large green letters which said 'THE MESS OF POTTAGE'. It suddenly seemed to him certain that he would find Donnie Macleod in there. He had no logical means of knowing this, only the mystical intuition of the great detective that he was.

He walked over to the building. Behind a glass screen sat a large woman who was wearing black lipstick.

'One ticket,' he said crisply. 'That will be enough.'

'Adult?' said the woman in a husky voice.

He disdained answering her; he had taken an instant dislike to her from the moment he saw her. But, more than that, he was suddenly struck by an intuition as he looked at her naked neck and almost naked breasts. He couldn't quite focus on what it was but it told him he had come to the right place.

He left the lobby and going through a door ahead he found himself in a large smoky room, in fact Sodom and Gomorrah. The noise was frightening. Dancers clung closely to each other. Some people were drinking at tables. On a stage a large, almost naked, woman was prancing. So this was what the Highlands had come to after the Clearances. So this was what the '45 had done to the people. So this was the result of the sheep runs and the deer forests.

If it hadn't been for his instinctive desire to pursue his investigations, he would have left at once. He touched his bowler hat as if for comfort.

As he stood there hesitating, a large woman wearing red lipstick and tottering on the sharp heels of her shoes (Armstrong and Brothers, Inverness) came up to him and said in a deep attractive voice, 'Are you not dancing, darling?' And before he could say anything he was dragged into the maelstrom of light and noise.

'Where do you come from?' asked his partner, against whose naked breast Sam's bowler hat bobbed like a cork in a stormy sea. He couldn't account for his hatred of her, but said sharply, 'Portree.'

'Portree, darling. Over the sea to Skye and so on.' (Her

cliché immediately offended him. Why, wherever one went nowadays, could one never get a really satisfactory religious discussion?) Her mouth yawned, surrounded by a red infernal line.

'Do you always wear a bowler hat when you are dancing?' she asked.

'Always,' said Sam.

'How flip, what an ironic comment you are making on our contemporary society,' said the large woman. 'You must be a satirist, rather like Juvenal.'

Not another pagan writer, thought Sam savagely. Why not one of the prophets such as Micah? But no one ever mentioned Micah or Jeremiah.

The large woman made as if to kiss Sam. He turned his head away from a breath that stank like garlic.

'Has "THE MESS OF POTTAGE" been here long? he forced himself to say, trying to wriggle away from her hand which rested on his rump. A thrill of horror pervaded him.

'Who knows, darling?' So many questions, so few answers.

Her shadowy chin bent over him and suddenly the solution to the case was as clear to him as a psalm book on a pew on a summer day. He withdrew rapidly from the woman's embrace and made his way to the exit, the sign for which hung green above his head.

'I knew it,' he said to the receptionist, 'I knew I had seen you before. The hair on your chest registered subconsciously.'

'It is true,' said Donnie. 'You have run me to ground. I suppose it was Annie who hired you . . . '

'It was indeed,' said Sam. (You ungrateful pervert, he muttered under his breath.) He wanted to crush Donnie into a pulp. So he had been right after all. That red spot beside the word 'enuff' had been lipstick, not blood.

'I couldn't stand it any longer,' the vicious serpent was saying. 'I was tired of hearing Leviticus and especially Numbers. You have no idea what it was like. If I had stayed I would have gone mad.' (You horrible atheist!) 'I couldn't distinguish between the Amalekites and the Philistines.' (You pathetic heretic!) 'When sitting at the table I would have an impulse to stab

Annie with a knife. I knew there was no future for us. I saw this job in the paper and applied for it.' (You belly-crawling snake!)

So this was why Donnie had said to that ineffable boring ferryman, 'A change is good for a man.' So this was why he had looked devilish.

'I won't go back,' said Donnie simply, 'I'm happy here. I love my new dresses. Pink was always my favourite colour.'

'You used to dress up in your bedroom,' said Sam.

'How did you know that?'

Sam ignored the question. After a while, Donnie said, 'You are a marvellous detective, the best in Portree. But you can tell Annie I will not go back. I have made a new life for myself here, and Jim and I have fallen in love. Tell her that if it hadn't been Leviticus it would have been someone else.'

Sam Spaid looked into Donnie's blue eyes, thinking many thoughts. His gaze rested on the rose in his corsage. Then he sighed deeply. 'I think you are taking the wrong course,' he said. 'But I cannot take you back by force, much as I would like to. You will have to give me something in your handwriting that will show Annie that I met you.'

'Yes indeed,' said Donnie, taking a pen from his purse of tinselly yellow. He wrote rapidly, and Sam read what he had written.

> *'Annie, you're a good woman. Too good for me. I shall think of you as a sister.*
>   *Signed Deborah.'*

'Deborah,' said Sam between his teeth.

'Yes, I have changed my name. Jim didn't like the name "Donnie".'

Sam put his hand out to Deborah (Donnie) while at the same time he was thinking that he should kick her (him) in the teeth.

'Goodbye,' he said. 'And may you learn more about those fleshpots than you know now.'

As he left 'THE MESS OF POTTAGE' he was thinking that he would not make much from this case – his fee, and his expenses, which were the rates for the ferry and the bus.

He would have to try and find some more complicated cases. Little did he know that there was one waiting for him which would be known as 'The Case of The Disappearing Pulpit' and which would push his logical powers to the limit, and bring him expenses to the devil-possessed village of Acharacle.

The Old Woman and the Rat

When the old woman went into the barn she saw the rat and she also saw the feathers of the little yellow chicken among which the rat was sitting. It was a large grey rat and its whiskers quivered. She knew that there was no way out for it but past her, for there was a hole between the door and the wall and she knew that this was the place where the rat had entered. She regretted that she had not filled this up before. It seemed that the rat was mocking her but certainly it knew that she was present. And it also knew that the chickens had belonged to her, those beautiful little chickens of bright yellow which she had nursed so carefully and which had seemed so much the sign of a new spring. The day was Easter Friday.

As she gazed at the rat she felt a ladder of distaste shudder up her spine climbed by many rats, but she stood where she was and then bent down slowly to pick up a plank of wood with nails at one end of it. Her back ached as she bent. The barn itself was large, spacious and clean with a stone floor. At the far end were the remains of the chickens and the hens. Above were the rafters on which hung an old mouldy saddle which her father had once had for the horses. It hung its wings on both sides of the rafter. She thought, and then quite deliberately she stuffed it, mouldy and breaking as it was, into the hole which the rat had entered by. All this while the rat watched her with bright intelligent eyes as if it knew perfectly well what she was up to. The arena was prepared, the large clean spacious arena. She made her way rather fearfully towards the rat. She felt rather unsteady but angry. After all, she was quite old and she had arthritis in her hands and she had varicose veins in her legs. The rat certainly was fitter than her, more agile, more swift. She advanced on the rat steadily with her plank, the nailed end foremost. It waited, almost contemptuously. She went up to it and thrust the plank at it. It moved rapidly away and crouched, looking at her, its long rat tail behind it, its whiskers quivering, its bright eyes moving hither and thither. Where have you been? she thought. Before the chickens, where have you been? She thought of her husband, dead in the cemetery, and closed her eyes. She deliberately made visions of flowers appear.

She thought. Then slowly she went over to a big disused table which she had put in the barn many years before and propped it up on end, to cut off part of the space. But that was useless for the rat immediately climbed up to its top and stood there slightly swaying and half smiling. For the first time as she looked up at it she thought that it might leap down at her from above and this frightened her. She was also frightened that her fear might be communicated to the rat which might then attack her. She backed away from the rat slowly, thinking. What a terrible thing to have this battle when she could be in church, but then some things were more important even than church. She backed towards the door still holding the short nailed plank ahead of her. She pulled the door slowly behind her and backed out, shutting the door quickly. She was determined that the rat would not escape. She almost felt the rat's claws in her back as she turned away but she knew that it was still there in the barn with the remains of its feast, its obscene supper. She went into the house and got a box of matches. Then she went round the side of the house in the great calm of the morning and got a lot of straw and grass, all of which was dry because of the blue cloudless weather. She felt happy now that she had something to do. But clutching her masses of grass and straw and with the box of matches in the pocket of her apron she was slightly frightened entering the bare arena again. Still it was better to be bare than not, for one knew where one was then. She felt in her mouth the tiny fragile bones of the chickens, and the taste of the blood. She slowly opened the door and edged in with all that grass and straw. The rat stayed where it was, licking its body. She threw the straw and the grass as far towards it as she could and then rapidly picked up the plank with the nails again, her back vibrating with terror. The rat watched her, more uneasily now, as if wondering what she was up to. She lit the match nervously and threw the lighted flame among the dry straw and the grass. The fire ran along it boiling like illuminated rats. The rat backed away into its corner, snarling. Smoke began to rise and billow round it, for there must have been some dampness at the centre of the straw somewhere. She backed towards the door. The rat rushed out through the smoke towards her, its teeth drawn back. Behind the rat she saw the flames rising and the smoke. It seemed to have emerged out of, been generated by, the fire. The rat made for the place where she had stuffed the remains of the broken winged saddle. As it did so she swiped at it with the nailed plank. It squirmed away, half hit. It turned and faced her snarling as if it knew that she was the only obstacle to its escape. Its face looked incredibly fierce and evil as if all the desire for life had been concentrated there. It wished to live at all costs. For a moment she was terrified at what she had done, at the smoking arena she was in. But she knew that the stone floor would prevent the fire from spreading. The rat launched itself at her, knowing that she was the enemy, that there was no going back through the smoke. She swung the nailed plank as its face, snarling and distorted, looked towards her, and she felt it hit the rat, felt the rat's claws scrabbling against it as if it wanted to get purchase on it, to grip it and climb towards her. She swung the plank against the floor and banged and banged. The rat's head and body squelched against the stone floor of the barn which had once been filled with sacks of corn. She banged and banged till the shudders left her back and breast and legs. She banged it so that it was a flat grey mess on the floor. Then after a while flushed and panting she opened the door on the wide day. She threw the plank as far away as she could into the undergrowth. There were bits of rat attached to it. No doubt the birds of the air would finish it off. She forced herself to get a spade to detach the smashed body from the floor. She threw the mashed carcass from the spade into the bushes as well and then fetched pail after pail of water which she splashed over the place where the body had been. She cleaned and cleaned till there was not even the shadow of the rat left. When the straw had finally burned itself out she took that away as well, and the remains of the chicken and the hens which had themselves got burnt. She spent a long time cleaning the barn, making it bright as new. When she had finished she went into the house and made herself strong tea. It was too late for church now. Still she could go there in the evening. Meanwhile she could sleep for a while by the window, for she felt empty and victorious. As she passed her mirror she saw that her face looked gaunt and fulfilled, and she hadn't felt so light for a long time.

The Crater

In the intervals of inaction it had been decided by the invisible powers that minor raids were feasible and therefore to be recommended. In the words of the directive: 'For reasons known to you we are for the moment acting on the defensive so far as serious operations are concerned but this should not preclude the planning of local attacks on a comparatively small scale . . . '

Like the rest of his men on that particular night, Lieutenant Robert Mackinnon blackened his face so that in the dugout eyes showed white, as in a Black Minstrel show. He kept thinking how similar it all was to a play in which he had once taken part, and how the jokes before the performance had the same nervous high-pitched quality, as they prepared to go out into the darkness. There was Sergeant Smith who had been directed to write home to the next of kin to relate the heroism of a piece of earth which had been accidentally shattered by shrapnel. His teeth grinned whitely beneath his moustache as he adjusted the equipment of one of the privates and joked, 'Tomorrow you might get home, lad.' They all knew what that meant and they all longed for a minor wound – nothing serious – which would allow them to be sent home honourably. And yet Smith himself had been invalided home and come back. 'I missed your stink, lads,' he had said when he appeared among them again, large and buoyant and happy. And everyone knew that this was his place where he would stay till he was killed or till the war ended.

'I remember,' he used to tell them, 'we came to this house once. It was among a lot of trees, you understand. I don't know their names so don't ask me. Well, the house was rotten with Boche and we'd fired at it all day. And the buggers fired back.

Towards evening – it might have been 1800 hours – they stopped firing and it got so quiet you could hear yourself breathing. One of our blokes – a small madman from Wales, I think it was – dashed across and threw a grenade or two in the door and the window. And there wasn't a sound from inside the house, 'part from the explosion of course, so he kept shouting, "The Boche are off, lads," in that sing-song Welsh of his. So we all rushed the place and true enough they'd mostly gone. Run out of ammunition, I suppose. We went over it for mines but there wasn't none. So we stood in the hall, I suppose you'd call it, all of us with our dirty great boots and our rifles and bayonets and there was these stairs going up, very wide. The windows were shot to hell and there was glass all over the place. And suddenly – this is God's truth – an old woman come down the stairs. Dressed in white she was, a lovely dress like you'd see in a picture. And her lips all painted red. You'd think she was dressed for a ball. Her eyes were queer, they seemed to go right through you as if you wasn't there. She came down the last steps and our officer stepped forward to help her. And do you know what she did? She put her arms around him and she started to waltz. He was so surprised he didn't know what to do – the fat bugger. And all the time there was this music. Well, in the end he got away from her and some people took her away. Well, we could still hear this music, see? So we goes upstairs – there was a dead Boche on the landing, he'd been shot in the mouth – and we goes into this room. There was a bed there with a pink what-do-you-call-it over it. And beside the bed there was this big dead Boche. And do you know what – there was a dagger with jewels in it stuck in his breastbone. And beside him on the floor there was this phonograph playing a French tune, one of the officers said. He said it was a dance tune. Someone said it was bloody lucky the little fat fellow wasn't wearing a grey uniform.'

'All present and correct, sir,' said Sergeant Smith.

'All right, let's go then,' said Lieutenant Mackinnon.

Down the trench they went, teeth and eyes grinning, clattering over the duckboards with their Mills bombs and their bayonets and their guns. 'What am I doing here?' thought Robert, and 'Who the hell is making that noise?' and 'Is the damned wire cut or not?' and 'We are like a bunch of actors,' and 'I'm leading these men, I'm an officer.'

And he thought again, 'I hope the guns have cut that barbed wire.'

Then he and they inched across No Man's Land following the line of lime which had been laid to guide them. Up above were the stars and the air was cool on their faces. But there were only a few stars, the night was mostly dark, and clouds covered the moon. Momentarily he had an idea of a huge mind breeding thought after thought, star after star, a mind which hid in daylight in modesty or hauteur but which at night worked out staggering problems, pouring its undifferentiated power over the earth.

On hands and knees he squirmed forward, the others behind him. This was his first raid and he thought, 'I am frightened.' But it was different from being out in the open on a battlefield. It was an older fear, the fear of being buried in the earth, the fear of wandering through eternal passageways and meeting grey figures like weasels and fighting with them in the darkness. He tested the wire. Thank God it had been cut. And then he thought, 'Will we need the ladders?' The sides of the trenches were so deep sometimes that ladders were necessary to get out again. And as he crawled towards the German trenches he had a vision of Germans crawling beneath British trenches undermining them. A transparent imagined web hung below him in the darkness quivering with grey spiders.

He looked at his illuminated watch. The time was right. Then they were in the German trenches. The rest was a series of thrustings and flashes. Once he thought he saw or imagined he saw from outside a dugout a man sitting inside reading a book. It was like looking through a train window into a house before the house disappears. There were Mills bombs, hackings of bayonets, scurryings and breathings as of rats. A white face towered above him, his pistol exploded and the face disappeared. There was a terrible stink all around him, and the flowing of blood. Then there was a long silence. Back. They must get back. He passed the order along. And then they wriggled back again avoiding the craters which lay around them, created by shells, and which were full of slimy water. If they fell into one of these they would be drowned. As he looked, shells began to fall into them sending up huge spouts of water. Over the parapet. They were over the parapet. Crouched they had run and scrambled and were over. Two of them were carrying a third. They stumbled down the trench. There were more wounded than he had thought. Wright ... one arm seemed to have been shot off. Sergeant Smith was bending over him. 'You'll get sent home all right,' he was saying. Some of the men were tugging at their equipment and talking feverishly. Young Ellis was lying down, blood pouring from his mouth. Harris said, 'Morrison's in the crater.'

He and Sergeant Smith looked at each other. They were both thinking the same: there is no point, he's had it. They could see each other's eyes glaring whitely through the black, but could not tell the expression on the faces. The shells were still falling, drumming and shaking the earth. All these craters out there, these dead moons.

'Do you know which one?' said Robert.

'I think so, sir, I ... Are you going to get him?'

'Sergeant Smith, we'll need our rifles. He can hang on to that if he's there. Harris, come with us.' They were all looking at him with sombre black faces, Wright divided between joy and pain.

'Sir.'

Then they were at the parapet again, shells exploding all around them.

'Which one is it?' And the stars were now clearer. Slowly they edged towards the rim. How had he managed to break away from the white lime?

They listened like doctors to a heartbeat.

'Are you there, Fred?' Harris whispered fiercely, as if he were in church. 'Are you there?' Lights illuminated their faces. There was no sound.

'Are you sure this is the right one?' Robert asked fiercely.

'I thought it was. I don't know.'

'Oh, Christ,' said Sergeant Smith.

'We'd better get back then,' said Robert.

'Are you going to leave him, sir?' said Harris.

'We can't do anything till morning. He may be in one of the shallower ones.' His cry of 'Morrison, are you there?' was drowned by the shriek of a shell.

'Back to the trench again,' he said, and again they squirmed along. But at that moment as they approached the parapet he seemed to hear it, a cry coming from deep in the earth around him, or within him, a cry of such despair as he had never heard in his life before. And it seemed to come from everywhere at once, from all the craters, their slimy green rings, from one direction, then from another. The other two had stopped as well to listen.

Once more he heard it. It sounded like someone crying 'Help'.

He stopped. 'All right,' he said. 'We're going for him. Come on.'

And he stood up. There was no reason for crawling any more. The night was clear. And they would have to hurry. And the other two stood up as well when they saw him doing so. He couldn't leave a man to die in the pit of green slime. 'We'll run,' he said. And they ran to the first one and listened. They cried fiercely, 'Are you there?' But there was no answer. Then they seemed to hear it from the next one and they were at that one soon too, peering down into the green slime, illuminated by moonlight. But there was no answer. There was one left and they made for that one. They screamed again, in the sound of the shells, and they seemed to hear an answer. They heard what seemed to be a bubbling. 'Are you there?' said Robert, bending down and listening. 'Can you get over here?' They could hear splashing and deep below them breathing, frantic breathing as if someone was frightened to death. 'It's all right,' he said, 'if you come over here, I'll send my rifle down. You two hang on to me,' he said to the others. He was terrified. That depth, that green depth. Was it Morrison down there, after all? He hadn't spoken. The splashings came closer. The voice was like an animal's repeating endlessly a mixture of curses and prayers. Robert hung over the edge of the crater. 'For Christ's sake don't let me go,' he said to the other two. It wasn't right that a man should die in green slime. He hung over the rim holding his rifle down. He felt it being caught, as if there was a great fish at the end of a line. He felt it moving. And the others hung at his heels, like a chain. The moon shone suddenly out between two clouds and in that moment he saw it, a body covered with greenish slime, an obscene mermaid, hanging on to his rifle while the two eyes, white in the green face, shone upward and the mouth, gritted, tried not to let the blood through. It was a monster of the deep, it was a sight so terrible that he nearly fell. He was about to say, 'It's no good, he's dying,' but something prevented him from saying it, if he said it then he would never forget it. He knew that. The hands clung to the rifle below in the slime. The others pulled behind him. 'For Christ's sake hang on to the rifle,' he said to the monster below. 'Don't let go.' And it seemed to be emerging from the deep, setting its feet against the side of the crater, all green, all mottled, like a disease. It climbed as if up a mountainside in the stench. It hung there against the wall. 'Hold on,' he said. 'Hold on.' His whole body was concentrated. This man must not fall down again into that lake. The death would be too terrible. The face was coming over the side of the crater, the teeth gritted, blood at the mouth. It hung there for a long moment and then the three of them had got him over the side. He felt like cheering, standing up in the light of No Man's Land and cheering. Sergeant Smith was kneeling down beside the body, his ear to the heart. It was like a body which might have come from space, green and illuminated and slimy. And over it poured the merciless moonlight.

'Come on,' he said to the other two. And at that moment Sergeant Smith said, 'He's dead.'

'Dead?' There was a long pause. 'Well, take him in anyway. We're not leaving him here. We'll take him in. At least he didn't die in that bloody lake.' They lifted him up between them and they walked to the trench. 'I'm bloody well not crawling,' said Robert. 'We'll walk. And to hell with the lot of them.' He couldn't prevent himself swearing and at the same time despising himself for swearing. What would Sergeant Smith think of him? It was like bringing a huge green fish back to the lines. 'To hell with them,' he shouted. 'This time we'll bloody well walk. I don't care how light it is.' And they did so and managed to get him back into the dugout. They laid him down on the floor and glared around them at the silent men.

'Just like Piccadilly it was,' said Harris, who couldn't stop talking. 'As bright as day.'

'Shut up, you lot,' said Sergeant Smith, 'and get some sleep.'

Robert was thinking of the man he had seen reading a book in a flash of light before they had gone in with their bayonets. He couldn't see properly whether it had been a novel or a comic. Perhaps it was a German comic. Did Germans have comics? Like that green body emerging out of the slime, that fish. He began to shiver and said, 'Give the men whisky if there is any.' But he fell asleep before he could get any himself, seeing page after page of comics set before him, like red windows, and in one there was a greenish monster and in another a woman dancing with a fat officer. Overhead the shells still exploded, and the water bounced now and again from the craters.

'The bloody idiot,' said Sergeant Smith looking down at him. 'He could have got us all killed.' Still, it had been like Piccadilly right enough. Full of light. It hadn't been so bad. Nothing was as bad as you feared.

The House

In Oban in Scotland there is an unfinished circular many-windowed tower which dominates the town. It was built by a local banking family in order to give employment to the townspeople at a time when there was not much work to be had. Modelled on the Colosseum, statues of the bankers were to be placed in the windows and possibly, for all one knows, illuminated at night. But in fact for some reason – it may be that there was not enough money or it may be that death intervened – the tower was never completed and remains to this day, an object of curiosity to the many tourists who come from all over the world. It is very high up and the walk there is long but pleasant. When one arrives inside the empty structure one can walk across the circular grassy floor and hear, if it is a day in spring or summer, the birds trilling close at hand, or one can perch on the sill of one of the windows and look down at the sea which glitters in the distance. It is said that a certain lady was once looking for the Colosseum in Italy and tried to find out where it was by describing it as that building which is modelled on McCaig's Tower in Oban.

But in fact in our own village when I was growing up there was a house which had been unfinished for a long time though of course it was not so large as this tower. It was being built by the family of the Macraes over many years and no one remembers when it was begun though there are legends about it. The first Macrae, it is said, spent his entire life gathering huge boulders from wherever he could find them and hammering away at them like a sculptor to prepare them for the house. He was, it is also said, a very large strong fellow who killed a man who made mock of his dream house, not a stone of which had actually been laid. The two men, the

Macrae and the other, fought, so it is said, for a whole day till eventually Macrae got his opponent on the ground and banged away at his head with a large stone which he was actually going to use in the building of the house. After that, no one made fun of his project. He died of a stroke with the hammer in his hand.

The next Macrae was a dreamier type of person. He himself didn't attempt any of the actual building but employed some workers to do it. The trouble was that he had so many ideas and plans, some appearing in his head simultaneously, that they had to pull down what they had built almost as soon as they had built it.

Also they drank and smoked when they should have been working and continually asked for higher wages which he refused to give them. At one time he would want the house to merge into the landscape, at another he would want it to stand out from it since he was subject to varying moods of submission and domination. They say that he would walk around dressed in very bright colours shouting at his workmen in fragments of Italian which he had picked up from a guidebook. The workers naturally thought that he was mad.

One of the inhabitants of the village – actually the schoolmaster – called him Penelope partly because of his dainty effeminate air, but also because he was pulling down each morning what had been erected the night before. But this Macrae, whose name was Norman, didn't care. He went his way, carried a whip, and liked nothing better than to order his workers about though they paid little attention to him. There seemed, otherwise, little purpose in his life. He didn't believe in God or the Bible and said once that things existed to be changed every day in order to prevent boredom. In fact he would have nothing to do with the detailed plans which his massive father had drafted out and wouldn't even look at them. He would sometimes say that he wasn't necessarily his father's son, a comment which caused some gossip in the village as in fact his father had been a man who liked women and was a bit of a Lothario.

When Norman died all that had been accomplished was that

half the gable had been built. Norman had wanted to have an engraving set in the stone which would show a horse with an eagle's head but had died before this could be started. The only reason he could give for creating such an engraving was that he liked eagles and horses, though in fact he had only seen an eagle once in his whole lifetime, and that was in a painting. The villagers didn't like him as much as they had liked his father, though he had harmed them less, and had not, like his father, fornicated with many of their pliant daughters. They didn't understand his statements for he could say that truth can be revealed as much in a green door as a red one, and that men's shoes are being worn out each day. However when there was a sickness in the village he had helped them out with corn and fish though he openly despised all of them and called most of them superfluous.

The next Macrae – Donald – was different again from Norman. He was a gloomy man who always wore dark clothes and spent most of his time reading his grandfather's plans in a small room of his house. He also hired workers but kept them at it. The trouble was that he could never find the exact kind of stone that he wanted for the house, and all the stone that he did find locally was, according to him, soft and inferior. He spent much money on importing stone and because it was so expensive he became poorer and poorer but succeeded at last in adding another wall in which a long narrow lugubrious window was set. Sometimes he would sit with his elongated head and body at this window gazing across the village or brooding or reading a theological book. He would tell the villagers that they must prepare for their deaths and that they were merely like the lilies of the field. It did not escape their notice however that he got as much money from them as he could. He said that the house he was building was like a temple which would last forever and that it would glorify them all, poor as they were. Did they not wish to see some solid building erected among their poor thatched houses? They would gaze down at the ground, their caps in their hands, but say nothing since they couldn't understand a word he was saying. What with his theological books and his stones he spent practically all his money and the family's money and he died at fifty years old, a religious recluse who would suddenly emerge from his house and shout at the workmen that they weren't worthy of their hire. Then he would mutter to himself and go back into his gloomy room where he would read till the early hours of the morning. No one had a good word to say for him for he would say things like, 'You have no sense of excellence' to their faces. At one time he even started a school in competition with the one already there, but after a while no one would attend it for he would never allow any of the pupils out during school hours in contrast to the teacher in the other school who used to take the children out to pick flowers and berries.

The Macrae I knew – the son of this one – was a large jovial fat man who dressed in a brown canvas blouse. Day after day he would set off with his wheelbarrow and bring back a huge boulder which he would lever on to the ground in order to add another part of the wall to the house, which by now had three walls and a stone floor and three windows. The trouble with Iain Macrae was that he liked children and when they danced round making fun of his house which would never in their opinion be finished, he would look at them with a merry smile and tell them stories. When he was doing this, his expression would become wonderfully tender and he would gaze into the distance over their heads as if he were seeing a most beautiful serene sight. He would completely abandon any work on his house and begin, 'Last night I was walking across the moor looking for a boulder when I saw an owl sitting on a stone reading a book.' The children would gather round him open-mouthed and cease to play pranks. He was really a very lazy fat man who seemed to move heavily like a large solid cloud. When he was asked why he didn't abandon the house altogether he would say, 'One must have something to do. Even if it's no good.' And he would smile a sad clownish smile. He was liked in the village as he would do anything for anyone at any time and would wholly neglect his own affairs in order to help. When he was on his death-bed he was making jokes about his coffin and saying that they must get him a large one. At one time he would say that it should be made of stone, but at other times he preferred wood since it changed so much, whereas stone never changed, and this was its weakness. In fact he didn't care about the quality of the stone he trundled along in his wheelbarrow and sometimes he would forget which stone he ought to have been using at a particular time. 'We all have something to do,' he would say, 'and this was what was left to me. I couldn't live in this house,' he would add, 'if it was finished. I would admire it from a distance.' And so another wall and another window would be slowly added in the interval of telling stories to the children. But the people grew used to seeing this unfinished structure and praised God that their own houses were wind and rain proof and tightly made. He also died as a result of wheeling a stone along. He fell on his face while torrents of blood poured out of his mouth, and stained the ground. He wasn't long on his death-bed where he grew very thin and meagre so that no one would ever have thought that he had weighed fifteen stone and could tell interesting stories to children, who as a mark of respect gathered a bunch of flowers and laid them on his grave.

His son was a brisker thinner man who decided that the house must be finished once and for all. He had grown up in the knowledge that his father had been, to a certain extent, a figure of fun and was determined that he himself would not be humorous or play the clown for anybody. For this reason he would rise early in the morning and start on the house. The village would resound to his hammering day after day. He never ceased working. He was also resolute that he would do all the work himself. It is true that he couldn't handle a hammer as well as his forebears but what he lost in skill he made up for in determination. 'One should never leave a job incomplete,' he would say, staring you straight in the eye. 'Never. It is immoral. Laziness is immoral.' And as most of the villagers were themselves lazy, standing at the corners of their houses with their hands in their pockets most of the day, he wasn't liked much. 'I have other things I must do after this is completed,' he would say. And so he would work like a slave. People said that he would kill himself but in fact he didn't. He seemed to be very tough physically and never once had an illness while he was building the house, though he worked in the rain and sometimes in the snow.

Eventually one morning he finished it. People thought that he would have a celebration party but he didn't. He wasn't the kind of man who cared for sentiment. But when the house was completed it was noticed that he would stand looking at it and then move onward and look at it from another angle. A depression hung over the village. The villagers had thought that they would be glad when the house was finished but they weren't. It was partly because it wasn't as good as they had expected (after all builders had been working at it for a hundred years at least and perhaps even longer than that) and in comparison with their dreams it looked more ordinary than they had expected. They didn't quite know what they had expected, but they had certainly expected a structure more elaborate and elegant than they got. It seemed to be saying that after all man's imagination is much the same everywhere.

But the real trouble was that they didn't have so much to talk about. In the past if there was a pause in the conversation they would start to tell some story about That House or if they didn't have actual stories about it they would invent some. In any case the village seemed to grow gloomier and gloomier. Some of them wanted to smash the house down so that it could be started all over again. But of course they wouldn't do that for they were all basically law-abiding people. But they grew to hate the last of the Macraes, who was called William. And as he sensed this he began to avoid them. He too grew tired of looking at the house in which he had begun to live. He had bought very ordinary furniture for it, and all the usual conveniences of a house, and in fact made it look very common and not to be distinguished from the other houses of the village except that it was a stone house. People would say how different he was from his forefathers and what fine ideas they had had, and what plans and ideals they had nursed. William tried to mix with them but not very successfully since, though he enquired about their families, they knew that fundamentally he wasn't interested. Obscurely they felt that they had been betrayed. Was all their legend-making to end up like this after all, with this very ordinary house which seemed to answer very trivial problems? Why, because it was lived in, the house didn't even have any ghosts! The villagers had even been cheated of that! They looked forward to William's death and for this reason hoped that he would not marry, since they would then have the freedom to do with the house what their imaginations wished. They actively discouraged any girl in the village from marrying him, though at the same time they were worried lest he should import a wife from somewhere else. But in fact he showed no sign of doing that. On the contrary, he would sit in the house brooding for hours and it was even rumoured that he wished to pull the house down and start again. But all the zest had left him – perhaps he had overworked too long – and he remained where he was in his ordinary house with the ordinary curtains and the ordinary carpets and furniture.

He died of some form of melancholia. After his death, all the furniture and carpets etc. were sold by a dull-looking niece of his from outside the island who had no intention of coming back. The house remained empty since there was no one who wanted to buy it and a satisfactory series of legends began to blossom around it, most of them having to do with mysterious lights at windows, men reading Bibles in a greenish light or telling stories to phantom children. Stories were freely invented and the best of them survived and the worst perished. The most mysterious statement they found was in one of the books which the second Macrae had kept. It read, 'When all the lies have been answered, other lies will have to be invented.' The villagers thought that in inventing legends they were being true to the early founders of the house and looked at it as women will stand at a church door watching the bride coming out and dreaming that she at least will begin a race of uncorrupted children, not realising that for this to happen she must be a virgin of the purest blood.

A September Day

It was a day in autumn when I came home from school in Stornoway, a town which was seven miles from the village. The sky was a perfect blue, and the corn was yellow and as yet uncut. I left the bus at the bottom of the road and walked the rest of the way home. I was eleven years old, and I wore short trousers and a woollen jersey both of which my mother had made for me. Even as I write, the movement of the fresh air on my legs returns to me, and the red radiance of the heather all about me. Every day I went to Stornoway on the bus and every day I came back. I began to think of myself as more sophisticated than the villagers. Didn't I know all about Pythagoras's Theorem and was I not immersed in the history of other nations as well as my own?

As I walked along the road I looked down at the thatched house where old Meg stayed. Sometimes one would see her coming from the shop with her red bloomers down about her big red fat legs. She went home to a house full of cats, hungry, ragged, vicious. Today there was no smoke from her chimney: perhaps she was lying in her bed. Her breath was much shorter than it used to be.

Outside his house old Malcolm was sharpening his scythe. I shouted, 'Hullo' to him and the scythe momentarily glittered in the sun as he turned towards me. His wife like a small figure on a Dutch clock came out and threw a basinful of water on the grass. 'Hullo,' I shouted as I felt myself coming home. Old Malcolm shouted in Gaelic that it was a fine day, and then spat on his hands.

The village returned to me again, every house, every wall, every ditch. It was so very different from Stornoway whose houses were crowded together, whose sea was thickly populated with fishing boats. I knew practically every stone in the village. At the same time I knew so much that didn't belong to the village at all.

Head bent over his scythe, Malcolm sharpened the blade, and I made my way home to the little house in which we lived. Very distantly I heard a cock crow in the middle of the afternoon, a traditional sign of bad luck. After it had crowed a dog barked and then another dog and then another one. Ahead of me stretched the sea, a big blue plate that swelled to the horizon on which a lone ship was moving.

'Huh, so you're home,' said my mother, 'you took your time.'

As my mother hardly ever went to town I came home to her as if from another land. She made me work at my books but the work I was doing was beyond her. Nevertheless she knew with a deep instinctive knowledge that learning was the road to the sort of reasonable life that she had never had.

'You're just in time to go out to the shop for me,' she said. 'You can have your tea when you come back. Get me some sugar and tea.'

I put my bag down on the oil-skinned table and took the money she gave me. I didn't particularly like to go to the shop, but at the same time I didn't strenuously object. As I was walking along the road I met Daial who had come home from the village school. Now that I had gone to the town school I was warier with him than I had been in the past. He asked me if I wanted a game of football and I said that I had to go on a message for my mother. He snorted and went back into his house.

When I had passed him, I met old deaf Mrs Macleod. She shouted at me as if against a gale, in Gaelic, 'And how is Iain today? You're the clever one, aren't you? Ask your mother if she wants to buy any milk. Anything going on in the town?'

I said I didn't know of anything. She came up and said, 'Your mother made that jersey, didn't she? I wonder what kind of wool it is. Your mother is a very good knitter.'

I squirmed under her hands. 'I'll have to get the pattern from her sometime,' she shouted into my ear. I almost felt my knees reddening with embarrassment.

When I left her I ran and ran, as if I wished to escape somewhere. Why were people always poking and probing? And yet I had been flattered when she said that I was the clever one.

I arrived at the shop and waited my turn. The shop sold everything from sugar to paraffin to methylated spirits for our Tilleys. Seonaid was talking to the woman who owned the shop and saying, 'Did you hear if war is declared yet? I'll take two loaves.'

'No,' said the other one.

I was gazing at the conversation sweets in the jars, and wished that I had money to buy some, but we were too poor.

'Nugget, did you say?' said the woman who owned the shop.

'Black,' said Seonaid. 'They won't wear brown shoes. Everything black or navy blue.'

'That's right,' said the shop owner. 'No, I never heard anything about the war.'

'That man Chamberlain always carries an umbrella,' said Seonaid. 'You'd think it was raining all the time.'

She turned to me and said, 'And how is Iain today? You're getting taller every time I see you. And are you doing well at the school?'

I murmured something under my breath but she soon forgot about me. I went to the door of the shop and I saw Peggy, a girl of my own age who was wearing a yellow dress. She also went to the village school.

'Hullo,' I said to her.

'Hullo,' she said, looking at me with a slant laughing eye.

She was wearing sandals and her legs were brown. It was a long time since I had seen her and now I couldn't think of anything to say to her. She had used to sit beside me in Miss Taylor's class. She was the prettiest girl in the school. Once I had even written notes to her which Miss Taylor had never seen.

'Did you hear if war is declared?' I asked her, trying to look very wise.

'No,' she said, staring at me as if I were mad. Then she began to rub one sandal against the other.

'Are you liking the town school?' she asked, looking at me aslant and half giggling.

'It's all right,' I said. And then again. 'It's OK. We gamble with pennies,' I added. 'The school is ten times as big as the village school.'

Her eyes rounded with astonishment, but then she said, 'I bet I wouldn't like it.'

At that moment I looked up into the sky and saw a plane passing.

'That's an aeroplane,' I said.

'I bet you don't know what kind it is,' said Peggy.

I was angry that I didn't know.

Suddenly Peggy dashed away at full speed shouting at the top of her voice, 'Townie, townie, townie.'

I went back into the shop lest anyone should see me. I was mad and ashamed, especially as I had loved Peggy so much in the past.

When I got home my mother said that I had taken my time, hadn't I? She began to talk about her brother who had been in a war in Egypt. 'He was a sergeant,' she said. 'But this time,' she continued, 'all the young ones will be in the war.'

I thought of myself as a pilot swooping from the sky on a German plane, my machine gun stuttering. I was the leader of a squadron of aeroplanes, and after I had shot the enemy pilot down I waggled the wings of my plane in final salute. He and I were chivalrous foes, though we would never recognise each other of because of the goggles.

'There's Tormod who'll have to go and Murchadh and Iain Beag.' She reeled off a list of names. 'There won't be anyone left in the village except old men and old women. I was in the First World War myself, at the munitions. Peggy was with me, and one time she pulled the communication cord of the train,' and she began to laugh, remembering it all, so that she suddenly looked very young and girlish instead of stern and unsmiling.

'The ones here will all go to the navy,' she said.

I hoped that the war wouldn't stop before I was old enough to join the RAF, or perhaps the army.

When I had finished my tea I went out. Daial was waiting and we went and played a game of football. Daial was winning and I said that one of the goals he claimed he had scored shouldn't be counted because the ball wasn't over the line. We glared at each other and were about to fight when he said he wouldn't count it after all. After we had stopped playing we began to wrestle and he had me pinned to the ground shouting, 'Surrender.' But I managed to roll away and then I had his arms locked and I was staring into his face while my legs rested on his stomach. Our two faces glared at each other, very close, so that I could see his reddening, and I could hear his breathing, Eventually I let him up and we ran a race, which he won.

I felt restless as if something was about to happen. It was as if the whole village was waiting for some frightening news. Now and again I would see two women talking earnestly together, their mouths going click, click, click.

I tried to do some homework but ships and planes came between me and my geometry. I was standing on the deck of a ship which was slowly capsizing, looking at the boats which were pulling away. Not far from me there was a German U-boat. I remained on the deck for I knew that a captain always went down with his ship. The U-boat commander saluted me and I saluted him back. The water began to climb over my sandals, and my teeth chattered with the cold. I knew that the rest of the British Navy would avenge my death and that my heroic resistance would appear in the story books.

I looked up and my mother was standing looking at me with an odd expression on her face. However, all she said was, 'Get on with your lessons.'

'You wait,' I thought, 'you will read about me someday. Your sergeant brother won't be in it.'

I went out to the door, and saw Tinkan hammering a post into the ground. The hammer rose and fell and it looked as if he had been hammering for ever, his head bald as a stone bent down so that he didn't see me. In the distance I heard someone whistling. Why had Peggy called me a townie: there was no reason for that. But I would show her. Some day she would hear that I had died bravely winning the Victoria Cross or perhaps the Distinguished Conduct Medal. She would regret calling me a townie and in fact she might even show some of our notes to the man who came to write about me. Displacing the adverts on the front page of the local paper would be massive headlines: 'Local Hero Goes Down Fighting.'

I went over to the house next door and talked to Big Donald who as usual was wearing a blue jersey. He told me, 'There's no doubt of it. There will be a war in a day or two. No doubt of it,' he said, spitting into the fire. The globs of tobacco spit sizzled for a moment and then died. 'No doubt of it,' he said. 'And you'll see this village bare.'

'Thank God I don't have to go,' he said. 'But if I had been younger . . . ' and he made a sign as if he were cutting someone's throat with a knife. 'The Boche,' he said, 'were all right. But I didn't like the Frenchies. You couldn't trust a Frenchie. The Boche were good soldiers.' And he sighed heavily. 'Sometimes,' he added, 'we called him Fritz. But there's no doubt. We'll be at war in two or three days.'

I left him and stood at the door of our house before going in. I felt that something strange was about to happen, as if some disturbance was about to take place. Another plane crossed the sky and I stared up at it. It looked free and glittering in the sky, a quaint insect that buzzed up there by itself.

'Why aren't you coming in?' said my mother.

'I'm coming,' I shouted back, and as I shouted a dog barked.

I felt obscurely that the village would never be the same again, and it seemed to me that the standing stones which stood out in silhouette against the sky a mile behind our house had moved in the gathering twilight, with a stony purposeful motion.

'I'm coming,' I shouted again.

I went in and my mother arose from the table at which she had been sitting. She suddenly looked helpless and old and I thought she had been crying. 'Bloody Germans,' I thought viciously.

Suddenly my mother clutched me desperately in her arms

and said, 'You'll have to carry on with your studying just the same.'

'Yes,' I said.

I trembled in her arms like the needle on a gauge. I was rocking in her arms like a ship in the waves. Ahead of me through the window I could see the red sun setting like a cannon ball.

The Painter

We only once had a painter in our village in all the time that
I can remember. His name was William Murray and he had
always been a sickly, delicate, rather beautiful boy who was
the only son of a widow. Ever since he was a child he had
been painting or drawing because of some secret compulsion
and the villagers had always encouraged him. He used to
paint scenes of the village at harvest time when we were all
scything the corn, or cutting it with sickles, and there is no
doubt that the canvas had a fine golden sheen with a light
such as we had never seen before. At other times he would
make pictures of the village in the winter when there was a lot
of snow on the moor and the hills and it was climbing up the
sides of the houses so that there was in the painting a calm
fairytale atmosphere. He would paint our dogs – who were
nearly all collies – with great fidelity to nature, and once he
did a particularly faithful picture of a sheep which had been
found out on the moor with its eyes eaten by a crow. He also
did paintings of the children dressed in their gay flowery
clothes, and once he did a strange picture of an empty sack of
flour which hung in the air like a spook.

We all liked him in those days and bought some of his
pictures for small sums of money since his mother was poor.
We felt a certain responsibility towards him also since he was
sickly, and many maintained that he wouldn't live very long,
as he was so clever. So our houses were decorated with his
colourful paintings and if any stranger came to the village we
always pointed to the paintings with great pride and mentioned
the painter as one of our greatest assets. No other village that
we knew of had a painter at all, not even an adult painter, and
we had a wonderful artist who was also very young. It is true

that once or twice he made us uncomfortable for he insisted on painting things as they were, and he made our village less glamorous on the whole than we would have liked it to appear. Our houses weren't as narrow and crooked as he made them seem in his paintings, nor did our villagers look so spindly and thin. Nor was our cemetery, for instance, so confused and weird. And certainly it wasn't in the centre of the village as he had placed it.

He was a strange boy, seeming much older than his years. He hardly ever spoke and not because there was anything wrong with him but because it seemed as if there was nothing much that he wished to say. He dressed in a very slapdash manner and often had holes in the knees of his trousers, and paint all over his blouse. He would spend days trying to paint a particular house or old wall or the head of an old woman or old man. But as we had a lot of old people in the village, some who could play musical instruments – especially the melodeon – extremely well, he didn't stand out as a queer person. There is, however, one incident that I shall always remember.

Our village of course was not a wholly harmonious place. It had its share of barbarism and violence. Sometimes people quarrelled about land and much less often about women. Once there was a prolonged controversy about a right of way. But the incident I was talking about happened like this. There was in the village a man called Red Roderick who had got his name because of his red hair. As is often the case with men with red hair he was also a man of fiery temper, as they say. He drank a lot and would often go uptown on Saturday nights and come home roaring drunk, and march about the village singing.

He was in fact a very good strong singer but less so when he was drunk. He spent most of his time either working on his croft or weaving in his shed and had a poor thin wife given to bouts of asthma whom he regularly beat up when it suited him and when he was in a bad temper. His wife was the daughter of Big Angus who had been a famous fisherman in his youth but who had settled down to become a crofter and who was famed for his great strength though at this time he was getting old. In fact I suppose he must have been about seventy years old.

His daughter's name was Anna and during the course of most days she seemed to be baking a lot without much result. You would also find her quite often with a dripping plate and a soggy dishcloth in her hand. She had seven children all at various stages of random development and with running noses throughout both summer and winter.

It must be said that, when sober, Red Roderick was a very kind man, fond of his children and picking them up on his shoulders and showing them off to people and saying how much they weighed and how clever and strong they were, though in fact none of them was any of these things, for they were in fact skinny and underweight and tending to have blotches and spots on their faces and necks. In those moments he would say that he was content with his life and that no one had better children or better land than he had. When he was sunny-tempered he was the life and soul of the village and up to all sorts of mischief, singing songs happily in a very loud and melodious voice which revealed great depth of feeling. That was why it seemed so strange when he got drunk. His whole character would change and he would grow violent and morose and snarl at anyone near him, especially the weakest and most inoffensive people.

One thing that we noticed was that he seemed very jealous of his father-in-law who had, as I have said, a reputation in the village for feats of strength. It was said that he had once pulled a cart loaded with peat out of a deep muddy rut many years before when he was in his prime, but now that he was ageing and wifeless he lived on more failingly from day to day, since after all what else is there to do but that?

Red Roderick in his drunken bouts would say that it was time the 'old devil' died so that he might inherit something through his wife, since there were no other relations alive. Red Roderick would brood about his inheritance and sometimes when he was drunk he would go past his father-in-law's house and shout insults at him. He brooded and grew angry, the more so since his father-in-law's land was richer than his own and better looked after, and also there were a number of sheep and cows which he coveted. I sometimes think that this must have been how things were in the days of the Old Testament, though it doesn't mention that people in those days drank heavily unless perhaps in Sodom and Gomorrah.

His whole mind was set on his inheritance mainly because he regretted marrying the old man's daughter who, in his opinion, had brought him nothing but a brood of children whom in his drunken moments he despised and punished for offences that they had never even committed. Yet, as I said, in his sunny moments there was no one as gay and popular as he was, full of fine interesting stories and inventions.

However, I am coming to my story. One day he went to town in the morning (which was unusual for him) and came home in the afternoon on the bus, very drunk indeed. This was in fact the first time he had been drunk during the day, as it were, in the village, and we all thought that this was rather ominous, especially as he began by prowling around his own house like a tiger, sending one of his children spinning with a blow to the face in full sight of the village. The trouble was that all the villagers were frightened of him since none of them was as strong as he was in those moments of madness.

After he had paced about outside his house for a while shouting and throwing things, he seemed to make up his mind and went down to the byre from which he emerged with a scythe. At first I thought – since I was his neighbour – that he was going to scythe the corn but this was not at all what was in his mind. No, he set off with the scythe in his hand towards his father-in-law's house. I remember as he walked along that the scythe glittered in his hand as if it was made of glass. When he got to the house he shouted out to the old man that it was time he came out and fought like a man, if he was as great as people said he had been in the past. There was, apart from his voice, a great silence all over the village which drowsed in the sun as he made his challenge. The day in fact was so calm that there was an atmosphere as if one was in church, and it seemed that he was disturbing it in exactly the same way as a shouting lunatic might do who entered a church during a service.

One or two people said that someone should go for a policeman but no one in fact did. In any case looking back on it now

I think that in a strange shameful way we were looking forward to the result of the challenge as if it would be a break in an endless routine. Nevertheless there was something really frightening and irresponsible about Red Roderick that day as if all the poison that seethed about his system had emerged to the surface as cloudy dregs will float upwards to the surface of bad liquor. Strangely enough – in response to the shouting, as in a Western – the old man did come out and he too had a scythe. He advanced towards Roderick, his eyes glittering with venom and hatred as if he too shared in the madness which was shattering the silence of the day. Then they began to fight.

As Red Roderick was drunk perhaps the advantage given him by relative youth was to a certain extent cancelled. There was however no doubt that he wished to kill the old man, so enraged was he, so frustrated by the life that tortured him. As they swung their scythes towards each other ponderously, it looked at first as if they could do little harm, and indeed it was odd to see them, as if each was trying to cut corn. However, after some time – while the face of the old man gradually grew more demoniac in a renewal of his youth – he succeeded at last in cutting his son-in-law's left leg so that he fell to the ground, his wife running towards him like an old hen, her skirts trailing the ground like broken wings.

But that was not what I meant to tell since the fight in itself, though unpleasant, was not evil. No, as I stood in the ring with the others, excited and horrified, I saw on the edge of the ring young William with his paint-brush and canvas and easel painting the fight. He was sitting comfortably on a chair which he had taken with him and there was no expression on his face at all but a cold clear intensity which bothered me. It seemed in a strange way as if we were asleep. As the scythes swung to and fro, as the faces of the antagonists became more and more contorted in the fury of battle, as their cheeks were suffused with blood and rage, and their teeth were drawn back in a snarl, he sat there painting the battle, nor at any time did he make any attempt to pull his chair back from the arena where they were engaged.

I cannot explain to you the feelings that seethed through me as I watched him. One feeling was partly admiration that he should be able to concentrate with such intensity that he didn't seem able to notice the danger he was in. The other feeling was one of the most bitter disgust as if I were watching a gaze that had gone beyond the human and which was as indifferent to the outcome as a hawk's might be. You may think I was wrong in what I did next. I deliberately came up behind him and upset the chair so that he fell down head over heels in the middle of a brush-stroke. He turned on me such a gaze of blind fury that I was reminded of a rat which had once leaped at me from a river bank, and he would have struck me but that I pinioned his arms behind his back. I would have beaten him if his mother hadn't come and taken him away, still snarling and weeping tears of rage. In spite of my almost religious fear at that moment, I tore the painting into small pieces and scattered them about the earth. Some people have since said that what I wanted to do was to protect the good name of the village but I must in all honesty say that that was not in my mind when I pushed the chair over. All that was in my mind was fury and disgust that this painter should have watched this fight with such cold concentration that he seemed to think that the fight had been set up for him to paint, much as a house exists or an old wall.

It is true that after this no one would speak to our wonderful painter; we felt in him a presence more disturbing that that of Red Roderick who did after all recover. So disturbed were we by the incident that we would not even retain the happy paintings he had once painted and which we had bought from him, those of the snow and the harvest, but tore them up and threw them on the dung heap. When he grew up the boy left the village and never returned. I do not know whether or not he has continued as a painter. I must say however that I have never regretted what I did that day and indeed I admire myself for having had the courage to do it when I remember that light, brooding with thunder, and see again in my mind's eye the varying expressions of lust and happiness on the faces of our villagers, many of whom are in their better moments decent and law-abiding men. But in any case it may be that what I was worried about was seeing the expression on my own face. Perhaps that was all it really was. And yet perhaps it wasn't that alone.

In Church

Lieutenant Colin Macleod looked up at the pure blue sky where there was a plane cruising overhead. He waved to the helmeted pilot. Here behind the lines the sound of the gunfire was faint and one could begin to use one's ears again, after the tremendous barrages which had seemed to destroy hearing itself. Idly he registered that the plane was a Vickers Gun Bus and he could see quite clearly the red, white and blue markings. The smoke rising in the far distance seemed to belong to another war. He had noticed often before how unreal a battle might become, how a man would suddenly spin round, throwing up his arms as if acting a part in a play: as in the early days when they had driven almost domestically to the front in buses, the men singing, so that he looked out the window to see if there were any shops at the side of the road. Released for a short while from the war he wandered into a wood whose trees looked like columns in a church.

He was thinking of the last bombardment by the Germans which had thrown up so much dust that the British gunners couldn't see what they were firing at and the Germans were on top of them before they knew what was happening. The only warning had been the mine explosion to their left. They had fought among trenches full of dead bodies, and grey Germans had poured out of the dust clouds, seeming larger than life, as if they had been resurrected out of the dry autumnal earth. It was after the plugging of the line with fresh troops that he and his company had been pulled out after what seemed like years in the trenches digging, putting up wire, in the eternal hammering of the German big guns, the artillery battles which were so much worse than local fights, for the death which came from the distant giants was anonymous and negligent as if gods were carelessly punching them out of existence.

He was grateful now for the silence and for the wood which had a certain semblance of order after the scarred ground worked over and over, continuously revised by shells, so that it looked like carbon paper scribbled over endlessly by a typewriter that never stopped.

He looked up again and as he did so he saw two birds attacking another one. They seemed to synchronise their movements and they were low enough for him to see their beaks quite clearly. The third tried to fly above them but they attacked, probing upwards from below. He could no longer see the plane, just the birds. The third bird was weakening. He couldn't make out whether it was a buzzard or a crow. The other two birds were zeroing in at it all the time, pecking and jabbing, going for the head.

He couldn't stand watching the fight any more and turned away into the wood, and it was then that he saw it – the church. It was completely intact though quite small and with gravestones beside it. It was strange to see it, like a mirage surrounded by trees whose brown leaves stirred faintly in the slight breeze. From the sky above, the birds had departed: perhaps the two had killed the third one or perhaps it had escaped. It reminded him of a dogfight he had seen between a German triplane and a British Sopwith Camel. After a long duel, the German triplane had destroyed the British plane but was in turn shot down by another British fighter. The triplane made a perfect landing. The British troops rushed up to find the pilot seated at the controls, upright, disciplined, aristocratic, eyes staring straight ahead, and perfectly dead. Later they found the bullet which had penetrated his back and come out at the chest.

He pushed open the door of the church and stood staring around him. He had never been in a church like this before with the large effigy of the Virgin Mary all in gold looking down at him, hands crossed. The stained glass windows had pictures of Christ in green carrying a staff and driving rather shapeless yellow sheep in front of him. In one of the panes there was another picture of him holding out his hands in either a helpless or a welcoming gesture. There were no Bibles or hymn books on the seats as if no one had been there for some time. At the side there was a curtained alcove which he thought might be a confessional. He pulled the curtains aside but there was no one there.

He sat down and gazed for a long time at the huge golden cross which dominated the front of the church. The silence was oppressive. It was not at all like the churches at home. There was more ornament, it was less bare, more decorated. The churches at home had little colour and less atmosphere than this. He could feel in his bones the presence of past generations of worshippers, and then he heard the footsteps.

He turned round to see a man in a black gown walking towards him. There was a belt of rope round his gown and his hands could not be seen as they seemed to be folded inside his gown. The face was pale and ill looking.

'What do you want, my son?' said the voice in English.

He was so astonished that he could think of nothing to say. To find a priest speaking English here seemed suddenly nightmarish. For some reason the thought came into his mind of the most macabre sight he had seen in the war, a horse wearing a gas mask. 'Childe Roland to the Dark Tower came ...'

'You are admiring the church?' said the minister or priest or whatever he was.

'It is very beautiful,' said Colin, and it seemed to him that his voice was echoing through the church.

'It is very old,' said the priest. 'How did you find it?'

'I was walking through the wood and I happened to ...'

'Alone? I see,' said the priest. 'Would you like to see the rest of it? There is more of it, you know.'

Colin looked round him uncomprehendingly.

'Oh, it's down below. There's a stair that leads downwards. I keep some wine down there, you understand. If you would care for a glass?'

'Well, I ...'

'It will only take a minute. I would be glad of the company.'

'If it's all ...'

'Certainly. Please follow me.'

Colin followed him down some stone steps to what appeared to be a crypt which was lit by candles. The priest walked with his hands folded in front of him as all priests seemed to walk, slow and dignified.

They arrived at a small room. 'Here is my bed, you see,' said the priest. 'And here . . . '

All over the floor, bones were scattered, and there seemed to be an assortment of bloody animal traps.

'Rabbit bones,' said the priest smiling. 'Bones of hares. It is not very . . . '

'You mean you . . . '

'This is how I live,' said the priest. 'I have no bread to offer you, I'm afraid. If you would please sit down?'

'I think I had better . . . '

'I said please sit down. I shall tell you about myself. I have lived now for a year by myself. Alone. What do you think of that?' The priest smiled showing blackened teeth. 'You see, I couldn't stand it any more.'

'Stand what?'

'The war, of course. I was in the trenches you see. And I couldn't stand it. I wasn't intended to be a soldier. I was studying for the ministry and they took me out here. I couldn't stand the people one got in the trenches. I couldn't stand the dirt and I couldn't stand all that dying. What do I live on? I eat rabbits, anything I can find. One morning, you see, I ran away. I didn't know where I was going. But I knew that I couldn't stay there any longer. And I found this place. Perhaps God directed me. Who knows? I was frightened that someone would find me. But no one did. I used to hide in the crypt here. But today I felt very alone so I thought I would talk to you. Do you know what it is to be alone? Sometimes I wish to go back but it is impossible now. To hear the sound of one human voice again! One human voice. I needn't have revealed I was here. If you had been German I wouldn't have come out. I don't speak German, you see, not at all. I'm not good at languages, though I did once study Hebrew. Now, shall we go up again?'

'If you wish.'

'I wish to preach. I have never preached. That is something I must do. Shall we go up? If you would go first? I was going to offer you something to eat but I think I should preach first. If you would please sit in the front row. You haven't brought anyone else with you, have you?'

Colin preceded him, knowing that he was in the presence of a madman. He sat down in the front seat and prepared to listen. He felt as if he were in a dream but then he had felt like that for a long time since he had taken the train south to join up in the first place.

The minister went up into the pulpit with great gravity and began to speak:

'I shall not pray because that would mean closing my eyes. God will understand. After all, while I was closing my eyes you might run away. I shall talk about war.

'Dearly beloved,' he began, his voice growing more resonant, not to say rotund, as he continued:

'May we consider who we are? What we are? When I was young I read books as so many of the young do about the legends of Greece and Rome. I believed in the gods. I believed that we are godlike. My favourite god was Mercury because of his great speed and power. Later my favourite hero was Hector because he was so vulnerable.

'I grew up innocent and hopeful. One night when I was sixteen years old I went to a prayer meeting. A visiting preacher spoke of Christ's sufferings and his mercy so vehemently, with such transparent passion, that I was transported into that world and I suffered the thorn and the vinegar in the land of Galilee. I thought that I should lay my life at the feet of a merciful God.

'At the age of eighteen I was forced into the army to fight for what they call one's country. I did not know what this was since my gaze was always directed inward and not outward. I was put among men whom I despised and feared – they fornicated and drank and spat and lived filthily. Yet they were my comrades in arms.

'I was being shot at by strangers. I was up to my knees in green slime. I was harassed by rats. I entered trenches to find the dead buried in the walls. Once, however, on a clear starry night at Christmas time we had a truce. This lasted into the following day. We – Germans and English – showed each other our photographs, though I had none. We, that is, the others, played football. And at the end of it a German officer came up to us and said: "You had better get back to your dugouts: we are starting a barrage at 1300 hours." He consulted his watch and we went back to our trenches after we had shaken hands with each other.

'One day I could bear no more of the killing and I ran away. And I came here, Lord. And now I should like to say something to you, Lord. I was never foolish enough to think that I understood your ways. Nevertheless I thought you were on the side of the good and the innocent. Now I no longer believe so. You may strike me dead with your lightning – I invite you to do so – but I think that will not happen. All these years, Lord, you have cheated me. You in your immense absence.' He paused a moment as if savouring the phrase. 'Your immense absence. As for me, I have been silent for a year without love, without hope. I have lived like an animal, I who was willing to give my all to you. Lord, do you know what it is to be alone? For in order to live we need language and human beings.

'I think, Lord, that I hate you. I hate you for inventing the world and then abandoning it. I hate you because you have not intervened to save the world.

'I hate you because you are as indifferent as the generals. I hate you because of my weakness.

'I hate you, God, because of what you have done to mankind.'

He stopped and looked at Colin as if he were asking him, Am I a good preacher or not?

'You have said,' said Colin after a long time, 'exactly what I would have said. I have no wish to . . . '

'Betray me? But you are an officer. It is your duty. What else can you do?'

He looked at Colin from the pulpit and for the first time his hands came out from beneath the gown. They were holding a gun.

In the moment before the gun was fired Colin was thinking: How funny all this is. How comical. Here I am in a church which is not like my own church with the golden cross and the effigy of the Virgin in front of me. Here I am, agreeing with everything he says. And it seemed to him for a moment as if the gold cross wavered slightly in the blast of the gun. But that might have been an illusion. In any case it was very strange to die in that way, so far from home, and not even on the battlefield. It was so strange that he almost died of the puzzle itself before the bullet hit him and spun him around in the wooden pew.

The Prophecy

I may say at the very beginning of this story that I am a very worried man for it had never occurred to me before that what is up there or somewhere around may very well be a joker. In fact to be perfectly honest I hadn't believed that there was anything much around at all. Some years ago I came to live in this village in Scotland (I am by the way an Englishman and my name is Wells). I have no connection at all with the Highlands: I am not an alien exploiter either. I am just a man who like others was fed up of the rat race as it is called reasonably correctly. In fact I am (or perhaps was) a psychologist. I am not very much now. Brilliance in psychology as in everything else belongs to a youth of energy and fire and by leaving the rat race I suppose I was signalling those days were over for me even though I thought of myself somewhat in the manner of those Chinese exiles from court who used to drink wine and write little poems in the cold mountains while they gazed at the road they would never travel again. I am also unmarried.

I worked in a university and quite frankly I got tired. If you wish to know what I got tired of I will tell you. I became enraged, literally enraged, by the contradictions which I saw in people's personalities every day and which they seemed implacably to be unaware of. Let me give you one or two instances. One man I knew was always talking of 'professional behaviour' and yet at the same time he was the worst, most consistently destructive and rabid gossip I have ever seen. Another, a hard drinker, lectured on alcoholism as the manifestation of ultimate weakness. Another, a so-called devotee of pure research, was leaping on to the barbaric bandwagon of the quick Penguin for the masses.

I became obsessed by this gap between the spoken word

and the reality of the personality. I was losing my balance. I found that I was checking myself continually against my own standard of consistency and in doing so making myself more and more vulnerable. In other words I was coming to the conclusion that these contradictions are necessary to life and that he who sets out deliberately to erase them is in fact destroying himself. I found in other words that there is an enmity between consistency and life. This discovery was so shattering that for a long time I was incapable of working at all. For if this were true then an attempt to seek consistency and truth was in fact suicidal. Many nights I have sat staring at a book completely oblivious of my surroundings, and when I woke up from my daydream I found that I was still at the same page. The discovery I had made seemed to me utterly shattering. My mind roamed pitilessly in all directions. It seemed to me quite clear for instance that Christ was both violent and peaceful in his nature and that theologians in trying to eliminate the one in order to reinforce the other so as to create a perfectly consistent being without flaw were, in fact, being false to reality. Life is not reasonable, to live is to be inconsistent. To be consistent is to cease to live. That was the logical converse.

Now, however it happened, I thought that I should try and find a place where there would be a greater simplicity than I had been used to and that there I would be able to test this new theory. In fact what of course had happened was very simple. My energy and fire had run out and I was merely escaping. That was the truth I was disguising in terms of my research and my love of truth. I understand perfectly why my love of truth is so great. I was brought up by possessive parents who married late and each day I was trying to justify myself to their unlimited love and pride. Never would it be possible for any human being to do that – to fill that gap with the continual victories of the virtuoso – but this did not mean that it was possible for me to stop trying. It was this hunger for justification that destroyed me. For it is clear to me now that an excessive consciousness is bound to be at the mercy of the mediocre and the satisfied. An immense hunger for truth and consistency is rare and cannot by its nature lead to happiness. Most men do not by a privileged mercy see their own contradictions. Gandhi was peaceful to the world but aggressive to his family. So was Tolstoy. Both these men among many others were impaled on the impossible attempt to make life consistent and truthful. This is impossible precisely because truth is abstract and static and life flows ceaselessly like a river.

I arrived therefore in this village, in this country, the Highlands. I didn't know very much of the Highlands when I came. Naturally I could appreciate its scenery, but scenery after all is only a reflection of the psyche. There were hills, lochs, rivers, broken fences and roads. It looked like a land to which much had been done, adversely. It looked a lonely land without sophistication or riches. It echoed with ghosts and waterfalls. It looked a broken land. And it suited me because that was what I was myself, a broken man. Quite literally, I was a signpost pointing nowhere. It wasn't, I suppose, at all extraordinary that the Highlanders accepted me or at least didn't show any hostility. I used to go out fishing and they would tell me the best bait. I was shown how to cut my own peats. I even used to tar and felt my own roof. All these things I learned from them. I imagine that what I was doing was using my psychological techniques so that they would like me. I took care not to offend them. The only thing was I never went to church but strangely enough they accepted that too on the grounds that a man must be loyal to his own church and since mine was presumably the Church of England I couldn't be expected to betray it simply because I had put a number of miles between it and myself.

I studied these people and their history. I knew what had made them and what they had become. I recognised their secretiveness and the reason for it. I sensed the balance of forces which is necessary to keep a village together. I recognised the need for rivalry between villagers. I was dimly aware of the vast spaces of their past and how they must be occupied. I noticed the economic differentiation between men and women. I was aware of the hidden rancours and joys. After all I had been a psychologist. These things were child's play to

me. I learned their language and read their books and poems.
I had plenty of time to read and I read a lot. The local
schoolmaster came to visit me.

And this is what happened. Now I am ready to tell my story
and I am sure that you must appreciate that it is a very odd
one.

This schoolmaster was a very odd psychological type. He
was immersed in his children, I mean his pupils. He believed
that his ideal work, what he was destined for, was to be among
them. He was really rather a child himself with his rosy face
and his impermeable surfaces. I could see what had happened
to him, but after all that is the terror with which a psychologist
must live, to see the gestures and know their real value and
weight and meaning, to track a joke to its stinking lair. The
schoolmaster was in fact one of the few people I could really
talk to on a certain level since he had in fact read a little
though in no sense deeply. Still he was useful to me since he
knew a great deal of the lore and literature of the people,
though of course not profoundly, being himself still inside
that lore.

One night we had a long discussion about predestination. It
was disordered and random and without penetration. My mind
had lost its edge and wandered vaguely round the edges of the
real problem like someone who roams round a field at night. I
knew that my mind had lost its edge and its conviction and it
disturbed me. I knew that my mind was not powerful enough
to make a proper analysis of such a concept though in relation
to his it was in fact the mind of a giant. We drank much sherry
since the schoolmaster would not drink whisky. I was sick of
myself and only half listening when suddenly he said, 'What
do you think of this? Many years ago, in fact it must be over a
hundred years ago, we had a prophet here who made some
odd prophecies.'

'And how many of them have come true?' I said indifferently,
purely automatically.

'Well,' he said, 'it is rather difficult to say. They are set in
such mysterious terms. For instance, he said that when the
river ate the land stones would be raised. Some people think

this refers to the storm of last year when that big wall was built.'

Mechanically, I said, 'That could be expected, surely, in a place which gets so much rain as this. I wouldn't place much reliance on that.' And I poured myself another sherry.

Anyway he told me some more of his mysterious sayings but only one stayed in my mind. There is a reason for this which I did not see at the time but which will appear later.

This saying went something like this: 'When the wood is raised at the corner then wills will crash.'

In my befuddled state I couldn't make any sense of this, especially the last part. The first part could refer to a wooden building and the corner was a clear enough sign since there is a place at the end of the village called the Corner but as for the second part I was bemused. I said to him and I remember this clearly, 'Surely that must really be "Wills will clash", not "crash".'

'That's how it has come down to us,' he said looking at me. And that was that. I was sure that there had been an error in the manuscript or whatever and later found out that the manuscript if it had existed no longer did so. For that matter, perhaps the man had never existed at all. The schoolmaster however was very sure of the prophet's existence and talked of him as a strange being who lived by himself, wore a beard and walked about in a dream most of the time.

Anyway, the night passed and the schoolmaster went home and I went to bed half thinking about the phrase 'Wills will crash' and pretty certain that the word should have been 'clash'. Otherwise the whole thing didn't make any sense and naturally I wanted it to make sense. After all that was what I was, a man who wanted to make sense of things. I slept a dreamless sleep but when I woke up in the morning I was still thinking of this saying. I am sure it would have passed smoothly into my mind leaving no trace if it hadn't contained what I considered to be a semantic inexactitude. I worried at it but could make no further sense of it. I tried to find out more about the prophet's sayings but could discover little about him, no more in fact than the schoolmaster had told me. As it was winter time I had time on my hands and pursued my investigations and came up with a blank. It was at this point that the idea came to me, as Relativity must have come to Einstein.

2

It was really a blindingly simple idea and I wondered why no one had thought of such a thing before. Maybe (I half considered) I had been sent to this place in order to arrive at the stunning conception I had now arrived at. Maybe I was predestined to meet the schoolmaster . . . At that time you see I had no idea of the intricacies that would enmesh me. Anyway my idea was this. Why didn't I raise the wood at the corner (that is, raise a shed there) and see what would happen? There was no reason why I couldn't do it if I wanted to. I had plenty of money. There were one or two unemployed people who would build the shed for me. I had no fears that permission would be refused me as I was quite popular and not thought of as an outsider. I reviewed my idea from all angles and there seemed nothing against it. It would give me an interest during the winter months and it would return me to a psychological or at least philosophical theme. I may say that as I have mentioned already I had no feeling for ghosts, spirits, stars, etc., at that time, and thought them easily explicable manifestations of the fallible human psyche.

Anyway, not to be too tedious about the business, I decided to build a wooden shed at the Corner. I had no doubt that this was the location mentioned since I gathered that the place had been so-called from time immemorial. I got hold of a middle-aged fellow called Buckie who was a builder but unemployed at the time. As he had a large family which consisted mostly of teenage girls who shrieked and screamed and presumably ate a lot, like seagulls, he was very glad to help me. The hut was to be fairly spacious. Buckie reported every morning in his blue overalls with his rule in his pocket and began to work on the fine new yellow wood. I often used to watch him but as he didn't say much at any time I ended by leaving him alone. He didn't even ask me why I wanted the shed built. Perhaps he thought I wanted a place where I could be absolutely quiet or perhaps he thought I intended to get some stuff which I would store there eventually.

In any case one fine day I went to the Corner and found that the shed had been built. As green is my favourite colour I decided to paint it green and this I did myself. For the rest it was a fairly spacious shed with two windows and one door. It was fairly warm inside but not too warm and there was plenty of room. The windows were quite large and looked out on to the road which travelled past the hut towards the town eight miles away. After the hut was finished I would go and sit there. I took a chair and table and I would read and so some writing. Otherwise I didn't use it much.

At nights I would lie awake and wonder why I had been so stupid as to build it. There it pointlessly stood for no reason that I or anyone else could offer. I had no clue as to what I was going to do with it. I couldn't offer it to anyone else, not even as a place for staying in, for no one would have made their home there as there was a tradition that there were ghosts at the Corner and the villagers were very superstitious. Thus the days passed and I waited. I had built the hut and the next move was up to the prophet, if there was to be any next move. Sometimes I felt like a girl waiting to be visited by a lover and impatient that he wasn't coming. If he had any sincerity or love why didn't he prove by his presence that his words were true?

Naturally some of the villagers asked me why I had built the hut and I told them some vague story about wanting a quiet place to study in. They seemed quite satisfied with this explanation as though I mixed with them, they didn't make any pretence of understanding me.

Then on a lovely spring evening the first move was made. There was a knock at the door and standing there was a young boy from the village whose name was John Macleod. He was a tall rather clumsy-looking fellow with a reddish face and large hands and he worked as a painter in the town coming home at nights on the bus. I was in a good mood at the time for some reason and I stood there at the window

looking out towards the glittering sea across the walls and
ditches and houses and fields.

The boy took a long time to come to the point (indeed if he
had had a cap he would have been twisting it in his hands) but
the gist of his request was that perhaps out of the goodness of
my heart I might lend the young people of the village the
hut for their weekend dances. Normally they conducted their
dances in the open air at the Corner but of course this
meant that there could be no dances on a rainy night. There
was really no problem since my hut was large enough to
accommodate all the young people who were likely to turn up
(about sixteen at the most). I thought about it very briefly and
then agreed, especially as the boy assured me that the hut
would be left spick and span after they had finished with it,
that there would be no damage at all as the village youth were
well-behaved, that he would return the key to me after they
had cleaned out the hut if it was necessary to do so. I myself
knew that the villagers were law-abiding and would not harm
the hut, so I agreed readily. And he went away quite excessively
happy. I dismissed the whole thing from my mind, glad that at
last a use had been found for my hut. Funnily enough, though,
I had a vague feeling at the back of my mind that I had made
some connection however tenuous with the prophet hovering
somewhere in the offing. It was an odd unaccountable feeling
and I soon got rid of it.

Nothing happened for four or five weeks. During the
successive Saturdays the dances in the hut went on, the key
was handed back to me and the place was left tidy as promised.
Unfortunately, though I didn't know it, the air around me was
rapidly darkening with omens. As everyone knows islanders
are not notable for speaking out, and no rumour at first
reached me till quite suddenly out of the blue the Rev. Norman
Black made his explosive attack in the pulpit on a particular
Sunday. As I wasn't in church I didn't hear his exact words but
I was given accounts of it. The Rev. Norman Black is a small
fiery man with a ginger moustache who holds the local people
in an iron grip. They go out and gather his peats for him, they
give him presents of meat and milk, and in return he exercises

dominion over them. They are in fact very frightened of him indeed. I cannot help admiring him in a way since his consciousness of his own rightness is so complete and utter. He bows the knee to no one and he flashes about in his small red car like a demon from the pit spitting sulphur and flame, and when he feels it is necessary he has no deference to the high and no mercy on the low. As far as I could gather the drift of his sermon, shorn of theological and ecclesiastical language, was as follows. The shed or hut was infested by young people intent on fornication: this was in fact the reason why the hut had been built in the first place. As long as the dancing took place in the open then one could see what was going on but when walls had been erected then privacy suitable for dalliance and immorality had been created. Also why was the hut painted green? This was very ominous indeed. Furthermore why had this hut been built by an Englishman who never attended church? Was it because he was bent on undermining the morality of the village? What other explanation could there be? Considered from that angle my enterprise did indeed look suspicious and cunning especially as I had no real explanation for the hut, and even if I were to offer one no one would believe me now. As for my true reason, who would believe that?

At first I was inclined to laugh at the whole thing but in fact there apparently had been some drinking. Some 'dalliance' had, in fact, taken place though it was, I am sure, quite innocent. Nevertheless people began to sidle past me. They began to wonder. Was I some thin end of the wedge? Had my previous civil behaviour been a mask? Cold shoulders were turned to me. My visitors dwindled. Anger grew. After all I had been extended hospitality and I was repaying it with lasciviousness cunningly disguised as philanthropy. I felt around me a rather chill wind. Neighbours began to slant off when I approached.

Steadily as the Rev. Norman Black blew on the flames and lashed his theological whip the village divided itself into two camps, that of the adults and that of the young. One night there was an attempt to set the place on fire. After that a guard was mounted over the hut for some time each night. Parents warned their children not to go to the dances and the young rebelled. I found myself at the centre of the cross fire. Messages were scrawled on my door in the middle of the night. The young expected me to stand up for them and I still gave them the key. Even the schoolmaster was divided in his mind and ceased to visit me. I was alone. My visits to the local shop became adventures into enemy country. The shop was often out of articles that I needed. My letters arrived late.

One day a group of youngsters came to the door and told me that some adults were intending to march on the green hut and burn it down.

Let me say at this point that I was faced with a particularly interesting scientific problem. I wished naturally to be merely an observer in the experiment I was conducting and for this reason I couldn't interfere on either side. However, I walked along with the youngsters towards the hut. When we arrived the adults had not yet reached it, and we waited outside the hut in a group. There was a number of boys and girls and many of them were very angry. They felt that they were defending not only a hut but a principle. They felt that the time had come when they must stand up for themselves against the rigid ideology which was demanding the destruction of their hut. My hut had in fact become a symbol.

We waited therefore and saw in complete silence the adults approaching. There was a large number of them and they carried axes and spades. They stopped when they saw us and the two groups faced each other in the fine sunshine. They were led, as one could see very quickly, by the fiery minister. This was indeed a clash or crash of wills that the prophet had foreseen. The minister came forward and said, 'Are you going to allow us to pull down peacefully this habitation of the devil?'

One of the boys who was home from university and whose name was John Maclean said, 'No, we're not. You have no right to pull the hut down. It doesn't belong to you.' He was studying, as I remember, to be a lawyer. I said nothing but remained an interested spectator. What was I expecting? That there would be an intervention from heaven?

The minister said no more but walked steadily forward with an axe in his hand. Now this posed another interesting problem. No one had ever laid hands on a minister before, certainly not in a country village. If anyone did, would there indeed be an intervention from heaven? The minister, small and energetic, advanced towards the hut. The group of youngsters interposed themselves. He pushed among them while one or two of the girls, their nerve breaking, rushed to the other side to join their fathers, who were waiting grimly to see the result of the minister's lone attack. I think they too were wondering what the youths would do. In his tight black cloth the minister moved steadily forward, axe in hand.

The youths were watching and wondering what I should do but I did nothing. How could I? After all I was a scientist engaged in an experiment. Some of them were clearly speculating on what would happen to them when their parents, many of them large and undeniably fierce, got them home again. In the sunshine the minister advanced. One could see from the expression on his face that for him this hut really was an abomination created by the devil, that its destruction had been ordered by the Most High, that he, the servant of God attired in his sober black, was going to accomplish that destruction. Interestingly enough I saw that among the adults was Buckie the builder placidly awaiting the destruction of the work of his own hands. Did I however glimpse for one moment a twitch of doubt on his face, a fear that he perhaps too was present at a personal surrender? I knew all the invaders, every single one of them, placid, hard-working men, good neighbours, heavy moral men, all bent on destroying my green hut which was at the same time both Catholic and demonic and perhaps life-enhancing. It was odd that such a construction should have caused such violent passions. But I had not met a man like this minister before. When he had finally arrived next to the youths he said in a slightly shrill voice (perhaps even he was nervous?), 'I have come here to lay this abomination to the ground. Shall any of you dare touch the servant of the Lord?' Quivering he raised his head, his moustache bristling. There was a long silence. It was clearly a moment permeated with significance. Were the young going to establish their independence once and for all? Or were they going to surrender? The village would never be the same again after this confrontation, no matter what happened.

The men waited. The minister pushed. And he slipped on the ground. I am not sure how it happened – maybe he slipped on a stone, or maybe he had done it with the unconscious deliberation and immense labyrinthine cunning that the service of the Lord had taught him. Anyway as if this had been what they waiting for, the men pushed forward in a perfect fury (would these sons of theirs defy their elders as represented by the minister?), impatiently pushed their sons and daughters aside and with axes held high hacked away at the hut. Thus in Old Testament days must men such as this have hacked to pieces the wooden gods of their enemies, coloured and magical and savage. Thus they splintered and broke my hut. Before they were finished the youngsters had left, giving me a last look of contempt. I was the fallen champion, the uncommitted one. I who had apparently been on the side of youth against the rigid structures of religion, had surrendered. When the men had accomplished their destruction, their penetration of the bastion of immorality, they too turned away from me as if in embarrassment that I had witnessed such an orgy, almost sexual in its force and rhythm. Without speaking to me they left.

After they had all gone, leaving an axe or two behind, I stood there beside my ruined hut, the shell which had been ripped open and torn. Not even the Bacchanalians had been so fierce and ruthless. Thinking hard, I poked among the fragments. Above me the sky was blue and enigmatic. No prophecy emerged from its perfect surface. I remembered the words, 'When the wood is raised at the Corner wills will crash.' Or rather 'will clash'. Suddenly in a moment of perfect illumination such as must have been granted to the prophets I realised that the words could also be 'walls will crash'. But even before I had assimilated that meaning another one so huge and comic and ironic had blossomed around me that I was literally staggered by the enormous terror of its implications and sat down with my head in my hands. For I now knew that I could not stay in the village. My time there had come to an end. I was ready to start afresh. My retreat had ended. I must return to the larger world and continue with my work. But then the final revelation had come, as I shivered suddenly in the suddenly hostile day. I thought of my discussion on predestination with the schoolmaster. I thought of his casual remarks about the prophet. I thought of how I had been led to this particular village to learn about the prophecy and this prophet. I thought of the hundred years the man had been dead. I thought of the last meaning of all which had just come to me and I laughed out loud at the marvellous joke that had been perpetrated on me, rational psychologist from an alien land. There the words stood afresh in front of my mind's eye as if written in monstrous letters, luminous and hilarious, in the sunny day of clear blue. It was as if the heavens themselves cracked, just like my hut, as if the vase, elegant and beautiful, had shown a crack running right down its side, as if I could see the joking face, the body doubled over in laughter. For the words that came to me at that moment, the last reading of all, were these: 'WHEN THE WOOD IS RAISED AT THE CORNER WELLS WILL CRASH.'

Do You Believe in Ghosts?

'I'll tell you something,' said Daial to Iain. 'I believe in ghosts.'

It was Hallowe'en night and they were sitting in Daial's
house – which was a thatched one – eating apples and cracking
nuts which they had got earlier that evening from the people
of the village. It was frosty outside and the night was very
calm.

'I don't believe in ghosts,' said Iain, munching an apple.
'You've never seen a ghost, have you?'

'No,' said Daial fiercely, 'but I know people who have. My
father saw a ghost at the Corner. It was a woman in a white
dress.'

'I don't believe it,' said Iain. 'It was more likely a piece of
paper.' And he laughed out loud. 'It was more likely a newspaper. It was the local newspaper.'

'I tell you he did,' said Daial. 'And another thing. They say
that if you look between the ears of a horse you will see a
ghost. I was told that by my granny.'

'Horses' ears,' said Iain laughing, munching his juicy apple.
'Horses' ears.'

Outside it was very very still, the night was, as it were,
entranced under the stars.

'Come on then,' said Daial urgently, as if he had been
angered by Iain's dismissive comments. 'We can go and see
now. It's eleven o'clock and if there are any ghosts you might
see them now. I dare you.'

'All right,' said Iain, throwing the remains of the apple into
the fire. 'Come on then.'

And the two of them left the house, shutting the door
carefully and noiselessly behind them and entering the calm
night with its millions of stars. They could feel their shoes

creaking among the frost, and there were little panes of ice on the small pools of water on the road. Daial looked very determined, his chin thrust out as if his honour had been attacked. Iain liked Daial fairly well though Daial hardly read any books and was only interested in fishing and football. Now and again as he walked along he looked up at the sky with its vast city of stars and felt almost dizzy because of its immensity.

'That's the Plough there,' said Iain, 'do you see it? Up there.'

'Who told you that?' said Daial.

'I saw a picture of it in a book. It's shaped like a plough.'

'It's not at all,' said Daial. 'It's not shaped like a plough at all. You never saw a plough like that in your life.'

They were gradually leaving the village now, had in fact passed the last house, and Iain in spite of his earlier protestations was getting a little frightened, for he had heard stories of ghosts at the Corner before. There was one about a sailor home from the Merchant Navy who was supposed to have seen a ghost and after he had rejoined his ship he had fallen from a mast to the deck and had died instantly. People in the village mostly believed in ghosts. They believed that some people had the second sight and could see in advance the body of someone who was about to die though at that particular time he might be walking among them, looking perfectly healthy.

Daial and Iain walked on through the ghostly whiteness of the frost and it seemed to them that the night had turned much colder and also more threatening. There was no noise even of flowing water, for all the streams were locked in frost.

'It's here they see the ghosts,' said Daial in a whisper, his voice trembling a little, perhaps partly with the cold. 'If we had a horse we might see one.'

'Yes,' said Iain still trying to joke, though at the same time he also found himself whispering. 'You could ride the horse and look between its ears.'

The whole earth was a frosty globe, creaking and spectral, and the shine from it was eerie and faint.

'Can you hear anything?' said Daial who was keeping close to Iain.

'No,' said Iain. 'I can't hear anything. There's nothing. We should go back.'

'No,' Daial replied, his teeth chattering. 'W–w–e w–w–on't go back. We have to stay for a while.'

'What would you do if you saw a ghost?' said Iain.

'I would run,' said Daial, 'I would run like hell.'

'I don't know what I would do,' said Iain, and his words seemed to echo through the silent night. 'I might drop dead. Or I might . . . ' He suddenly had a terrible thought. Perhaps they were ghosts themselves and the ghost who looked like a ghost to them might be a human being after all. What if a ghost came towards them and then walked through them smiling, and then they suddenly realised that they themselves were ghosts.

'Hey, Daial,' he said, 'what if we are . . . ' And then he stopped, for it seemed to him that Daial had turned all white in the frost, that his head and the rest of his body were white, and his legs and shoes were also a shining white. Daial was coming towards him with his mouth open, and where there had been a head there was only a bony skull, its interstices filled with snow. Daial was walking towards him, his hands outstretched, and they were bony without any skin on them. Daial was his enemy, he was a ghost who wished to destroy him, and that was why he had led him out to the Corner to the territory of the ghosts. Daial was not Daial at all, the real Daial was back in the house, and this was a ghost that had taken over Daial's body in order to entice Iain to the place where he was now. Daial was a devil, a corpse.

And suddenly Iain began to run and Daial was running after him. Iain ran crazily with frantic speed but Daial was close on his heels. He was running after him and his white body was blazing with the frost and it seemed to Iain that he was stretching his bony arms towards him. They raced along the cold white road which was so hard that their shoes left no prints on it, and Iain's heart was beating like a hammer, and then they were in the village among the ordinary lights and now they were at Daial's door.

'What happened?' said Daial panting, leaning against the door, his breath coming in huge gasps.

And Iain knew at that moment that this really was Daial, whatever had happened to the other one, and that this one would think of him as a coward for the rest of his life and tell his pals how Iain had run away. And he was even more frightened than he had been before, till he knew what he had to do.

'I saw it,' he said.

'What?' said Daial, his eyes growing round with excitement.

'I saw it,' said Iain again. 'Didn't you see it?'

'What?' said Daial. 'What did you see?'

'I saw it,' said Iain, 'but maybe you don't believe me.'

'What did you see?' said Daial. 'I believe you.'

'It was a coffin,' said Iain. 'I saw a funeral.'

'A funeral?'

'I saw a funeral,' said Iain, 'and there were people in black hats and black coats. You know?'

Daial nodded eagerly.

'And I saw them carrying a coffin,' said Iain, 'and it was all yellow, and it was coming straight for you. You didn't see it. I know you didn't see it. And I saw the coffin open and I saw the face in the coffin.'

'The face?' said Daial and his eyes were fixed on Iain's face, and Iain could hardly hear what he was saying.

'And do you know whose face it was?'

'No,' said Daial breathlessly. 'Whose face was it? Tell me, tell me.'

'It was your face,' said Iain in a high voice. 'It was your face.' Daial paled.

'But it's all right,' said Iain. 'I saved you. If the coffin doesn't touch you you're all right. I read that in a book. That's why I ran. I knew that you would run after me. And you did. And I saved you. For the coffin would have touched you if I hadn't run.'

'Are you sure,' said Daial, in a frightened trembling voice. 'Are you sure that I'm saved?'

'Yes,' said Iain. 'I saw the edge of the coffin and it was almost touching the patch on your trousers and then I ran.'

'Gosh,' said Daial, 'that's something. You must have the

second sight. It almost touched me. Gosh. Wait till I tell the boys tomorrow. You wait.' And then as if it had just occurred to him he said, 'You believe in ghosts now, don't you?'

'Yes, I believe,' said Iain.

'There you are then,' said Daial. 'Gosh. Are you sure if they don't touch you you're all right?'

'Cross my heart,' said Iain.

A Day in the Life of . . .

She paid off the taxi she had taken from the railway station and went into the hotel. She felt sweaty and the palm of her right hand slid along the handle of the red case. She put the case down and waited for the girl at the reception desk to stop phoning. She had been in the hotel three or four times before in the past two years but she didn't expect that anyone would recognise her, and this girl seemed new as if she were a school-girl working there during holiday time. As she waited she looked around her. There were some chairs with olive green covers at one side of the lobby and on one an old man lying asleep, his mouth open, his feet stretched out, and what looked like a guidebook fallen open on the floor beside him. Her eyes traversed him, following the wall upward to the high ceiling with its white edgings like wedding cake. She turned back to the girl who was looking at her enquiringly. She was a very pretty girl with dark pigtails and bare tanned arms.

'A single room,' she said. 'Have you a single room?'

'I think we can manage that,' said the girl brightly, turning to a plan of the hotel hung up on a sheet on the wall. 'Room 5,' she said, 'or would you like one with a bath? There's 31.'

'I'll take 5.'

'Righto. If you would please sign?'

She signed 'Miriam Hetherington', hesitating as she always did whether to put 'Scottish' or 'British' and finally deciding as she always did to put 'British'. She took the key attached to the large blue block and went to the room which was on the ground floor. She opened the door and entered.

It was like all the other hotel rooms in which she had stayed. There was a dressing table, a wardrobe, a wash basin with towels, a phone, a card with a list of hotel charges, a large notice about what to do in the event of fire, a Gideon Bible, a bed with electric blanket, a large glass ashtray and a small gold-coloured box of matches stamped with the name of the hotel. She lay down on the bed and fell asleep.

When she woke she found by a glance at her small silver wrist watch that she had slept two hours and that it was five o'clock in the afternoon. She got off the bed, looking down vaguely at her red shoes which matched the case. Then she opened the latter and took out her clothes – two dresses, a hat, four pairs of stockings, a pair of shoes, three sets of under-garments, two pairs of pyjamas, shoe brushes and shoe polish and various other odds and ends including a sewing kit and a number of paperbacks. She packed them neatly into her wardrobe and dressing chest. When she had done this she took off her blouse and began to wash her face and neck, rubbing the cold water briskly into her eyes.

The face that looked back at her from the mirror was the face of a woman of about thirty-five whose skin at the corner of the eyes was beginning to wrinkle. The eyes themselves had a questioning look as if, confronted with the world, they had found it rather puzzling, not to say unintelligible. The nose was rather long, the upper lip narrow and severe, the lower lip full and red. Her teeth were still her own and fairly white. The forehead was narrow and high and lightly veined and the hair cut into a boyish crop. In short she had the appearance of someone who might have been passionate but whose passion had been mastered by a relentless severity. Her colourful red blouse and red shoes seemed like a late desperate blossoming of her buried personality. But she wasn't ugly and, given rouge and lipstick and relaxation of mind, she would in certain circumstances appear pretty.

When she had washed herself and used rouge and lipstick she thought for a moment and then going out of the room and leaving the key at the desk she went out into the dazzling sunlight.

The streets were crowded with people – men in shirt sleeves, women bare-armed in blouses – all strolling along in an easy, relaxed manner. The road was dense with traffic and it took her some time to cross, but she waited till the sign 'Cross' appeared and then half ran across the street. On the opposite side was a restaurant which she entered. She sat down at a table in the shade and when the waitress came she ordered fruit juice and a gammon steak. At a table beside her there was a boy and a girl holding hands and gazing into each other's eyes. At another table there was a large man with a moustache eating fish and squeezing juice from a lemon on to his plate. He had a newspaper propped against the tea-pot.

She drank her juice and waited for her gammon steak. She didn't feel at all hungry but decided that she ought to eat something since that was what people did at that time of day. Since her parents had died and she had started living on her own she sometimes skipped meals but on holiday one ought to eat, she told herself. She remembered that her mother used always to be very keen on her eating a lot, and would pile her plate high with meat and vegetables which weren't really very well cooked. Her father of course ate steadily and gravely, not seeming to mind what was set in front of him, but as if he were filling himself with necessary fuel. He reminded her of a large squat car which was being pumped full of petrol. Of course he had been a large man and he needed the food. Her mother on the other hand was thin and stringy.

She ate the gammon, carefully putting aside the chips. The man with the newspaper was chewing rapidly and reading at the same time. The young couple were preparing to leave. They had eaten, she noted, some of the cheapest stuff, sausage and egg, but had wiped their plates clean. It took her a long time to eat the gammon but she succeeded and got up. She didn't want any sweet as it might fatten her too much. The waitress hoped that the gammon had suited her and she said yes. The waitress said that if she cared to come back tomorrow they would have something special on the menu. She didn't reply. Again she went out into the sunshine.

For a while she walked along the streets looking in the shop windows. It was a good area of the town with a large number of jewellers' shops, good food shops, and furniture shops. She looked at the rings in the windows and noted that they were very expensive. There were also some quite splendid Russian watches. She remembered giving away her father's watch to her uncle but she had kept her mother's watch and was still wearing it. Her father's watch had been a large golden one, of the kind that men used to carry in their waistcoat pockets. She still had his Masonic ring in a box in the house.

She went into a supermarket and walked around for a bit. There was nothing there that she wanted to buy except possibly two large red footballs which she might take to the neighbours' boys who were mad keen on football. It was always a good idea to take something home to them: one never knew when one might need help from a neighbour, for example if one was ill with 'flu and couldn't get out, especially in the winter time. There were various perfumes which she was tempted to buy but didn't. Later on she went into a large bookshop and studied the books. She read a lot but not as much as she used to. Her mother had always told her that she read too much. 'Too much reading is a weariness to the flesh,' she would say, quoting from the Bible, or what she thought was the Bible. Her mother had hardly read a book in her life except the Bible and the People's Friend, and couldn't understand why people should want to read books at all: it seemed such a waste of time when they could be doing something useful. She herself thought she might buy a book called *Emerging Africa* to help her with her geography but decided against it. Holiday time wasn't the right time to read serious books. One read detective stories or thrillers. Half ashamedly she looked at a book on horoscopes and found that she ought to keep a tight grip on financial matters that week and not mix very much with strangers. She put the book down and went out again into the sun.

As she walked down the street she came to a cinema which was showing a film called *The Cowboys* starring John Wayne. She decided to go in and bought a ticket for the balcony. When she sat down it disturbed her to find that she was the only person in the whole cinema. Not only was there no one in the balcony seats, there was no one – not even children – in the stalls. She felt rather frightened and wished that she had not come in till later but after all she had paid her money and couldn't go out again. The red curtains were still drawn and for a long time there was nothing but music to which she listened impatiently, now and again looking behind her as if expecting that someone would come in and attack her. Eventually the music stopped and there were some advertisements, one of which showed a young girl riding a horse through a mountain stream and which after all turned out to be an advertisement for cigarettes. 'Cool as a mountain stream,' breathed the sexy voice of the sponsor. She herself didn't smoke. Her mother hadn't believed in girls smoking: her father however smoked a pipe. When he was finished working for the day in the distillery he would read the paper for a while and smoke his pipe and then fall asleep. She herself was the only child and had perhaps loved her father more than her mother who had often told him that he ought to have a better job with his abilities though as a matter of fact his abilities weren't all that extraordinary except that he was good with his hands. He could make or repair anything. He had made a chair for her when she was a child and later he would make toys for her, wooden animals of all kinds. Her favourite was a squirrel which would climb the chair on its clockwork machinery.

The credits came on the screen for the big picture and she realised that she had read a review of the film in the *Observer* which she bought every Sunday. She also bought the *Sunday Times*. Her father and mother used to get the *Sunday Post* and they would spend the whole week reading it, not missing a single story. In her own job as a teacher she would use the Sunday Supplements for projects. One of her projects was on the Motor Car, though she couldn't drive.

The film turned out to be rather a good one, at least at the beginning. The title *The Cowboys* had to be taken literally for it was about boys, not about men. John Wayne, a rancher whose cowhands abandoned him in order to join a gold rush, was a stern man who had lost two sons partly because he had been too strict with them. The film showed him becoming attached to the boys and learning how to handle them in a human manner with the help of a coloured cook. On the drive too the boys learned to become men. They were attacked by some ex-jailbirds who killed the unarmed Wayne after he had refused to kow-tow to them and had then driven off his cattle. The last part of the film she wasn't sure of. It showed the boys setting off grim-faced after the killers and one by one detaching them and murdering them and finally manoeuvring the survivors into a trap where they shot them all. The leader of the killers had got his legs entangled in his horse's stirrups and pleaded to be freed but one of the boys fired a shot into the air which so frightened the horse that it dragged its rider along through a river till he was drowned. She wasn't sure about this last part. Nothing surely could condone violence and if there had been someone with her she would have argued about it. But there was no one there.

Many years before while her parents were still alive she had fallen in love with a man who owned a shop at the time. He was very handsome and very glib but what she took for cleverness her parents took for falsity. He used to take her out a lot especially to the cinema but most of the time she had to pay for their outings. She didn't mind this as she thought that he was making his way in the business. The first time he had tried to seduce her she had been very cold, so cold that she had managed to put him off. It had been in a wood where he had taken her in his new car: she could remember the brown autumnal leaves, and the river flowing through the glen with a desolate sound. He had been very persuasive using all the common arguments such as that it was good for one to have sex. He had been very handsome with his fair hair and fine blue eyes but she had not succumbed. She thought that innocence was important and felt that if she had given in she would have carried for a long time a load of guilt. In fact the sequence which showed the girl riding through the mountain stream had reminded her of the episode. He had been very passionate and also persuasive. He used to take her to parties and she had been so much in love or so infatuated that she had defied her parents and come into the house in the early hours of the morning, still remembering the dancing round the record player in the grey streamers of cigarette smoke. Once she had come in at four o'clock in the morning, only to find her mother, toothless, still awake and waiting for her. 'After all we have done for you,' hissed her mother through a mouth without dentures, 'and you are just a common prostitute.' As a matter of fact it hadn't been like that at all. The party had been exciting and they had all danced to the music of the latest pop songs. She could still remember them with a certain bitterness. Not that she was the kind of person who was very interested in pop songs; she was more interested in classical music and conversation. But coming back in the whiteness of the morning under the million stars had been an experience, for during most of her life she had gone to bed at eleven at the latest, drawing the curtains carefully before removing her clothes.

In any case the whole romance had finished when she discovered that the man to whom she had been engaged had been seeing another girl all the time, a very common girl who really liked pop songs and worked in a supermarket. She had found it shattering that he should have preferred this girl to her. In fact this was the most painful part of the whole episode, that the girl should have such a cheap mind, and that her mother had been right all along. 'It was lucky for you that you found out in time,' her mother would say to her. For a long time she didn't feel like going out but she had to since she was teaching and otherwise people would talk. So she had put on a brave face and pretended that the whole thing had been trivial but for weeks she would burst out crying for no particular reason. After all he had been very entertaining and they had gone to so many different places. What struck her most was that afterwards she would analyse the whole relationship and realise that without her knowing it he had been incredibly selfish. For instance he would only go to places which he himself suggested, football matches for instance because he was interested in football or pubs because he liked to drink. She would have much preferred to visit museums and art galleries but he didn't like that so she had remained silent about her preferences. If once in a while they did go to an art gallery he would fidget and make rude remarks about the paintings. One thing she did discover during their relationship. At the beginning of it she liked representational paintings, at the end she preferred surrealist ones.

Before she started going out with him she had idealistic illusions about love and marriage. She wanted to have children, but legitimately. She imagined herself staying at home looking after the garden and watching her children playing among the flowers while he earned their living. But in fact he let the shop go to ruin and lived extravagantly because his mother would do anything for him and never saw any of his faults. His mother was a woman with blue rinsed hair who played cards a lot.

So that episode had ended ingloriously and the worst of it was that her ideas about love and marriage had been irretrievably soured. If ever a man showed any intention of taking her out she would analyse his motives quite coolly and in the end decide that she would prefer to be on her own. All the passion had been drained out of her. Most of the time after school she stayed in the house and prepared her lessons for the following day. She transferred all her love to her pupils who were all young children. And of course her parents were growing old. Her father had a stroke one day after he had been out working in the garden on a very hot summer's day. Her mother had great difficulty tending him since she didn't want to send him to hospital and eventually she herself had fallen ill. Her father had died first and then her mother and then she was left alone.

After the initial grief which had lasted for a long time she had felt free. She thought that with the money which she had carefully saved she would go to places that she had only read about but which she felt that she ought to visit. There would be no one peering over her shoulder, no one wondering when she would come home at night, she could come and go as she pleased. She had always wanted to go to Greece because she couldn't believe that places such as Parnassus had ever existed or that Homer had ever lived. She could believe in the existence of all other places but not the places in Greece. But in fact she had cancelled her reservations because when it came to the point she couldn't go alone. She had however gone to places nearer home and hadn't enjoyed her holidays at all in spite of her freedom.

Gradually she came to the conclusion that total freedom is an unmitigated evil. There ought to be someone waiting up for one, there ought to be someone with whom one could communicate, even quarrel. But there was no one. She found herself moving in the world like a shadow. And she didn't visit much. There was no one really she wanted to visit and she felt that people might be sorry for her. So she tended to stay in the house a great deal. At first she passed the time by reading but this soured on her. Later she would knit and sew a lot but after a while she thought there was no particular reason for that either. Then she took to going to night classes and she would attend courses such as 'Pre-Raphaelitism' and 'Inflation and How to Deal with it'. But she found the same small earnest women at these courses, not understanding what the lecturer was saying, but only going there because they couldn't bear to stay in the house. And so she had stopped going to these courses as well.

But the long summer holidays were the biggest problem of all. She couldn't stay at home then all the time. She had to go away for a while and therefore she usually took a holiday of about a week. Before she left she carefully turned off the water and the electricity and worried sometimes even after she had reached her destination whether the fire or the immersion had been left on. She was very careful with the doorkey, which she hung round her neck. One of her greatest nightmares was to find herself at the door and not be able to find her key. Once she had left the house lights on all night after going to bed, and a neighbour in the block of flats opposite had come over in the morning wondering if there was anything wrong. They did think about her and they did worry about her. But of course they couldn't be expected to understand what it was to be lonely.

She came out of the cinema, not waiting for the cartoon (she didn't like cartoons) and went outside again. The sun was still hot and there were still as many people on the street as there had been before. It was only eight o'clock and she didn't want to go back to the hotel as early as that. People in hotels noticed you and summed you up, even receptionists. For instance that young girl had asked her if she had a car and she had to confess that she hadn't. Things like that marked you out, made you different. And the more there were of these absences, of these differences, the more wary people became of you. If there were enough differences they would avoid you altogether.

She made her way to the Gardens and sat down on a bench. Even as late as this – eight o'clock in the evening – the sun was still hot though not intolerably so. She sat in the shadow of a tree on a bench on which no one else was sitting. She crossed her legs and automatically pulled her skirt down. Her skirt was of medium length, there was no point in her wearing one of those very short skirts. And she simply watched the people passing. There were young couples with their arms round each other, an Indian girl of quite astonishing beauty who wore clothes the colour of a peacock, accompanied by two grave children – a girl and a boy – who also wore very bright clothes and looked like two perfect statues walking. They wore yellow socks, red shoes and lilac jerseys. A lone Negro went past and a boy on the back of whose blouse was written the number and name 15784 *Pentonville*. Two small girls rolled on the grass till the park-keeper blew a whistle and when he began to stride towards them they ran away. On the bench next to hers an oldish woman was sitting by herself throwing bread to the fat blue pigeons who waddled towards her, interrupted now and then by diminutive birds which would fly away with large morsels almost as big as themselves.

It occurred to her that most of her life she had been watching other people pass by as if she herself had no life but were the spectator of the lives of others. Other people often astonished her. So many of them walked instinctively into the future without thinking as if they expected that the water would buoy them up and that nothing would ever happen to them that they could not foresee. They accepted the motions of the present in a way that she could never do. They laughed and played in a forgetfulness which they seemed to be able to summon at will. For instance, she herself found it difficult to sit still on the bench. She wanted to walk about and at that moment she did so. She took a path which deviated from the main road and again sat under a tree. Here it was darker and there was more vegetation, truncated tree trunks and so on. It was some time before she noticed that only a few yards away from her a boy naked to the waist was lying on top of a girl who was also naked to the waist. It was some time too before she pulled her eyes away from them: not that she found the sight disgusting but that she wondered what it was like. She felt stirring within her a motion of regret, an irretrievable absence. But she got up again in case they would see her looking at them and went back to where she had been before.

She took out a magazine which she began to read. It was a romantic magazine which had stories of love found and lost in hospitals, factories and offices. This was her secret vice. She thought of herself as an intellectual who would attend concerts, the better films and plays, but who would never descend to reading trashy love stories. And yet this was what she was doing. And also she was looking up her sign in the horoscope to find out what was to happen to her. She was in fact Capricorn, remote, cold, miserly, determined. She read quickly but with only half her mind. The park was so beautiful, so crowded with people, and she was so alone. An old unshaven man who carried a paper bag sat down at the end of her bench. He slumped forward, his hands on his knees, staring down at the ground. Beside him on the bench he had placed an old greasy cap. His lips mumbled some words which he was apparently addressing to himself. She couldn't make out what he was saying. Eventually he got up and this time she heard him say, 'Bugger everything, bugger everything,' as if it were some meaningful litany. She drew in her legs as he passed her. Then she put down her book and watched the children playing.

She liked children. Since her parents died she often thought that it was the children who had saved her. They were so nice, so innocent, so willing to learn, so willing to engage themselves in plays, concerts, projects, so alive and so loving. She believed that her own mother had never liked children. She herself had been born – she worked out – when her father had been unemployed and when her mother must have been very worried about the future. The coldness of her own personality must have been because her mother had never lavished enough love upon her. Surely that must be the reason. What other reason could there be?

But perhaps the reason why she liked children was that she wanted to mould them to be like herself. Was that it? No, it couldn't be that. Children were so spontaneous, perhaps it was their very spontaneity that she loved. They would come up to her and tell her stories of what had happened to them, and she would listen attentively. They wrote nice little poems which had fine feeling and a directness which moved her. She was lucky in a way to have them. And yet there was something which she was missing. She couldn't think what it was but it was something which kept reality at a remove from her as if she were looking at it through a plate glass window. Children weren't like that. Children moved unselfconsciously through reality.

Her father had that kind of unselfconsciousness. He would sit down in a chair and seem able to endure time without terror. He would move about in a very slow heavy manner as if he were at home in the world. He would eat carefully as if he were drawing from what he ate sustenance for some work which it was necessary for him to do. He talked little and slowly. He would look out of the window and say, 'It's going to be a good day,' and in some way the statement seemed final and exact. He never discussed anything profound or philosophical. Her mother from that point of view was the same. But she was also much more ambitious, much more jagged and edgy. She had even gone to see her daughter capped at the university though she had never been such a long distance from home before. She herself had tried to stop her from going in case she would utter idiocies to her friends but she hadn't in fact done so and had behaved very circumspectly. She had also, strangely enough, chosen the right clothes to wear.

But her mother had said something to her once which she remembered. 'I don't know what will happen to you if you are ever left alone.' She remembered this as if it were some prophecy of disaster.

She put down her book and got up. It was time to return to the hotel. In the hotel there were some sandwiches and tea laid on a table in the lounge. She took some tea but no sandwiches and sat for a bit watching the TV. The only other people in the room were an old man with a white moustache and his wife who sat on the sofa together, not speaking, gazing at the screen with the same kind of look as they might have had if they were looking at fish in an aquarium. The screen seemed to be showing a gangster story for shortly after she sat down a small thin quivering man was shot and the seeping blood reddened the screen. After a while she got up and looked at some magazines which were lying around. One was the *Scottish Field*, another the *Countryside*. There was an unfinished crossword which she looked at without much interest. At one time she had used to do a lot of crosswords but she had given that up.

As she sat there, there came to her the extraordinary feeling that she had ceased to live properly, that at some time she had left a road and was slowly going down a side track where she would find herself on abandoned sidings among old railway carriages in a blaze of yellow flowers. For a moment she suffered intense panic but then the panic subsided and the two old people were still there watching the TV as silently as ever.

Her father hardly ever watched TV. When someone switched it on he went outside and did some job. Her mother would watch it avidly. Sometimes she used to think that the announcers were smiling at her when they signed off for the night. She even seemed to have fallen in love with the man who did the weather forecast. Her face suddenly became schoolgirlish and illuminated by an autumnal pathos.

When her father had died her mother had acted very practically, doing all the necessary things but then, after all the business was over, relapsing into herself. She seemed to lose all her energy and would fall asleep in the chair even at midday. She also gave up cooking as if all those years she had really been cooking for her husband and for no one else, her husband who had done everything she had wanted him to do, who had never drunk even though he worked in a distillery, who had always been there, quiet, silent and strong. She had ceased visiting people's houses. She had even ceased to watch TV and would say, 'What rubbish they are showing there.'

Two large blue policemen burst into a red room and there were gun shots. She rose and went to her room. She took off her clothes, laying them down on the chair, and then got into bed. She took out a paperback and began to read it. One of the things she had always dreaded was that she would become an insomniac but in fact she slept quite well. One of the teachers in her school was an insomniac. His name was Ross and he had told her that he only slept an average of an hour a night. He would stay up most of the night making tea and reading. He had got through the whole of Dostoevsky and Tolstoy in one spell of six months. Now he was getting to work on Dickens. She couldn't imagine what it would be like to be an insomniac. She was sure she would go off her head but thanked God that at least she could sleep at nights. She looked at her watch which told her that it was ten o'clock. She closed the book and then her eyes, even though outside she could hear quite clearly the roar of the traffic and somewhere in the hotel the sound of conversation and crockery and trays. She fell asleep almost immediately.

She dreamed that she was in a park full of Greek statues of boys with short cropped hair like American athletes. In the middle of the night the statues began to move and to dance as if during the day they had been waiting patiently so that they could do precisely that. Their hollow eyes assumed expression and intelligence, they moved as if to a music which she herself could not hear. All round them bits of paper and other litter as well as fallen leaves swirled in a wind which had blown up. In the storm of leaves the statues remained solid and the expressions on the faces were both smiling and cruel as if they belonged to a royal supercilious race which despised the human. Then she saw in her dream the park-keeper unlocking the gate and the statues became immobile and blank again.

The following morning she woke new and refreshed and in the blaze of white sunlight that illuminated the room felt inexplicably the same kind of large hope that she used to feel

when she was a girl, when suddenly she would throw off the
bed-clothes and walk about the silent house as if waiting for
something dramatic to happen.

She washed quickly and went down to her breakfast. The
waitress was an old woman with a limp who had a pleasant
smile, and asked her whether she would like one egg or two as
if she really wanted to give her the two. When she had finished
her breakfast she went outside, her handbag over her shoulder.
The morning was still cool and she felt confident and happy as
she walked along. She knew exactly what she was going to do.
She would tour the High Street and look at the museums and
other sights and she might even have a look at the Castle later.

All around her she could see the crenellated outlines of old
houses, solid and heavy, houses that had been in existence for
centuries and between which were lanes and steps that had
known many secrecies which at the time appeared trembling
and immediate. She could see the spires of large churches that
had seen many congregations which had flowed into them and
flowed out again in their changing dresses. She found herself
on ancient winding stairs at which people had once stood and
talked in their short red flaring cloaks. The whole area was a
place of romance and mystery. She walked up the steps till she
arrived at a library which was advertising an exhibition of old
manuscripts. She entered and went into a room which was off
to the right and in which a man in blue uniform was sitting at
a desk looking rather bored. He said good morning and turned
back to whatever he was doing. She walked around looking at
the old manuscripts, most of them beautiful illuminated Bibles
such as she had never seen before. The pages were embellished
with colourful Virgin Marys, green fields, and omnipresent
angels. She couldn't read the writing, most of which appeared
to be in Latin. In one section she saw Mary, Queen of Scots'
last letter written in ancient French in which she seemed not
to show so much fear as an imperious hauteur. But it was the
lovely illuminated Bibles with their populace of angels that
captivated her. What patience and faith and sense of vocation
these monks must have had to create these works! She imagined
them in gardens, surrounded by trees inhabited by birds, pains-

takingly drawing and painting. She compared their colours to those of the TV screen and smiled to herself. The world which they revealed seemed so natural and so real though in fact the angels were descending on to the earth that we know. One showed Sarah, Abraham's wife, being greeted by the two young men who were really angels and the whole picture was so ordinary and almost banal and everyday that it comforted her. Imagine a time when angels came to talk to human beings in such an unremarkable manner, descending and ascending ladders that led from heaven to earth like painters on the street. She thought what her mother would have said. 'Nothing but candles and masses,' she would have said. 'Heathenism.'

As she was going out the old librarian was standing at the door. He said, 'We have millions of books here. Millions. Down below,' he said, pointing.

'Do any of them ever get stolen?' she asked.

'Sometimes,' he said. 'We have a lot of manuscripts here. Some valuable ones get stolen.'

'I suppose a lot of them go to America,' she said.

'They go where the money is. But I don't know much about that.' They talked for a little longer and then she went out into the sunshine.

She continued down the long street. After a while she came to a museum and went inside after she had paid ten pence. She stayed for some time at a case which showed old spectacles worn by people in the past. One pair reminded her of the ones her grandmother used to wear when she visited her as a child. She remembered her grandmother as a twinkling old woman who seemed always to be sitting knitting at a window looking out on to a field full of flowers and inhabited by one wandering cow with soft resentful eyes. As she looked at the spectacles she seemed to see her grandmother again holding a needle up to her eyes and peering through her steel-rimmed glasses.

She left the case with the glasses and had a look at one with old coins, and later one with old stones which were labelled with the name of the finders. There were also ancient stone axes and stone jewellery.

There was a case which showed a wild cat with its claws sunk in the dead body of a rabbit, and another one of a large eagle with flashing yellow eyes. In a corner there were some old guns. There were powder horns richly decorated and domestic implements of various kinds.

One section had a complete reconstruction in shaded orange light of a cottage of the nineteenth century. There was an old woman wearing a shawl sitting on a chair looking into a peat fire. In one corner there was a herring barrel and in another a creel. There was an old clock on a mantelpiece and an iron grille for holding oat cakes. There were old candles and by the fire an old teapot and kettle. Beside the old woman there was a cradle with a doll lying in it imitating a sleeping child. There was a churn and a dressing table. There was a flail and a table. The old woman, long-nosed and shawled, seemed to be dreaming as she looked into the imitation fire. Again she was reminded of her grandmother as this woman too had a pair of spectacles on her nose.

How long ago it all was. How apparently calm it had all been. How pastoral and tranquil that existence behind glass. Had it really been like that? Day after day of peaceful existence without challenge, surrounded by the furniture and routine of a life without significant history. If she broke the glass and entered that world how would she find it? Would she find it peaceful or boring, a world without radio or TV or ballet or art or music, but a world with children and animals and work? How much one could lack and how much one could have. Faintly in the distance she heard the roar of the traffic. What about her own mother? Had she been happy in her routine? She didn't think so, though her father had apparently been. Did she love her father more than she loved her mother? She couldn't say: perhaps they were both part of her, the restless and the tranquil. The fire flamed in front of the old woman showing a red landscape. What was she thinking of as she looked into it? What a strange motionless world really. What a distant motionless world.

She turned away and went outside again. She sat down on a bench and rested in the coolness of the morning.

Men and women were going in and coming out of a bar

opposite but she herself never went into a bar alone. At one time she used to go to pubs with Phil and she would sit there sipping a tomato juice. She never said much but Phil was always the centre of attention, open and generous. Not that he was particularly witty, he was just energetic and lively. She sometimes wondered whether this was what was important in life, energy, but at other times she thought that it was courage that was important. Phil wasn't particularly courageous. In fact in many ways he was weak. She had heard that he had left the shop and gone off to London and wasn't doing very well there. He was the kind of person who would become very dull and complaining when he felt that his youth was over, she was sure of that.

She decided that she would go to the Castle after all, since there was nothing else to do. She got up and walked slowly up the brae and when she got to the entrance bought her ticket and joined the queue which was waiting for the guide to take them round. Standing at the gate were two soldiers dressed in tartan trews who, with rifles beside them, stared unwinkingly ahead of them as if they were mechanical dolls. The guide who was carrying a stick and who looked like an ex-sergeant major – strong and red-cheeked – led them off. She half listened to his practised commentary, watching the people ahead of her, most of them foreign. There was a Japanese girl and a boy, some crew-cut Americans, a group who spoke German and a Frenchman with a moustache. The guide told them about the defences of the castle and she thought that every day he would be making the same speech and stopping at the same places for laughter. He made a few jokes about the English and she saw some people laughing: she thought that they were probably English.

After a while she left the party and entered a small chapel which was dedicated to St Margaret. There was a portrait of her in colour with folded hands set in the window, and a Bible on the table. She had a certain tranquillity about her such as she had already seen in the illuminated manuscripts. What was a saint? she wondered. How did one become a saint? Was it when all anger left one, when all passion was drained away, when one was utterly transparent and all life moved in front of one as in pictures? And were saints saints all the time, or only at particular moments?

She left the chapel and went into the museum which contained all sorts of stuff, uniforms, helmets, guns. She stayed for a long time staring at a black Prussian cap which was shaped like a skull. Once she saw the uniform of a British soldier which had a charred hole in the breast where the bullet had entered. There were pictures on the wall of battle scenes. One showed a British soldier in the act of driving his sword through a French standard bearer at Waterloo. She shuddered. What was it like to kill a man with a sword? It would be easier to do it with a gun. She couldn't imagine herself killing anyone with bare steel, it would be an impossibility.

She wandered about studying waterbottles, guns, powder-horns, armour. She read the names of those who had been killed in wars and read the memorial to the unknown dead. She had a look at the Scottish jewellery, the Honours of Scotland. It looked tawdrier than she expected.

When she came out she sat down on a bench near the black cannon wondering what she would do next. From where she was sitting she could look down into the mouths of the cannon and above them the roofs of the city, on which gangs had written with chalk words like groovy and so on. Eventually she got up and left the Castle and walked down the brae and into a restaurant where she had her lunch.

It was two o'clock when she came out and she was at a loss what to do next. She thought that perhaps she might go and sit in the Gardens. So that was what she did. She sat on a bench and half read a book and half snoozed. There were a number of people on the putting green and others lying in the sun, their arms about each other, while in the Pavilion a religious singer sang with great fervour a song about Jesus's saving blood.

All around her was movement and laughter. She tried to concentrate on her book, which was a paperback copy of Rebecca, but she couldn't, and finally she laid it down. It was as if she was feeling a change coming over her, a mutation, but she couldn't imagine what it was and she felt dizzy and slightly frightened. She got up again and walked over to the Information Bureau which was quite near. She discovered that there was a play on that night and decided that she would go. It was about Hitler but she didn't know what to expect. Time passed very slowly. She bought an evening paper but most of it seemed to be about cricket and tennis. There was, however, a story about a man and his wife who had picked up a hitch-hiker in their car. After they had been travelling for some time the hitch-hiker had dragged the wife into a wood threatening the husband that if he said anything he would kill him. She nodded over the paper and fell asleep. When she woke up it seemed to be cooler and the place slightly more empty. She got up and went along for her tea. It was now five o'clock.

It occurred to her as she walked along that she ought to have more friends, people she could go and stay with. The previous summer she had actually gone to stay with a friend of hers, a college friend called Joan, who had recently married. But she had found the stay constricting and tedious as Joan had become very dull and respectable and responsible since her marriage, and she had left earlier than she had intended. It was odd how people changed. Before her marriage Joan had been very gay and exciting; now she looked as if she were carrying the weight of the whole world on her shoulders. She also worried a lot about money though her husband had a good job and was making at least three thousand a year.

She went into a restaurant and had some tea. By this time she was almost getting tired of eating. After her tea, which she prolonged till half past five, she went down and sat in the station waiting-room for a while, till the play would begin. She thought about being married and being single. When one was married there were all sorts of things one had to do: the world became untidy. One had to adjust to a husband, then one had to cope with noisy children. She could do this all right in the school because the children she taught were not her own. She saw them to a certain extent at their best, not when they were screaming for attention, or harassing one when one was tired. On the other hand, to be single was not a particularly good state to be in. One gradually lost contact with people unless one was one of those women who served on committees or started art clubs or went to church with flowered hats or made endless jars of preserves.

She sat on a leather seat in the waiting room as if she were waiting for a train. She could imagine herself going to London or any other part of Britain. Better still would be an airport lounge: there one could imagine oneself going to Europe or Africa or Asia. She had only been on a plane once and it had been just like being on a bus, not at all exciting, just looking out of a window and seeing banks of white clouds below one.

It was funny how she fell asleep so often nowadays if she sat down for a long time. Perhaps that was a good thing: on the other hand it might mean that there was something wrong with her. It might be psychological also. She ought really to try and keep awake.

She read some of her book and then went out and walked about the station. She noticed a number of telephone kiosks some of which had been smashed and had gang slogans written on them in chalk. The dangling useless phones somehow looked symbolic. The unharmed booths were occupied by people talking excitedly into black mouthpieces.

Everywhere she went it was the same, people talking to each other, laughing, gesturing, sometimes shouting at each other, as once she had seen a gipsy and his wife quarrelling. It had ended with the man hitting his wife across the face so that blood poured out of her lip. A bony dog barked at their heels and in the background smoke rose slowly out of their camp.

You never saw so many gipsies now. Her mother would never give them anything when they came whining to the door, nor would she listen to the Jehovah's Witnesses who tried to hand out what she called heathenish magazines. Her mother would get rid of such people briskly and effectively. She herself would listen to them in an embarrassed manner while they, that is the religious people, would talk about

Darwin and God, referring closely like automata to verses in the Bible. Invariably she bought one of their magazines which her mother would immediately throw in the bin.

As she sat in the waiting-room, watching through the window trains coming and going, pictures of all kinds passed before her eyes. She remembered a holiday she had once had in a desolate glen in the Highlands. She could visualise clearly the mountains veined with stone, the deer that grazed by fences, the foaming rivers, the abandoned cottages, the blaze of yellow gorse, the horses nuzzling each other on the sands. She had liked that place. It seemed suited to her personality. But one day she had seen, sitting in front of a caravan, a large fat lady dressed in red trousers and painting the glen, and the illusion of contentment had been destroyed.

At five past seven she started to walk to the theatre. Now that she had an aim she was happy but at the same time she thought that she would have difficulty in filling the hours of the following day. She had already exhausted quite a lot of the sights she had intended to see, unless perhaps she went on a bus tour. She would have to check on that in the morning, or perhaps they had a brochure in the hotel.

Her feet were already getting sore as she had done a lot of walking but she didn't want to spend money on a taxi. She didn't like taxis. They reminded her of hearses and she was always sure she was being cheated. They would always take one the long way round and she was sure the drivers recognised strangers to the town instinctively.

At twenty past seven she reached the theatre which was a very small one, seating perhaps sixty people or so, on cushions round the central area which formed the stage. There were strong lights blazing down which made the place hot: she imagined interrogations taking place there in a concentrated hot dazzle. She had bought a programme which gave very little information about the actual play: all that she gathered was that it seemed very avant garde. She didn't know what exactly to expect, perhaps a dramatisation of the rise of Hitler, with reference to the SS and the Jews and the concentration camps. She didn't often go to the theatre, preferring the cinema, but there was nothing else on that evening. She also didn't like avant-garde stuff.

She noticed that the audience was predominantly youthful, girls wearing slacks and Indian headbands, most of them probably students. The theatre was a small and intimate one and she could hear some of them talking in a brittle know-ledgeable way before the play started. She sat in the front row on her cushion wishing that it was a chair and feeling rather tired because there was no support for her back.

It was certainly not a conventional play. It began with a sinister music on drums which went on and on, exerting a hypnotic dark rhythm. In a mirror high above she could see the drummers with their long hair reflected. Then a young man came into the central space and stood there motionless for a long time while the music played.

Suddenly he became a dying German soldier with glazed eyes, greatcoat, rifle and dull boots. Children came in and danced around him, among them a girl who appeared to be a spastic. The beating drums seemed to draw one into the dying festering mind of the German soldier by their rhythmic com-pulsion, as he was slowly resurrected, pulling himself to his feet against the wind of death and the beat of the drums. He made an appointment with the spastic girl who at night went into a wood to meet him, the dead German soldier. The lights all dimmed, there was only the wood created by the words, and the girl trying to find the German soldier on her macabre tryst, while the music played, the music of dark Nazism, the music of the terrible haunted wood, where everything was eerie and festering, and the animals crawled and killed. The scene was electrifying. It made her feel excited and disgusted at the same time, that wood where all desires were waiting, buried, but rising as if reflected in the manic glasses of the murdering German soldier. The girl crawled into the wood. The music quickened and then there was the interval, a sane blaze of lights.

She stood up, shaken. She hardly knew where she was. She left the theatre knowing that she couldn't bear to watch. She walked out into the hurting daylight. She walked down the brae steadily till she came to the park again. There she sat down on a bench among all the people. Behind her she could hear the tolling of a church bell. Ahead of her she could see the glasshouse where all the flowers were – the wide red flowers – and the plants, the Mexican cacti which she had once seen and which could exist on so little water.

She sat on the bench and as she did so she thought to herself: I can't bear this total freedom any more. I can't, I can't. I don't know what to do. I cannot live like this. She got up restlessly and walked into the wood. She looked down at a stretch of water where the polluted river flowed past. There were some boys wearing towels round their waists who seemed to have just emerged from the dirty stream, which was not at all like the clean streams to which she herself had been accustomed and where you could see right down to the bottom where the white stones were.

As she stood there she saw a little girl in checked skirt and checked blouse walking into the wood by herself to pick flowers. Dazed she watched her. To her right she could hear the shouting of the boys. Without knowing precisely what she was doing she began to follow the little girl. As she did so she was amazed to discover that a transformation had taken place in her as if she had found a role which she could perform, as if the total freedom had narrowed and come to a focus. She didn't know what she was going to do but it was as if she felt it right whatever it would turn out to be. She followed the little girl into the wood.

Murdo and Calvin

One day Murdo went into the police station.

'I wish,' he said, 'to report something.'

'And what is that, sir?' said the sergeant, who was large, polite, and red-faced.

'I wish to report,' said Murdo feverishly, 'a sighting of Calvin.'

He paused impressively.

'And which Calvin is that, sir?' said the sergeant quietly. 'And why should you report him?'

'Calvin, Sergeant, is a dangerous lunatic. He is responsible for the Free Church, for the state of Scottish literature, and for many other atrocities too numerous to mention. And especially the Kailyard,' he added in a low voice.

'Kailyard, sir?'

'That's right, Sergeant. One of his grossest inventions. I want him arrested.'

'But, sir,' said the sergeant, 'I can't . . .'

'I haven't finished yet,' said Murdo in a penetrating voice. 'I believe him also to have committed the greatest sin of all. I can only tell you in a whisper. I believe him to have invented the Bible.'

'Invented the Bible, sir?'

'That's right, sergeant. I have always suspected that the Bible was the invention of one man, a man with a colossal ego and a criminal mind. Let me ask you this. If the Bible had been invented by God would it contain all the mistakes that it contains. For instance,' he said rapidly, 'how is it that God is supposed to have created light before making the sun or the moon? You can read of that error in Genesis. That is only one example. Another example is this. What woman was supposed to have married Cain when there was no other woman alive on the face of the deep but his own mother Eve? They suggest to me the inventions of a man who was not naturally creative and, as we know, Calvin – like Francis Bacon, another treacherous man – was a lawyer.

'Listen, in the Bible there's a man called Amraphel, one called Ashteroth, and another one called Chedorlaomer. There are the names invented by a tired mind. Also, he made other slips in this gigantic enterprise. He said that Reu lived after he begat Serug two hundred and seven years. All this suggests a man engaged in the creation of a stupendous best-seller whose mind flickered at the typewriter. Have you any idea, Sergeant, how many copies of this vast book have been sold in the last thousand years? It is the most bizarre plot in human history.'

'But, sir, I . . . ' the sergeant tried to intervene.

'And that is not all by any means,' said Murdo, his eyes assuming a supernatural sharpness and directness. 'If you will allow me to continue. There is also this fact which I think is almost conclusive. A book of such magnitude must have taxed even the greatest brain. And so we find whole chapters which are feverish outpourings making no sense at all, either that or these are space fillers pure and simple. How else can one explain whole chapters which run as follows?

'And Shem lived after he begat Arphaxad five hundred years, and Arphaxad lived three and thirty years and begat Salah, and Arphaxad lived after he begat Salah four hundred and three years. And this, mark you, Sergeant, is the lowest limit of some of the ages. Think, Sergeant, of the huge amounts of money that would have to be paid in old age pensions if that were true. Think of the drain on the Health Service, the hospitals required, the Social Security, the guide dogs, the food, the drink, the white sticks, the geriatric wards. How could any economy have sustained such a vast number of the ancient, especially before television was invented. Look, sergeant, it cannot be denied that there is at least here a basis for investigation.'

The sergeant's round reddish eyes gazed at him.

'All the oxen and the asses,' continued Murdo relentlessly,

'that one could covet. Is there not something there too? Crimes unimaginable. A fiction of such remarkable cunning that it is difficult for us to understand the ramifications of its plot. The sex, the murders, the casual examples of incest, sodomy, black magic and theft. The silences on important matters like justice and religion. It has been clear to me for many years that at the back of all this was Calvin. Tell me this,' said Murdo earnestly, 'if you were going to investigate a criminal would you not ask yourself certain questions? Ah, I see that you would. Who, you ask, gains by such an immense crime. And you must answer if you look around your country today that the only person to gain must be Calvin. Wasn't it he and his church who became triumphant? Who therefore would be more likely to bring such a result about? Ah, you are now going to ask me the most penetrating question. Opportunity. Did Calvin in fact have the opportunity? You may say reasonably enough that Calvin lived centuries ago but was not so old as the Bible. That puzzled me for a while too, till eventually I saw the solution to it. And I found the solution, as commonly happens, in his own work. You remember that he mentioned a number of people who lived to the age of eight hundred. I believe that Calvin lived to the almost unimaginable age of 22,000 years five months and two days. He waited and waited, keeping his manuscript intact, till one day the printing press was invented and he pounced (is it a coincidence by the way that Calvin differs from Caxton by only three letters?).

'I can tell you, sergeant, that on that day Calvin was in his element. Imagine what it must have been like for him to know that his book, once a scroll, would be read all over the world, that boats would ferry his best-seller to the ignorant Africans, Asians and the Scots. Imagine the size of the royalties.

'And now he is here and I have seen him. He will hardly leave his house (for his cunning is supernatural) and I only saw him briefly while he was completing his toilet on the moor. He will speak to no women and if any come near him he will shake his stick at them and mutter words like, "Impudent whores, prostitutes of the deepest dye." And that is another thing,' said Murdo vigorously, boring his eyes towards the crab-red eyes of the sergeant. 'A writer can be told by his convictions, by his mannerisms. Calvin hated women and this appears in the Bible. In nearly every case the women are either treacherous or boring. He hated sheep as well: think of the number that he sacrificed. Who is this man then, this woman-hater, this sheep-hater-genius who has deceived so many million people, ambitious inventor of strange names? What other evidence do you need?'

He stopped and the silence lasted for a long time.

'But I have not,' Murdo continued, 'reached the highest point of my deductions yet. It came to me as a bolt from the blue as bolts often do. The beauty of it is breathtaking. Let me list those things again: a man who hates women, who deceives men, who lives thousands of years, who will stop at nothing for gain, who has come out of hiding at this present disturbed time, who wears a bowler hat, whose sense of humour is so impenetrable that no one can understand it, who imposes such colossal boredom on the world that no one can stay awake in his presence, a man who uses boredom as a weapon. Who, I repeat, is this man? I will tell you,' and he lowered his voice again. 'I believe that this man is the Devil.' He leaned back in triumph. 'There, I have said it. Think how many problems that solves at a stroke. Think how the knots untie themselves, if we once understand that Calvin is the Devil. Everything that was opaque to us before is now crystal clear. All the questions that we need to ask are answered. You must,' he said decisively, 'send a Black Maria for him at once, or a green one or even a blue one, before he can start on more books of such length. Is he planning to come out of hiding to demand his royalties? Think of our country. How could it withstand such a demand? Surely you of all people can see that . . . Ah, I understand, you aren't going to do anything. I was afraid of that. Well, don't say that I didn't warn you when the consequences of his arrival here become clear.' He backed towards the door, the sergeant leaning across the desk towards him. 'Remember that I warned you. You have my phone number, my fingerprints. I have nothing to gain. We know who has something to gain.' He screamed as he went round the door.

'Put him in a cell or he'll destroy us all. Bring him in on suspicion of loitering, of parking on a double yellow line, of singing at the Mod.'

The sergeant strode towards the door and locked and bolted it. He was breathing heavily. And even yet he thought that he could hear that voice shouting, ' . . . for being a hit man for the Educational Institute of Scotland.'

After the Dance

I had met her at a dance and we went to her house at about eleven o'clock at night. It was in a tenement and the steps up to her door were wide and large and clean as if they had been newly washed. The road, I remember, was very slippery as it was winter and, walking along in her red leather coat and red gloves, she looked like an ageing heroine out of a fairy story.

When we opened the door and went in she said in a whisper, 'You'll have to be quiet. My father is asleep.' The room blossomed into largeness in the light and one's first impression was of whiteness, white wallpaper and white paint. Above the mantelpiece there was a rectangular mirror with a flowery border. There were rooms leading off the one we were in and the whole flat seemed much more spacious than one might have expected.

She took off her coat and gloves and laid them on the table and sat down. The fire had gone out but there were still a few bits of charred wood remaining in it. A large dog got up and greeted her and then lay down in a corner munching a bone. A white-faced clock ticked on the mantelpiece.

'Would you like some tea?' she asked.

I said 'Yes,' and she went to the blue cooker and put the kettle on. She got out a tin of biscuits.

'My father will be trying to listen,' she said. 'But he's in the far end room. He doesn't sleep very well. There's no one to look after him but me. No one else. I have four sisters and they're all married and they won't look at him. Does one abandon him?' She looked at me wearily and now that she had removed her red coat her face appeared more haggard and her throat more lined. 'Or does one sacrifice oneself? He says to me, "Why did you never marry like your sisters and your brothers?" He taunts me with not marrying and yet he knows that if I married he would be left alone. Isn't that queer? You'd think he wouldn't say things like that, I mean in his own defence. You'd think he'd have more sense. But he doesn't have any sense. He spends a lot of his time doing jigsaws. They never come out right of course. A bit of a castle or a boat, something like that, but most of the time he can't be bothered finishing them. And another thing he does; he puts ships in bottles. He spends hours trying to get the sails inside with bits of string. He used to be a sailor you see. He's been all over the world. But most of the time he cuts wood. He goes down to the shore and gathers wood and chops it up in the woodshed. He makes all sorts of useless ornaments. He's got an axe. And lots of tools. In the summer he spends all his time in the shed chopping up wood. There's a wood-shed down below on the back lawn and in the summer there are leaves all round it. He sits there. But he's always hacking away with that axe. Day after day. But what can one do with the old?'

She poured the hot water into the tea-pot and took it over to the table. She poured the tea into two large blue mugs and milked it.

'It's a problem, isn't it, what to do with the old? If one wasn't so good-hearted – some people aren't like that at all. Do you take sugar? One? Some people can go away and forget. My sisters always make excuses for not having him. They say they haven't got enough space with the children. Or they say they haven't got enough money. Or they say he wouldn't be good for the children. It's funny how they can be so forgetful and yet he wasn't any better to me than he was to them. In fact he treated me worse.'

She looked at me as if she expected me to say something. I murmured something unintelligible through the biscuit I was chewing, thinking that it all did sound really like a fairy tale. I wondered why she wore red. I had been reading something in one of the Sunday colour supplements about colour being a betrayal of one's personality but then everything was a betrayal of one's personality. Even conversation. I myself preferred blue but she wore red gloves, a red coat and she even had a red ribbon in her hair.

She was an odd mixture. At the dance she had danced very freely as they do in *Top of the Pops*, swaying like an unconscious flower, in a hypnotic trance of complete surrender to the body.

The dog crunched his bone in the corner and the clock ticked on.

'I don't understand why I'm so soft-hearted,' she said, crushing a biscuit in her hand.

I looked at the TV set. 'Is there anything on TV?' I said, 'or would that disturb your father?'

'There's a *Radio Times* there,' she said carelessly. 'If we shut the door he won't hear it. I don't watch it much.' The set was of white wood and I had a vision of her father hacking it up for firewood with his trusty axe.

I found the *Radio Times* among a pile of romantic magazines, some of which lay open with rings of black ink round horoscopes.

'There's a series about Henry VIII,' I said. 'It's been going on for a week or two. Have you seen any of it?'

'No,' she said, 'but if you want it. So long as it isn't too loud.'

I switched on the TV and waited for the picture to declare itself. How did people exist before TV? What did they talk about? She rested her elbow on the table and drank her tea.

The picture clarified itself. It showed Anne Boleyn going to the scaffold. She was being prepared by her maids in attendance in the prison while the sunlight shone in straight shafts through the barred window. She told them that she wasn't frightened though some of them were crying and their hands shaking as they tied the ribbon in her hair.

The scene shifted to the execution block and showed a large man in black who was wearing a black mask: he was carrying a huge axe in his hand. The wooden block lay below. She came forward and lay down as if she were a swimmer, her hair neatly tied. Her motion had an eerie aesthetic quality as if she were taking part in a ballet dance, swanning forward, the axe falling. As the axe cut the head from the neck there was a roar of applause from the people.

I turned towards her. She was looking very pale. 'I don't like these TV programmes,' she said, and I switched it off. 'They're all so violent.'

'I'd better be going,' I said looking at the clock. 'It's getting late.'

'Yes, I suppose you'd better,' she said. 'I enjoyed the dance.'

I went out into the darkness, at first unable to see, and closing the main door of the tenement behind me. Then as my eyes focused and the sky came into view and defined itself, I saw the white stars. They were like the bones the dog had been crunching.

I walked very carefully along the glassy road almost slithering at times.

Funny about the tall man with the mask and the axe. It had reminded me of something in its extraordinary blatant brutality. The axe and the wood. But the picture I remembered most clearly was that of Anne Boleyn in the sunlight looking out of the narrow barred window on to the lawn. I really hoped that she had meant it when she said that she wasn't afraid. But she had certainly acted as if she meant it. And I was sure she did. For that particular moment in time she had meant it and that was something. One could not be expected to mean it for all moments, even on TV.

Mother and Son

His clothes were dripping as he came in. The water was streaming down his cheeks, a little reddened by the wind and the rain. He shook back his long hair and threw his jacket on the bed post, then abruptly remembering, he looked through the pockets for a box of matches. The house was in partial darkness, for, though the evening was not dark, the daylight was hooded by thick yellow curtains which were drawn across the width of the window. He shivered slightly as he lit the match : it had been a cold, dismal afternoon in the fields. The weather was extraordinarily bad for the time of year and gathering the sheaves into stacks was both monotonous and uncomfortable. He held the match cupped within his hands to warm them and to light his way to the box where he kept the peats. The flickering light showed a handsome face. The forehead was smooth and tanned, the nose thin though not incisive, the mouth curved and petulant, and the chin small and round. It was a good-looking face, though it was a face which had something childish about it. The childishness could be seen by a closer look, a look into the wide blue eyes which were rather stolid and netted by little red lines which divided them up like a graph. These eyes were deep and unquestioning as a child's, but they gave an unaccountable impression that they could be as dangerous and irresponsible as a child's. As the match flickered and went out with an apologetic cough, he cursed weakly and searched his pockets. Then he remembered he had left the box on the table, reached out for it impatiently, and lit another match. This he carried over to the lamp which lay on the table. The light clung to the wick, and he put the clean globe gently inside the brackets. When the lamp was lit, it showed a moderately sized kitchen, the walls of which were painted a dull yellow. The dresser was surmounted by numerous shelves which held numerous dishes, some whole, some broken. A little china dog looked over the edge as if searching for crumbs: but the floor was clean and spotless, though the green linoleum looked a bit worn. Along one wall of the room was a four-poster bed with soiled pillows and a coverlet of some dark, rough material. In the bed was a woman. She was sleeping, her mouth tightly shut and prim and anaemic. There was a bitter smile on her lips as if fixed there; just as you sometimes see the insurance man coming to the door with the same smile each day, the same brilliant smile which never falls away till he's gone into the anonymity of the streets. The forehead was not very high and not low, though its wrinkles gave it an expression of concentration as if the woman were wrestling with some terrible witch's idea in dreams. The man looked at her for a moment, then fumbled for his matches again and began to light a fire. The sticks fell out of place and he cursed vindictively and helplessly. For a moment he sat squatting on his haunches staring into the fire, as if he were thinking of some state of innocence, some state to which he could not return : a reminiscent smile dimpled his cheeks and showed in eyes which immediately became still and dangerous again. The clock struck five wheezingly and, at the first chime, the woman woke up. She started as she saw the figure crouched over the fire and then subsided: 'It's only you.' There was relief in the voice, but there was a curious hint of contempt or acceptance. He still sat staring into the fire and answered dully: 'Yes, it's only me!' He couldn't be said to speak the words: they fell away from him as sometimes happens when one is in a deep reverie where every question is met by its answer almost instinctively.

'Well, what's the matter with you!' she snapped pettishly, 'sitting there moping with the tea to be made. I sometimes don't know why we christened you John' – with a sigh. 'My father was never like you. He was a man who knew his business.'

'All right, *all* right,' he said despairingly. 'Can't you get a new record for your gramophone. I've heard all that before,' as if he were conscious of the inadequacy of this familiar retort – he added: 'hundreds of times.' But she wasn't to be stopped.

'I can't understand what has come over you lately. You keep mooning about the house, pacing up and down with your hands in your pockets. Do you know what's going to happen to you, you'll be taken to the asylum. That's where you'll go. Your father's people had something wrong with their heads, it was in your family but not in ours.' (She had always looked upon him as her husband's son, not as her own: and all his faults she attributed to hereditary weaknesses on his father's side.)

He pottered about, putting water in the kettle, waiting desperately for the sibilant noise to stop. But no, it took a long time to stop. He moved about inside this sea of sound trying to keep detached, trying to force himself from listening. Sometimes, at rarer and rarer intervals, he could halt and watch her out of a clear, cold mind as if she didn't matter, as if her chatter which eddied round and round, then burst venomously towards him, had no meaning for him, could not touch him. At these times her little bitter barbs passed over him or through him to come out on the other side. Most often however they stung him and stood quivering in his flesh, and he would say something angrily with the reflex of the wound. But she always cornered him. She had so much patience, and then again she enjoyed pricking him with her subtle arrows. He had now become so sensitive that he usually read some devilish meaning into her smallest utterance.

'Have you stacked all the sheaves now?' she was asking. He swung round on his eddying island as if he had seen that the seas were relenting, drawing back. At such moments he became deferential.

'Yes,' he said joyously. 'I've stacked them all. And I've done it all alone too. I did think Roddy Mason would help. But he doesn't seem to have much use for me now. He's gone the way the rest of the boys go. They all take a job. Then they get together and laugh at me.' His weakness was pitiful: his childish blue eyes brimmed with tears. Into the grimace by which he sought to tauten his face, he put a murderous determination:

but though the lines of his face were hard, the eyes had no steadiness: the last dominance had long faded and lost itself in the little red lines which crossed and recrossed like a graph.

'Of course Roddy doesn't want to help you. He's got enough to do as it is. Anyway he's got his day's work to do and you haven't.'

'It isn't my fault I haven't.' He spoke wearily. The old interminable argument was beginning again: he always made fresh attacks but as often retired defeated. He stood up suddenly and paced about the room as if he wanted to overawe her with his untidy hair, his thick jersey, and long wellingtons.

'You know well enough,' he shouted, 'why I haven't my day's work. It's because you've been in bed there for ten years now. Do you *want* me to take a job? I'll take a job tomorrow . . . if you'll only say!' He was making the same eternal argument and the same eternal concession: 'If you'll only say.' And all the time he knew she would never say, and she knew that he would never take any action.

'Why, you'd be no good in a job. The manager would always be coming to show you what you had done wrong, and you'd get confused with all those strange faces and they'd laugh at you.' Every time she spoke these words the same brutal pain stabbed him. His babyish eyes would be smitten by a hellish despair, would lose all their hope, and cloud over with the pain of the mute, suffering animal. Time and time again he would say to her when she was feeling better and in a relatively humane mood: 'I'm going to get a job where the other fellows are!' and time and time again, with the unfathomable and unknowable cunning of the woman, she would strike his confidence dead with her hateful words. Yes, he was timid. He admitted it to himself, he hated himself for it, but his cowardice still lay there waiting for him, particularly in the dark nights of his mind when the shadow lay as if by a road, watching him, tripping behind him, changing its shape, till the sun came to shine on it and bring its plausible explanations. He spoke again, passing his hand wearily over his brow as if he were asking for her pity.

'Why should anybody laugh at me? They don't laugh at the

other chaps. Everybody makes mistakes. I could learn as quickly as any of them. Why, I used to do his lessons for Norman Slater.' He looked up eagerly at her as if he wanted her to corroborate. But she only looked at him impatiently, that bitter smile still upon her face.

'Lessons aren't everything. You aren't a mechanic. You can't do anything with your hands. Why don't you hurry up with that tea? Look at you. Fat good you'd be at a job.'

He still sat despairingly leaning near the fire, his head on his hands. He didn't even hear the last part of her words. True, he wasn't a mechanic. He never could understand how things worked. This ignorance and inaptitude of his puzzled himself. It was not that he wasn't intelligent: it was as if something had gone wrong in his childhood, some lack of interest in lorries and aeroplanes and mechanisms, which hardened into a wall beyond which he could not go through – paradise lay yonder.

He reached up for the tea absent-mindedly and poured hot water into the tea-pot. He watched it for a while with a sad look on his face, watched the fire leaping about it as if it were a soul in hell. The cups were white and undistinguished and he felt a faint nausea as he poured the tea into them. He reached out for the tray, put the tea-cup and a plate with bread and jam on it, and took it over to the bed. His mother sat up and took the tray from him, settling herself laboriously back against the pillows. She looked at it and said:

'Why didn't you wash this tray? Can't you see it's all dirty round the edges?' He stood there stolidly for a moment, not listening, watching her frail, white-clad body, and her spiteful, bitter face. He ate little but drank three cups of tea. Then he took out a packet of cigarettes and lit one nervously and self-consciously.

'Cigarettes again? Don't you know that there's very little money coming into the house. If it weren't for your father's pension where would you be . . . you who's never done a day's work in your life? Answer me!' she screamed. 'Why are you sitting there like a dummy, you silly fool!' He took no notice, but puffed at his cigarette. There was a terrible weariness in his eyes. Nowadays he seldom felt his body tired: it was always his mind. This voice of hers, these pettinesses of hers, were always attacking his mind, burrowing beneath it, till he felt himself in a dark cave from which there was never to be any escape. Sometimes words came to him to silence her, but between the words leaving his mind and leaving his lips they had changed: they had lost their import, their impact, and their usefulness.

His mind now seemed gradually to be clearing up, and he was beginning to judge his own actions and hers. Everything was clearing up: it was one of his moments. He turned round on his chair from a sudden impulse and looked at her intensely. He had done this very often before, had tried to cow her into submission: but she had always laughed at him. Now however he was looking at her as if he had never seen her before. Her mouth was open and there were little crumbs upon her lower lip. Her face had sharpened itself into a birdlike quickness: she seemed to be pecking at the bread with a sharp beak in the same way as she pecked cruelly at his defences. He found himself considering her as if she were some kind of animal. Detachedly he thought: how can this thing make my life a hell for me? What is she anyway? She's been ill for ten years: that doesn't excuse her. She's breaking me up so that even if she dies I won't be any good for anyone. But what if she's pretending? What if there is nothing wrong with her? At this a rage shook him so great that he flung his half-consumed cigarette in the direction of the fire in an abrupt, savage gesture. Out of the silence he heard a bus roaring past the window, splashing over the puddles. That would be the boys going to the town to enjoy themselves. He shivered inside his loneliness and then rage took hold of him again. How he hated her! This time his gaze concentrated itself on her scraggy neck, rising like a hen's out of her plain white night-gown. He watched her chin wagging up and down: it was stained with jam and flecked with one or two crumbs. His sense of loneliness closed round him, so that he felt as if he were on a boat on the limitless ocean, just as his house was on a limitless moorland. There was a calm, unspeaking silence, while the rain beat like a benediction on the roof. He walked over to the bed, took the tray from her as she held it out to him. He had gone in answer to words which he hadn't heard, so hedged was he in his own thoughts.

'Remember to clean the tray tomorrow,' she said. He walked back with the tray fighting back the anger that swept over him carrying the rubbish and debris of his mind in its wake. He turned back to the bed. His mind was in a turmoil of hate, so that he wanted to smash the cup, smash the furniture, smash the house. He kept his hands clenched, he the puny and unimaginative. He would show her, avenge her insults with his unintelligent hands. There was the bed, there was his mother. He walked over.

She was asleep, curled up in the warmth with the bitter, bitter smile upon her face. He stood there for a long moment while an equally bitter smile curled up the edge of his lips. Then he walked to the door, opened it, and stood listening to the rain.

An American Sky

He stood on the deck of the ship looking towards the approaching island. He was a tall man who wore brownish clothes: and beside him were two matching brown cases. As he stood on the deck he could hear Gaelic singing coming from the saloon which wasn't all that crowded but had a few people in it, mostly coming home for a holiday from Glasgow. The large ship moved steadily through the water and when he looked over the side he could see thin spitlike foam travelling alongside. The island presented itself as long and green and bare with villages scattered along the coast. Ahead of him was the westering sun which cast long red rays across the water.

He felt both excited and nervous as if he were returning to a wife or sweetheart whom he had not seen for a long time and was wondering whether she had changed much in the interval, whether she had left him for someone else or whether she had remained obstinately true. It was strange, he thought, that though he was sixty years old he should feel like this. The journey from America had been a nostalgic one, first the plane, then the train, then the ship. It was almost a perfect circle, a return to the womb. A womb with a view, he thought and smiled.

He hadn't spoken to many people on the ship. Most of the time he had been on deck watching the large areas of sea streaming past, now and again passing large islands with mountain peaks, at other times out in the middle of an empty sea where the restless gulls scavenged, turning their yellow gaunt beaks towards the ship.

The harbour was now approaching and people were beginning to come up on deck with their cases. A woman beside him was buttoning up her small son's coat. Already he could see red buses and a knot of people waiting at the pier. It had always been like that, people meeting the ship when it arrived at about eight, some not even welcoming anyone in particular but just standing there watching. He noticed a squat man in fisherman's clothes doing something to a rope. Behind him there was a boat under green canvas.

The ship swung in towards the harbour. Now he could see the people more clearly and behind them the harbour buildings. When he looked over the side he noticed that the water was dirty with bits of wooden boxes floating about in an oily rainbowed scum.

After some manoeuvring the gangway was eventually laid. He picked up his cases and walked down it behind a girl in yellow slacks whose transistor was playing in her left hand. Ahead of her was a man in glasses who had a BEA case with, stamped on it, the names of various foreign cities. There were some oldish women in dark clothes among the crowd and also some girls and boys in brightly coloured clothes. A large fat slow man stood to the side of the gangway where it touched the quay, legs spread apart, as if he had something to do with the ship, though he wasn't actually doing anything. Now and again he scratched a red nose.

He reached the shore and felt as if the contact with land was an emotionally charged moment. He didn't quite know how he felt, slightly empty, slightly excited. He walked away from the ship with his two cases and made his way along the main street. It had changed, no doubt about it. There seemed to be a lot of cafés, from one of which he heard the blare of a jukebox. In a bookseller's window he saw *From Russia with Love* side by side with a book about the Highlands called *The Misty Hebrides*. Nevertheless the place appeared smaller, though it was much more modern than he could remember, with large windows of plate glass, a jeweller's with Iona stone, a very fashionable-looking ladies' hairdressers. He also passed a supermarket and another bookseller's. Red lights from one of the cafés streamed into the bay. At the back of the jeweller's shop he saw a church spire rising into the sky. He came to a cinema which advertised Bingo on Tuesdays, Thursdays and Saturdays. Dispirited trailers for a Western filled the panels.

He came to a Chinese restaurant and climbed the steps, carrying his two cases. The place was nearly empty and seemed mostly purplish with, near the ceiling, a frieze showing red dragons. Vague music – he thought it might be Chinese – leaked from the walls. He sat down and, drawing the huge menu towards him, began to read it. In one corner of the large room an unsmiling Chinaman with a moustache was standing by an old-fashioned black telephone and at another table a young Chinese girl was reading what might have been a Chinese newspaper. A little bare-bottomed Chinese boy ran out of the kitchen, was briefly chased back with much giggling, and the silence descended again.

For a moment he thought that the music was Gaelic, and was lost in his dreams. The Chinese girl seemed to turn into Mary who was doing her homework in the small thatched house years and years before. She was asking their father about some arithmetic but he, stroking his beard, was not able to answer. At another table an old couple were solidly munching rice, their heads bowed.

The music swirled about him. The Chinese girl read on. Why was it that these people never laughed? He had noticed that. Also that Chinese restaurants were hushed like churches. A crowd of young people came in laughing and talking, their Highland accents quite distinct though they were speaking English. He felt suddenly afraid and alone and slightly disorientated as if he had come to the wrong place at the wrong time. The telephone rang harshly and the Chinaman answered it in guttural English. Perhaps he was the only one who could speak English. Perhaps that was his job, just to answer the phone. He had another look at the menu, suddenly put it down and walked out just as a Chinese waitress came across with a notebook and pencil in her hand. He hurried downstairs and walked along the street.

Eventually he found a hotel and stood at the reception desk. A young blonde girl was painting her nails and reading a book. She said to the girl behind her, 'What does "impunity" mean?' The other girl stopped chewing and said, 'Where does it say that?' The first girl looked at him coolly and said, 'Yes,

Sir?' Her voice also was Highland.

'I should like a room,' he said. 'A single room.'

She leafed rapidly through a book and said at last, 'We can give you 101, Sir. Shall I get the porter to carry your bags?'

'It's not necessary.'

'That will be all right then, Sir.'

He waited for a moment and then remembered what he was waiting for. 'Could I please have my key?' he asked.

She looked at him in amazement and said, 'You don't need a key here, Sir. Nobody steals anything. Room 101 is on the first floor. You can't miss it.' He took his cases and walked up the stairs. He heard them discussing a dance as he left.

He opened the door and put the cases down and went to the window. In front of him he could see the ship and the bay with the red lights on it and the fishing boats and the large clock with the greenish face.

As he turned away from the window he saw the Gideon Bible, picked it up, half smiling, and then put it down again. He took off his clothes slowly, feeling very tired, and went to bed. He fell asleep very quickly while in front of his eyes he could see Bingo signs, advertisements for Russian watches, and seagulls flying about with open gluttonous beaks. The last thought he had was that he had forgotten to ask when breakfast was in the morning.

2

The following day at two o'clock in the afternoon he took the bus to the village that he had left so many years before. There were few people on the bus which had a conductress as well as a driver, both dressed in uniform. He thought wryly of the gig in which he had been driven to the town the night he had left; the horse was dead long ago and so was his own father, the driver.

On the seat opposite him there was sitting a large fat tourist who had a camera and field-glasses slung over his shoulder and was wearing dark glasses and a light greyish hat.

The driver was a sturdy young man of about twenty or so.

He whistled a good deal of the time and for the rest exchanged badinage with the conductress who, it emerged, wanted to become an air stewardess. She wore a black uniform, was pretty in a thin, sallow way, and had a turned-up nose and black hair.

After a while he offered a cigarette to the driver who took it. 'Fine day, Sir,' he said and then, 'Are you home on holiday?'

'Yes. From America.'

'Lots of tourists here just now. I was in America myself once. I was in the Merchant Navy. Saw a baseball team last night on TV.'

The bus was passing along the sparkling sea and the cemetery which stood on one side of the road behind a grey wall. The marble of the gravestones glittered in the sun. Now and again he could see caravans parked just off the road and on the beach men and children in striped clothing playing with large coloured balls or throwing sticks for dogs to retrieve. Once they passed a large block of what appeared to be council houses, all yellow.

'You'll see many changes,' said the driver. 'Hey, bring us some of that orangeade,' he shouted to the conductress.

'I suppose so.'

But there didn't seem all that many in the wide glittering day. The sea, of course, hadn't changed, the cemetery looked brighter in the sun perhaps, and there were more houses. But people waved at them from the fields, shielding their eyes with their hands. The road certainly was better.

At one point the tourist asked to be allowed out with his camera so that he could take a photograph of a cow which was staring vaguely over a fence.

If the weather was always like this, he thought, there wouldn't be any problem ... but of course the weather did change ... The familiar feeling of excitement and apprehension flooded him again.

After a while they stopped at the road end and he got off with his two cases. The driver wished him good luck. He stood staring at the bus as it diminished into the distance and then taking his case began to walk along the road. He came to the ruins of a thatched house, stopped and went inside. As he did so he disturbed a swarm of birds which flew out of the space all round him and fluttered out towards the sky which he could see quite clearly as there was no roof. The ruined house was full of stones and bits of wood and in the middle of it an old-fashioned iron range which he stroked absently, making his fingers black and dusty. For a moment the picture returned to him of his mother in a white apron cooking at such a stove, in a smell of flour. He turned away and saw carved in the wooden door the words MARY LOVES NORMAN. The hinges creaked in the quiet day.

He walked along till he came to a large white house at which he stopped. He opened the gate and there, waiting about ten yards in front of him, were his brother, his brother's daughter-in-law, and her two children, one a boy of about seventeen and the other a girl of about fifteen. They all seemed to be dressed in their best clothes and stood there as if in a picture. His brother somehow seemed dimmer than he remembered, as if he were being seen in a bad light. An observer would have noticed that though the two brothers looked alike the visitor seemed a more vivid version of the other. The family waited for him as if he were a photographer and he moved forward. As he did so his brother walked quickly towards him, holding out his hand.

'John,' he said. They looked at each other as they shook hands. His niece came forward and introduced herself and the children. They all appeared well dressed and prosperous.

The boy took his cases and they walked towards the house. It was of course a new house, not the thatched one he had left. It had a porch and a small garden and large windows which looked out towards the road.

He suddenly said to this brother, 'Let's stay out here for a while.' They stood together at the fence gazing at the corn which swayed slightly in the breeze. His brother did not seem to know what to say and neither did he. They stood there in silence.

After a while John said, 'Come on, Murdo, let's look at the barn.' They went into it together. John stood for a while inhaling the smell of hay mixed with the smell of manure. He

picked up a book which had fallen to the floor and looked
inside it. On the fly-leaf was written:

Prize for English
John Macleod

The book itself in an antique and slightly stained greenish
cover was called Robin Hood and His Merry Men. His brother
looked embarrassed and said, 'Malcolm must have taken it off
the shelf in the house and left it here.' John didn't say anything.
He looked idly at the pictures. Some had been torn and
many of the pages were brown with age. His eye was caught
by a passage which read, 'Honour is the greatest virtue of all.
Without it a man is nothing.' He let the book drop to the floor.

'We used to fight in that hayloft,' he said at last with a smile,
'and I think you used to win,' he added, punching his brother
slightly in the chest. His brother smiled with pleasure. 'I'm
not sure about that,' he answered.

'How many cows have you got?' said John looking out
through the dusty window.

'Only one, I'm afraid,' said his brother. 'Since James died . . . '
Of course. James was his son and the husband of the woman
he had met. She had looked placid and mild, the kind of wife
who would have been suited to him. James had been killed in
an accident on a ship: no one knew very much about it. Perhaps
he had been drunk, perhaps not.

He was reluctant for some reason to leave the barn. It
seemed to remind him of horses and bridles and bits, and in
fact fragments of corroded leather still hung here and there
on the walls. He had seen no horses anywhere: there would be
no need for them now. Near the door he noticed a washing
machine which looked quite new.

His brother said, 'The dinner will be ready, if it's your
pleasure.' John looked at him in surprise, the invitation sounded
so feudal and respectful. His brother talked as if he were John's
servant.

'Thank you.' And again for a moment he heard his mother's
voice as she called them in to dinner when they were out playing.

They went into the house, the brother lagging a little behind.

John felt uncomfortable as if he were being treated like royalty when he wanted everything to be simple and natural. He knew that they would have cooked the best food whether they could afford it or not. They wouldn't, of course, have allowed him to stay at a hotel in the town during his stay. That would have been an insult. They went in. He found the house much cooler after the heat of the sun.

3

In the course of the meal which was a large one with lots of meat, cabbages and turnip and a pudding, Murdo suddenly said to his grandson:

'And don't you forget that Grandfather John was very good at English. He was the best in the school at English. I remember in those days we used to write on slates and Mr Gordon sent his composition round the classes. John is very clever or he wouldn't have been an editor.'

John said to Malcolm, who seemed quietly unimpressed: 'And what are you going to do yourself when you leave school?'

'You see,' said Murdo, 'Grandfather John will teach you . . . '

'I want to be a pilot,' said Malcolm, 'or something in science, or technical. I'm quite good at science.'

'We do projects most of the time,' said his sister. 'We're doing a project on fishing.'

'Projects!' said her grandfather contemptuously. 'When I was your age I was on a fishing boat.'

'There you are,' said his grandson triumphantly. 'That's what I tell Grandfather Murdo I should do, but I have to stay in school.'

'It was different in our days,' said his grandfather. 'We had to work for our living. You can't get a good job now without education. You have to have education.'

Straight in front of him on the wall, John could see a photograph of his brother dressed in army uniform. That was when he was a corporal in the Militia. He had also served in Egypt and in the First World War.

'They don't do anything these days,' said Murdo. 'Nothing. Every night it's football or dancing. He watches the TV all the time.'

'Did you ever see Elvis Presley?' said the girl who was eating her food very rapidly, and looking at a large red watch on her wrist.

'No, I'm sorry, I didn't,' said John. 'I once saw Lyndon Johnson though.'

She turned back to her plate uninterested.

The children were not at all as he had expected them. He thought they would have been shyer, more rustic, less talkative. In fact they seemed somehow remote and slightly bored and this saddened him. It was as if he were already seeing miniature Americans in the making.

'Take some more meat,' said his brother, piling it on his plate without waiting for an answer.

'All we get at English,' said Malcolm, 'is interpretations and literature. Mostly Shakespeare. I can't do any of it. I find it boring.'

'I see,' said John.

'He needs three Highers to get anywhere, don't you, Malcolm,' said his mother, 'and he doesn't do any work at night. He's always repairing his motor bike or watching TV,'

'When we got the TV first,' said the girl giggling, 'Grandfather Murdo thought . . . '

'Hist,' said her mother fiercely, leaning across the table, 'eat your food.'

Suddenly the girl looked at the clock and said, 'Can I go now, Mother? I've got to catch the bus.'

'What's this?' said her grandfather and at that moment as he raised his head, slightly bristling, John was reminded of their father.

'She wants to go to a dance,' said her mother.

'All the other girls are going,' said the girl in a pleading, slightly hysterical voice.

'Eat your food,' said her grandfather, 'and we'll see.' She ate the remainder of her food rapidly and then said, 'Can I go now?'

'All right,' said her mother, 'but mind you're back early or you'll find the door shut.'

The girl hurriedly rose from the table and went into the living room. She came back after a while with a handbag slung over her shoulder and carrying a transistor.

'Goodbye, Grandfather John,' she said. 'I'll see you tomorrow.' She went out and they could hear her brisk steps crackling on the gravel outside.

When they had finished eating Malcolm stood up and said, 'I promised Hugh I would help him repair his bike.'

'Back here early then,' said his mother again. He stood hesitating at the door for a moment and then went out, without saying anything.

'That's manners for you,' said Murdo. 'Mind you, he's very good with his hands. He repaired the tractor once.'

'I'm sure,' said John.

They ate in silence. When they were finished he and his brother went to sit in the living room which had the sun on it. They sat opposite each other in easy chairs. Murdo took out a pipe and began to light it. John suddenly felt that the room and the house were both very empty. He could hear quite clearly the ticking of the clock which stood on the mantelpiece between two cheap ornaments which looked as if they had been won at a fair.

Above the mantelpiece was a picture of his father, sitting very upright in a tall narrow chair, his long beard trailing in front of him. For some reason he remembered the night his brother, home from the war on leave, had come in late at night, drunk. His father had waited up for him and there had been a quarrel during which his brother had thrown the Bible at his father calling him a German bastard.

The clock ticked on. His brother during a pause in the conversation took up a *Farmers' Weekly* and put on a pair of glasses. In a short while he had fallen asleep behind the paper, his mouth opening like that of a stranded fish. Presumably that was all he read. His weekly letters were short and repetitive and apologetic.

John sat in the chair listening to the ticking of the clock

which seemed to grow louder and louder. He felt strange again as if he were in the wrong house. The room itself was so clean and modern with the electric fire and the TV set in the corner. There was no air of history or antiquity about it. In a corner of the room he noticed a guitar which presumably belonged to the grandson. He remembered the nights he and his companions would dance to the music of the melodeon at the end of the road. He also remembered the playing of the bagpipes by his brother.

Nothing seemed right. He felt as if at an angle to the world he had once known. He wondered why he had come back after all those years. Was he after all like those people who believed in the innocence and unchangeability of the heart and vibrated to the music of nostalgia? Did he expect a Garden of Eden where the apple had not been eaten? Should he stay or go back? But then there was little where he had come from. Mary was dead. He was retired from his editorship of the newspaper. What did it all mean? He remembered the night he had left home many years before. What had he been expecting then? What cargo was he bearing with him? And what did his return signify? He didn't know. But he would have to find out. It was necessary to find out. For some reason just before he closed his eyes he saw in the front of him again the cloud of midges he had seen not an hour before, rising and falling above the fence, moving on their unpredictable ways. Then he fell asleep.

4

The following day which was again fine he left the house and went down to a headland which overlooked the sea. He sat there for a long time on the grass, feeling calm and relaxed. The waves came in and went out, and he was reminded of the Gaelic song *The Eternal Sound of the Sea* which he used to sing when he was young. The water seemed to stretch westward into eternity and he could see nothing on it except the light of the sun. Clamped against the rocks below were the miniature helmets of the mussels and the whelks. He remembered how he used to boil the whelks in a pot and fish the meat out of them with a pin. He realised as he sat there that one of the things he had been missing for years was the sound of the sea. It was part of his consciousness. He should always live near the sea.

On the way back he saw the skull of a sheep, and he looked at it for a long time before he began his visits. Whenever anyone came home he had to visit every house, or people would be offended. And he would have to remember everybody, though many people in those houses were now dead.

He walked slowly along the street, feeling as if he were being watched from behind curtained windows. He saw a woman standing at a gate. She was a stout large woman and she was looking at him curiously. She said, 'It's a fine day.' He said, 'Yes.'

She came towards him and he saw her red beefy face. 'Aren't you John Macleod?' she asked. 'Don't you remember me?'

'Of course I do,' he replied. 'You're Sarah.'

She shouted jovially as if into a high wind, 'You'll have to speak more loudly. I'm a little deaf.' He shouted back, 'Yes, I'm John Macleod,' and it seemed to him as if at that moment he were trying to prove his identity. He shouted louder still, 'And you're Sarah.' His face broke into a large smile.

'Come in, come in,' she shouted. 'Come in and have a cup of milk.'

He followed her into the house and they entered the living room after passing through the scullery which had rows of cups and saucers and plates on top of a huge dresser. In a corner of the room sat a man who was probably her son trapped like a fly inside a net which he was repairing with a bone needle. He was wearing a fisherman's jersey and his hands worked with great speed.

'This is George,' she shouted. 'My son. This is John Macleod,' she said to George. George looked up briefly from his work but said nothing. He was quite old, perhaps fifty or so, and there was an unmarried look about him.

'He's always fishing,' she said, 'always fishing. That's all he does. And he's very quiet. Just like his father. We're going to give John a cup of milk,' she said to her son. She went into the scullery for the milk and though he was alone with George the latter didn't speak. He simply went on repairing his net. This room too was cool and there was no fire. The chairs looked old and cracked and there was an old brown radio in a corner. After a while she came back and gave him the milk. 'Drink it up,' she instructed him as if she were talking to a boy. It was very cold. He couldn't remember when he had last drunk such fine milk.

'You were twenty-four when you went away,' she said, 'and I had just married. Jock is dead. George is very like him.' She shouted all this at the top of her voice and he himself didn't reply as he didn't want to shout.

'And how's that brother of yours?' she shouted remorselessly. 'He's a cheat, that one. Two years ago I sold him a cow. He said that there was something wrong with her and he got her cheap. But there was nothing wrong with her. He's a devil,' she said approvingly. 'But he was the same when he was young. After the penny. Always asking if he could run messages. You weren't like that. You were more like a scholar. You'd be reading books sitting on the peat banks. I remember you very well. You had fair hair, very fair hair. Your father said that you looked like an angel. But your brother was the cunning one. He knew a thing or two. And how are you?'

'I'm fine,' he shouted back.

'I hope you've come to stay,' she shouted again. He didn't answer.

'You would be sorry to hear about your mother,' she shouted again. 'We were all fond of her. She was a good woman.' By 'good' she meant that she attended church regularly. 'That brother of yours is a devil. I wonder if your mother liked him.' George looked at her quickly and then away again.

He himself shouted, 'Why do you ask that?' She pretended not to hear him and he had to shout the words again.

'It was nothing,' she said. 'I suppose you have a big job in America.'

He was wondering what she had meant and felt uneasy, but he knew that he wouldn't get anything more out of her.

'They've all changed here,' she shouted. 'Everything's

changed. The girls go about showing their bottoms, not like in my day. The boys are off to the dances every night. George here should get married but I wouldn't let him marry one of these trollops. And you can't visit your neighbours any more. You have to wait for an invitation. Imagine that. In the old days the door would be always open. But not any more. Drink up your milk.'

He drank it obediently as if he were a child.

'Jock died, you know. A stroke it was. It lasted for three years. But he never complained. You remember Jock.'

He didn't remember him very well. Was he the one who used to play football or the one who played tricks on the villagers? He couldn't summon up a picture of him at all. What had she meant by his mother and his brother? He had a strange feeling as if he were walking inside an illusion, as if things had happened here that he hadn't known of, though he should have. But who would tell him? They would all keep their secrets. He even had the feeling that this large apparently frank woman was in fact treacherous and secretive and that behind her huge façade there was lurking a venomous thin woman whose head nodded up and down like a snake's.

She laughed again. 'That brother of yours is a businessman. He is the one who should have gone to America. He would have got round them all. There are no flies on him. Did you not think of coming home when your mother died?'

'I was . . . I couldn't at the time,' he shouted.

George, entrapped in his corner, the net around his feet, plied his bone needle.

'It'll be good to come home again,' she shouted. 'Many of them come back. Donny Macdonald came back seven years ago and they hadn't heard from him for twenty years. He used to drink but he goes to church regularly now. He's a man of God. He's much quieter than he used to be. He used to sing a lot when he was young and they made him the precentor. He's got a beautiful voice but not as good as it was. Nobody knew he was coming home till he walked into the house one night off the bus. Can you imagine that? At first he couldn't find it because they had built a new house. But someone showed it to him.'

He got up and laid the cup on the table.

'Is Mr Gordon still alive?' he shouted. Mr Gordon was his old English teacher.

'Speak up, I can't hear you,' she said, her large bulging face thrust towards him like a crab.

'Mr Gordon?' he shouted. 'Is he still alive?'

'Mr Gordon,' she said. 'Yes, he's alive. He's about ninety now. He lives over there.' She took him over to the window and pointed out a house to him. 'Oh, there's the Lady,' she said. 'He's always sitting on the wall. He's there every day. His sister died, you know. She was a bit wrong in the head.'

He said goodbye and she followed him to the door. He walked out the gate and made his way to where she had pointed. The day seemed heavy and sleepy and he felt slightly drugged as if he were moving through water. In the distance a man was hammering a post into the ground. The cornfields swayed slightly in the breeze and he could see flashes of red among them. He remembered the days when he would go with a bucket to the well, and smelt again the familiar smell of flowers and grass. He expected at any moment to see the ghosts of the dead stopping him by the roadway, interrogating him and asking him, 'When did you come home? When are you going away?' The whole visit, he realised now, was an implicit interrogation. What it was really about was: What had he done with his life? That was the question that people, without realising it, were putting to him, simply because he had chosen to return. It was also the question that he himself wanted answered.

Ahead of him stretched the moors and in the far distance he could see the Standing Stones which could look so eerie in the rain and which had perhaps been used in the sacrifice of children in Druid times. Someone had to be knifed to make the sun appear, he thought wryly. Before there could be light there must be blood.

He made his way to see Mr Gordon.

5

Gordon recognised him immediately: it was almost as if he had been waiting for him. He came forward from behind a table on which were piled some books and a chessboard on which some pieces were standing, as if he had been playing a game.

'John,' he said, 'John Macleod.'

John noticed that standing beside the chair was a small glass in which there were the remains of whisky.

'Sit down, sit down,' said Gordon as if he hadn't had company for a long time. He was still spry, grey-haired of course, but thin in the body. He was wearing an old sports jacket and a shirt open at the neck. There was a slightly unshaven look about him.

'I play chess against myself,' he said. 'I don't know which of us wins.' His laugh was a short bark. John remembered himself running to school while Gordon stood outside the gate with a whistle in his hand looking at his watch impatiently.

'I suppose coming from America,' he said, 'you'll know about Fischer. He's about to do the impossible, beat the Russian World Champion at chess. It's like the Russians beating the Americans at baseball – or us at shinty,' he added with the same self-delighting barking laugh. 'He is of course a genius and geniuses make their own rules. How are you?'

'Very well. And how are you?' He nearly said 'Sir' but stopped himself in time.

'Oh, not too bad. Time passes slowly. Have you ever thought about time?' Beside his chair was a pile of books scattered indiscriminately. 'I belong to dozens of book clubs. This is a book on Time. Very interesting. From the point of view of physics, psychiatry and so on.' He pointed to a huge tome which looked both formidable and new. 'Did you know, for instance, that time passes slowly for some people and rapidly for others? It's a matter of personality, and the time of year you're born. Or that temperature can affect your idea of time? Very interesting.' He gave the impression of a man who devoured knowledge in a sterile way.

John looked out of the window. Certainly time seemed to pass slowly here. Everything seemed to be done in slow motion as if people were walking through water, divers with lead weights attached to them.

'Are you thinking of staying?' said Gordon, pouring out a glass of whisky for his guest.

'I don't know that yet.'

'I suppose you could buy a house somewhere. And settle down. Perhaps do some fishing. I don't do any myself. I read and play chess. But I suppose you could fish and do some crofting. Though I don't remember that you were particularly interested in either of these.'

'I was just thinking,' said John, 'of what you used to tell us when we were in your English class. You always told us to observe. Observation, you used to say, is the secret of good writing. Do you remember the time you took us out to the tree and told us to smell and touch it and study it and write a poem about it? It was a cherry tree, I recall. We wrote the poem in the open air.'

'I was in advance of my time,' said Gordon. 'That's what they all do now. They call it Creative Writing. But of course they can't spell nowadays.'

'And you always told us that exactitude was important. Be observant and exact, you said, above all be true to yourselves.'

'Drink your whisky,' said Gordon. 'Yes, I remember it all. I've kept some of your essays. You were gifted. In all the years I taught I only met two pupils who were really gifted. How does one know talent when one sees it? I don't know. Anyway, I recognised your talent. It was natural, like being a tiger.'

'Yes, you kept telling us about exactitude and observation. You used to send us out of the room and change objects in the room while we were out. You made Sherlock Holmeses out of us.'

'Why do you speak about that now? It was all so long ago.'

'I have a reason.'

'What is your reason?' said Gordon sharply.

'Oh, something that happened to me. Some years ago.'

'And what was that? Or don't you want to talk about it?'

'I don't see why not. Not that it's very complimentary to me.'

'I have reached the age now,' said Gordon, 'when I am not concerned with honour, only with people.'

'I see,' said John, 'but suppose you can't separate them. Well, I'll tell you anyway.' He walked over to the window, standing with his back to the room and looking out at the empty road. It was as if he didn't want to be facing Gordon.

'I was an editor for some time as you know,' he said. 'Your training stood me in good stead. It was not a big paper but it was a reasonable paper. It had influence in the largish town in which I stayed. It wasn't Washington, it wasn't New York, but it was a largish town. I made friends in this town. One was a lecturer in a university. At least that is what we would call it here. As a matter of fact, he wasn't a lecturer in English. He was a lecturer in History. It was at the time of the McCarthy trials when nobody was safe, nobody. Another of my friends went off his head at that time. He believed that everyone was persecuting him and opening his mail. He believed that planes were pursuing him. In any case this friend of mine, his name was Mason, told me that files had been dug up on him referring to the time when he was a student and had belonged to a left wing university club. Now there were complaints that he was indoctrinating his students with communism and, of course, being a History lecturer, he was in a precarious position. I told him that I would defend him in my paper, that I would write a hard-hitting editorial. I told him that I would stand up for principles, humane principles.' He stretched out his hand for the whisky and decided against drinking it. 'I left him on the doorstep at eleven o'clock on a Monday night. He was very disturbed because of course he was innocent, he wasn't a communist and anyway he had great integrity as a teacher and lectured on communism only theoretically as one ideology among others. But the McCarthy people of course were animals. You have no conception. Not here. Of the fog of lies. Of the quagmire. No conception.' He paused. A cow outside had bent its head to the grass and was eating.

'Anyway this was what happened. I walked home because I needed the exercise. The street was deserted. There were lampposts shining and it was raining. A thin drizzle. I could hear the echo of my feet on the road. This was the kind of thing you taught us, to remember and listen and observe, to be aware of our surroundings sensuously. By then it had become a habit with me.

'As I was walking along two youths came towards me out of the shadow, from under the trees. I thought they were coming home from the cinema or from a dance. They wore leather jackets and were walking towards me along the sidewalk. They stayed on the sidewalk and I made as if to go round them since they were coming straight for me without deviating. One of them said, "Daddy." I stopped. I thought he was going to ask me for a light. He said, "Your wallet, daddy." I looked at him in amazement. I looked at the two of them. I couldn't understand what was going on. And something happened to me. I could feel everything very intensely, you see. At that moment I could have written a poem, everything was so clear. They were laughing, you see, and they were very casual. They walked like those cowboys you see on the films, physically at ease in their world. And their eyes sparkled. Their eyes sparkled with pure evil. I knew that if I protested they would beat me up. I knew that there was no appeal. None at all. One of them had a belt, and a buckle on it sparkled in the light. My eyes were at the level of the buckle. I took out my wallet and gave them the money. I had fifty dollars. I observed everything as you had trained us to do. Their boots which were shining except for the drizzle: their neckties: their leather jackets. Their legs which were narrow in the narrow trousers. And their faces which were looking slightly upwards and shining. Clear and fine almost, but almost innocent though evil. A rare sort of energy. Pure and bright. They took the wallet, counted the money and gave me back the wallet. They then walked on. The whole incident took perhaps three minutes.

'I went into the house and locked the door. The walls seemed very fragile all of a sudden. My wife had gone to bed and I stood downstairs thinking, now and again removing a book from the shelves and replacing it. I felt the house as thin as the shell of an egg: I could hear, I thought, as far away as San

Francisco. There was a tap dripping and I turned it off. And I
didn't write the editorial, I didn't write anything. Two weeks
after that my friend killed himself, with pills and whisky.'

The whisky which Gordon had given him was still untouched.

'Observation and exactitude,' he said, 'and elegance of
language.' There was a long silence. Gordon picked up a
chess piece and weighed it in his hand.

'Yes,' he said, 'and that's why you came home.'

'Perhaps. I don't know why I came home. One day I was
walking along a street and I smelt the smell of fish coming
from a fish shop. And it reminded me of home. So I came
home. My wife, of course, is dead.'

'Many years ago,' said Gordon, still holding the chess piece
in his hand, 'I was asked to give a talk to an educational society
in the town. In those days I used to write poetry though of
course I never told anyone. I was working on a particular
poem at the time: it was very difficult and I couldn't get it to
come out right. Well, I gave this talk. It was, if I may say so
myself, a brilliant talk for in those days I was full of ideas. It
was also very witty. People came and congratulated me afterwards as people do. I arrived home at one o'clock in the
morning. When I got home I took out the poem and tried to
do some work on it. But I was restless and excited and I
couldn't get into the right mood. I sat and stared at the clock
and I knew quite clearly that I would never write again. Odd,
isn't it?'

'What are you trying to say?'

'Say? Nothing. Nothing at all. I don't think you'd better
stay here. I don't think this place is a refuge. People may say so
but it's not true. After a while the green wears away and you
are left with the black. In any case I don't think you'd better
settle here: that would be my advice. However, it's not my
business. I have no business now.'

'Why did you stay here?' said John slowly.

'I don't know. Laziness, I suppose. I remember when I was
in Glasgow University many years ago we used to take the
train home at six in the morning after the holiday started. At
first we were all very quiet, naturally, since we were half-

asleep, most of us. But then as the carriages warmed and the sun came up and we came in sight of the hills and the lochs we began to sing Gaelic songs. Odd, and Glasgow isn't that far away. What does it all mean, John? What are you looking at?'

'The broken fences.'

'Yes, of course. There's a man here and he's been building his own house for ten years. He carries stone after stone to the house and then he forgets and sits down and talks to people. Time is different here, no doubt about it.'

'I had noticed.'

'If you're looking for help from me, John, I can't give you any. In the winter time I sit and look out the window. You can see the sea from here and it can look very stormy. The rain pours down the window and you can make out the waves hitting the islands out there. What advice could I give you? I have tried to do my best as far as my work was concerned. But you say it isn't enough.'

'Perhaps it wasn't your fault.'

John made his way to the door.

'Where are you going?'

'I shall have to call on other people as well. They all expect one to do that, don't they?'

'Yes, they still feel like that. That hasn't changed.'

'I'll be seeing you then,' said John as he left.

'Yes, yes, of course.'

He walked towards the sea cliffs to a house which he had visited many times when he was a boy, where he had been given many tumblers of milk, where later in the evening he would sit with others talking into the night.

The sea was large and sparkling in front of him like a shield. No, he said automatically to himself, it isn't like a shield, otherwise how could the cormorants dive in and out of it? What was it like then? It was like the sea, nothing else. It was like the sea in one of its moods, in one of its sunny gentle moods. As he walked pictures flashed in front of his eyes. He saw a small boy running, then a policeman's arm raised, the baton falling in a vicious arc, the neon light flashing from his shield. The boy stopped in midflight, the picture frozen.

6

He knocked at the door of the house and a woman of about forty, thin and with straggly greying hair, came to the door.

She looked at him enquiringly.

'John, John Macleod,' he said. 'I came to see your mother.' Her face lighted up with recognition and she said, 'Come in, come in.' And then inexplicably, 'I thought you were from the BBC.'

'The BBC?'

'Yes, they're always sending people to take recordings of my mother singing and telling stories, though she's very old now.'

He followed her into a bedroom where an old white-faced white-haired woman was lying, her head against white pillows. She stretched out her prominently veined hand across the blankets and said, 'John, I heard Anne talking to you. There's nothing wrong with my hearing.'

They were left alone and he sat down beside the bed. There was a small table with medicine bottles and pills on it.

'It's true,' she said, 'the BBC are always sending people to hear me sing songs before I die.'

'And how are you?'

'Fine, fine.'

'Good, that's good.' Her keen wise eyes studied his face carefully. The room had bright white wallpaper and the windows faced the sea.

'I don't sleep so well now,' said the old woman. 'I waken at five every morning and I can hear the birds twittering just outside the window.'

'You look quite well,' he said.

'Of course I'm not well. Everybody says that to me. But after all I'm ninety years old. I can't expect to live forever. And you're over sixty but I can still see you as a boy.' She prattled on but he felt that all the time she was studying him without being obvious.

'Have you seen the BBC people? They all have long hair and they wear red ties. But they're nice and considerate. Of course everybody wears long hair now, even my daughter's son. Would you like to hear my recording? My grandson took it down on a tape.'

'I would,' he said.

She tapped on the head of the bed as loudly as she could and her daughter came in.

'Where's Hugh?' she asked.

'He's outside.'

'Tell him to bring in the machine. John wants to hear my recording.' She turned to John and said, 'Hugh is very good with his hands, you know. All the young people nowadays know all about electricity and cars.'

After a while a tall, quiet, long-haired boy came in with a tape recorder. He plugged it into a socket beside the bed, his motions cool and competent and unflurried. He had the same neutral quizzical look that John had noticed in his brother's two grandchildren. They don't want to be deceived again, he thought. This generation is not interested in words, only in actions. Observation, exactitude, elegance. The universe of the poem or the story is not theirs, their universe is electronic. And when he thought of the phrase 'the music of the spheres' he seemed to see a shining bicycle moving through the heavens, or the wheels of some inexplicable machine.

Hugh switched on the tape recorder and John listened.

'Tonight,' the announcer began, 'we are going to hear the voice of a lady of ninety years old. She will be telling us about her life on this far Hebridean island untouched by pollution and comparatively unchanged when it is compared with our own hectic cities. This lady has never in all her life left the island on which she grew up. She has never seen a train. She has never seen a city. She has been brought up in a completely pastoral society. But we may well ask, what will happen to this society? Will it be squeezed out of existence? How can it survive the pollution of our time, and here I am speaking not simply of physical but of moral pollution? What was it like to live on this island for so many years? I shall try to elicit some answers to that question in the course of this programme. But first I should like you to hear this lady singing a Gaelic traditional song. I may interpolate at this point that many

Gaelic songs have apparently been anglicised musically, thus losing their traditional flavour. But Mrs Macdonald will sing this song in the way in which she was taught to, the way in which she picked it up from previous singers.'

There followed a rendering of *Thig Tri Nithean Gun Iarraidh* ('Three things will come without seeking . . . '). John listened to the frail voice: it seemed strange to hear it, ghostly and yet powerful in its own belief, real and yet unreal at the same time.

When the singing was over the interviewer questioned her:

INTER. And now, Mrs Macdonald, could you please tell me how old you are?

MRS M. I am ninety years old.

INTER. You will have seen a lot of changes on this island, in this village even.

MRS M. Oh yes, lots of changes. I don't know much about the island. I know more about the village.

INTER. You mean that you hardly ever left the village itself?

MRS M. I don't know much about the rest of the island.

INTER. What are your memories then of your youth in the village?

MRS M. Oh, people were closer together. People used to help each other at the peat gathering. They would go out with a cart and they would put the peats on the cart. And they would make tea and sing. It was very happy times especially if it was a good day.

INTER. Do they not do that any more? I mean, coal and electricity . . .

MRS M. No, they don't do that so much, no. Nowadays. And there was more fishing then too. People would come to the door and give you a fish if they had caught one.

INTER. You mean herring?

MRS M. No, things like cod. Not herring. They would catch them in boats or off the rocks. Not herring. The herring were caught by the drifters. And the mackerel. We used to eat herring and potatoes every day. Except Sunday of course.

INTER. And what did you eat on Sunday?

MRS M. We would always have meat on Sunday. That was always the fashion. Meat on Sundays. And soup.

INTER. I see. And tell me, when did you leave school, Mrs Macdonald?

MRS M. I left school when I was fourteen years old. I was in Secondary Two.

INTER. It was a small village school, I take it.

MRS M. Oh, yes, it was small. Perhaps about fifty pupils.

Perhaps about fifty. We used to write on slates in those days and the children would bring in a peat for a fire in the winter.

Every child would bring in a peat. And we had people called pupil-teachers.

INTER. Pupil-teachers? What were pupil-teachers?

MRS M. They were young people who helped the teacher. Pupils. They were pupils themselves.

INTER. Then what happened?

MRS M. I looked after my father and mother. We had a croft too. And then I got married.

INTER. What did your husband do?

MRS M. He was a crofter. In those days we used to go to a dance at the end of the road. But the young people go to the town now. In those days we had a dance at the end of the road.

INTER. Did you not know him before, your husband I mean?

MRS M. Yes but that was where I met him, at the dance.

INTER. What did they use for the dance?

MRS M. What do you mean?

INTER. What music did they use?

MRS M. Oh, you mean the instrument. It was a melodeon.

INTER. Can you remember the tunes, any of the tunes, any of the songs?

MRS M. Oh yes, I can remember *A Ribhinn Oig bheil cuimhn' agad?*

INTER. Could you tell our listeners what that means, Mrs Macdonald?

MRS M. It's a love song. That's what it is, a sailors' song. A love song.

INTER. I see. And do you think you could sing it?

And she proceeded to sing it in that frail voice. John listened to the evocation of nights on ships, moonlight, masts, exile, and he was strangely moved as if he were hearing a voice speaking to him from the past.

'I think that will be enough,' she said to the boy. He switched off the tape recorder without saying anything, put it in its case and took it away, closing the door behind him.

John said, 'You make it all sound very romantic.'

'Well, it was true about the peats.'

'But don't you remember the fights people used to have about land and things like that?'

'Yes but I remember the money they collected when Shodan was drowned.'

'But what about the tricks they used to play on old Maggie?'

'That was just young boys. And they had nothing else to do. That was the reason for it.'

There was a silence. A large blue fly buzzed in the window. John followed it with his eyes. It was restless, never settling, humming loudly with an angry sound. For a moment he nearly got up in order to kill it, he was so irritated by the booming sound and its restlessness.

'Would you like to tell me about my mother?' said John.

'What about your mother?'

'Sarah said something when I was speaking to her.'

'What did she say?'

'I felt there was something wrong, the way she talked. It was about my brother.'

'Well you know your brother was fond of the land. What did you want to know?'

'What happened. That was all.'

'Your mother went a bit odd at the end. It's quite common with old people. Perhaps that's what she was talking about. My own brother wouldn't let the doctor into the house. He thought he was poisoning him.'

'You say odd. How odd?'

'She accused your brother of wanting to put her out of the house. But I wouldn't pay any attention to that. Old people get like that.'

'I see.'

'You know your brother.'

'Yes. He is fond of land. He always was. He's fond of property.'

'Most people are,' she said. 'And what did you think of my singing?'

'You sang well. It's funny how one can tell a real Gaelic singer. It's not even the way they pronounce their words. It's something else.'

'You haven't forgotten your Gaelic.'

'No. We had societies. We had a Gaelic society. People who had been on holiday used to come and talk to us and show us slides.' The successful and the failed. From the lone shelling of the misty island. Smoking their cigars but unable to go back and live there. Since after all they had made their homes in America. Leading their half lives, like mine. Watching cowboys on TV, the cheapness and the vulgarity of it, the largeness, the spaciousness, the crowdedness. They never really belonged to the city, these Highlanders. Not really. The skyscrapers were too tall, they were surrounded by the works of man, not the works of God. In the beginning was the neon lighting ... And the fake religions, the cheap multitudinous sprouting so-called faiths. And they cried, some of them, at these meetings, in their large jackets of fine light cloth, behind their rimless glasses.

He got up to go.

'It's the blood, I suppose,' she said.

'Pardon.'

'That makes you able to tell. The blood. You could have seen it on my pillow three months ago.'

'I'm sorry.'

'Oh, don't be sorry. One grows used to lying here. The blood is always there. It won't allow people to change.'

'No, I suppose not.'

He said goodbye awkwardly and went outside. As he stood at the door for a moment, he heard music coming from the side of the house. It sounded American. He went over and looked. The boy was sitting against the side of the house patiently strumming his guitar, his head bent over it. He sang the words in a consciously American way, drawling them affectedly. John moved quietly away. The sun was still on the water where some ducks flew low. He thought of the headland where he was standing as if it were Marathon. There they had combed each other's long hair, the effeminate courageous ones about to die.

As he walked back he couldn't get out of his mind an article about Billy Graham he had read in an American magazine not long before. It was all about the crewcut saint, the electric blue eyed boy perched in his mountain eyrie. The Victorian respect shown by the interviewers had been, even for him with a long knowledge of American papers, nauseating. Would you like these remarks off the record, and so on. And then that bit about his personal appearances at such shows as *Laugh-in* where the conversation somehow got round to Jesus Christ every time! In Africa a corps of black policemen, appointed to control the crowd, had abandoned their posts and come forward to make a stand for Jesus!

Mad crude America, Victorian and twentieth century at the one time. Manic country of the random and the destined. What would his father or his mother have thought of Billy Graham? The fundamentalist with the stereophonic backing. For the first time since he came home he laughed out loud.

7

It was evening when he got back to his brother's house and the light was beginning to thicken. As he turned in at the gate his brother, who must have seen him coming, walked towards it and then stopped: he was carrying a hammer in his right hand as if he had been working with posts. They stood looking at each other in the half-light.

'Have you seen everybody then,' said his brother. 'Have you visited them all?' In the dusk and carrying the hammer he looked somehow more authoritative, more solid than his brother.

'Most of them. Sarah was telling me about the cow.'

'Oh, that. There was something wrong with the cow. But it's all right now. She talks too much,' he added contemptuously.

'And also,' said John carefully, 'I heard something about our mother.'

'What about her? By God, if that bitch Sarah has been spreading scandal I'll . . . ' His hands tightened on the hammer and his whole body seemed to bulge out and bristle like a fighting cock. For a moment John had a vision of a policeman with a baton in his hand. John glimpsed the power and energy that had made his brother the dominant person in the village.

After a while he said, 'I didn't want to worry you.'

'About what?' said John coldly.

'About our mother. She went a bit queer at the end. She hated Susan, you see. She would say that she was no good at the housework and that she couldn't do any of the outside work. She accused her of smoking and drinking. She even said she was trying to poison her.'

'And?'

'She used to say to people that I was trying to put her out of the house. Which of course was nonsense. She said that I had plotted to get the croft, and you should have it. She liked you better, you see.'

'Why didn't you tell me any of this?'

'I didn't want to worry you. Anyway I'm not good at writing. I can dash off a few lines but I'm not used to the pen.' For that moment again he looked slightly helpless and awkward as if he were talking about a gift that he half envied, half despised.

John remembered the letters he would get – 'Just a scribble to let you know that we are well and here's hoping you are the same . . . I hope you are in the pink as this leaves me.' Clichés cut out of a half world of crumbling stone. Certainly this crisis would be beyond his ability to state in writing.

'She was always very strong for the church. She would read bits of the Bible to annoy Susan, the bits about Ruth and so on. You know where it says, "Whither thou goest I will go . . . " She would read a lot. Do you know it?'

'I know it.'

John said, 'I couldn't come back at the time.'

'I know that. I didn't expect you to come back.'

As he stood there John had the same feeling he had had with Sarah, only stronger, that he didn't know anything about people at all, that his brother, like Sarah, was wearing a mask, that by choosing to remain where he was his brother had been the stronger of the two, that the one who had gone to America and immersed himself in his time was really the weaker of the two, the less self-sufficient. He had never thought about this before, he had felt his return as a regression to a more primitive place, a more pastoral, less exciting position, lower on the scale of a huge complex ladder. Now he wasn't so sure. Perhaps those who went away were the weaker ones, the ones who were unable to suffer the slowness of time, its inexorable yet ceremonious passing. He was shaken as by a vision: but perhaps the visions of artists and writers were merely ideas which people like his brother saw and dismissed as of no importance.

'Are you coming in?' said his brother, looking at him strangely.

'Not yet. I won't be long.'

His brother went into the house and John remained at the gate. He looked around him at the darkening evening. For a moment he expected to see his mother coming towards him out of the twilight holding a pail of warm milk in her hand. The hills in the distance were darkening. The place was quiet and heavy.

As he stood there he heard someone whistling and when he turned round saw that it was Malcolm.

'Did you repair the bike?' said John.

'Yes, it wasn't anything. It'll be all right now. We finished that last night.'

'And where were you today, then?'

'Down at the shore.'

'I see.'

They stood awkwardly in each other's presence. Suddenly John said, 'Why are you so interested in science and maths?'

'It's what I can do best,' said Malcolm in surprise.

'You don't read Gaelic, do you?'

'Oh, that's finished,' said Malcolm matter-of-factly.

John was wondering whether the reason Malcolm was so interested in maths and science was that he might have decided, perhaps unconsciously, that his own culture, old and deeply rotted and weakening, was inhibiting and that for that reason he preferred the apparent cleanness and economy of equations without ideology.

'Do you want to go to America?' he asked.

'I should like to travel,' said Malcolm carelessly. 'Perhaps America. But it might be Europe somewhere.'

John was about to say something about violence till it suddenly occurred to him that this village which he had left also had its violence, its buried hatreds, its bruises which festered for years and decades.

'I want to leave because it's so boring here,' said Malcolm. 'It's so boring I could scream sometimes.'

'It can seem like that,' said John. 'I shall be leaving tomorrow but you don't need to tell them that just now.'

He hadn't realised that he was going to say what he did till he had actually said it.

Malcolm tried to be conventionally regretful but John sensed a relief just the same.

They hadn't really said anything to each other.

After a while Malcolm went into the house, and he himself stood in the darkening light thinking. He knew that he would never see the place again after that night and the following morning. He summoned it up in all its images, observing, being exact. There was the house itself with its porch and the flowers in front of it. There was the road winding palely away from him past the other houses of the village. There was the thatched roofless house not far away from him. There were the fields and the fences and the barn. All these things he would take away with him, his childhood, his pain, into the shifting world of neon, the flashing broken signals of the city.

One cannot run away, he thought to himself as he walked towards the house. Or if one runs away one cannot be happy anywhere any more. If one left in the first place one could never go back. Or if one came back one also brought a virus, an infection of time and place. One always brings back a judgment to one's home.

He stood there for a long time before going into the house. He leaned over the fence looking out towards the fields. He could imagine his father coming towards him, in long beard and wearing wellingtons, solid, purposeful, fixed. And hadn't his father been an observer too, an observer of the seasons and the sea?

As he stood thinking he saw the cloud of midges again. They were rising and falling in the slight breeze. They formed a cloud but inside the cloud each insect was going on its own way or drifting with the breeze. Each alive and perhaps with its own weight, its own inheritance. Apparently free yet fixed, apparently spontaneous yet destined.

His eyes followed their frail yet beautiful movements. He smiled wryly as he felt them nipping him. He'd have to get into the house. He would have to find out when the bus left in the morning. That would be the first stage of the journey: after that he could find out about boats and trains and planes.

Murdo & the Mod

At the time of the Mod, Murdo tended to get into long arguments about Mod medallists. He would say, 'In my opinion Moira Mcinally was the best medallist there ever was. Her timbre was excellent.' Most people wouldn't know what timbre was, and Murdo would repeat the word. On the other hand, he would say that though her timbre was excellent her deportment wasn't as good as that of Norma McEwan who became a bus conductress on the Govan route.

Such arguments would go on into the early hours of the morning, and as many as eighty Mod medallists might be mentioned with special reference to their expression when they sang their songs, as well as their marks in Gaelic and music. Murdo would sometimes say, '97 out of 100 is not enough for a medallist since I myself used to get more than that in Geometry.'

'However,' he would add, 'Mairi MacGillivary got 99 out of 100 for her timbre, though she only got 7 out of 100 for her Gaelic since in actual fact she was a learner and was born in Japan.

'Her expression,' he would add, 'was enigmatic.'

At one Mod he offered protection for adjudicators. This was a service which consisted of whisking them off to an armoured taxi immediately they had given their adjudication. For he said, 'Haven't you realised the number of threats those adjudicators get? Not so often from the contestants themselves but from their close relatives, especially their mothers who have carefully trained these contestants for many years in expression, timbre, and the best method of wearing the kilt. No one has any idea of what is involved in producing a gold medallist. His Gaelic must be perfection itself as far as expression is concerned and must be taken from the best islands. Furthermore, he must stand in a particular way with his hand on his sporran, and his expression must be fundamentally alert, though not impudent, though for the dreamier songs he may close his eyes. Now a mother who has brought up such a contestant cannot but be angry when an adjudicator, who doesn't even come from her island, presumes to make her son fifth equal in a contest which moreover only contains fifth equals. There have been death threats in the past. Some adjudicators have disguised themselves as members of the Free Church and carry Bibles and wear black hats and black ties, but this isn't enough as everyone knows that the Free Church doesn't like Mods, since they are not mentioned in the Bible. The *Comunn Gaidhealach* have even produced very thin adjudicators who, as it were, melt into the landscape when their adjudication is over, but even this has not prevented them from being assaulted. These mothers will stand in freezing rain outside adjudicators' houses and shout insults at them and sometimes the more ambitious of them have fired mortar shells into the living-room.'

Thus Murdo's 'Adjudicators Rescue Service', knows as ARS for short, was in great demand, and for an extra pound the adjudicator could make faces at frenzied mothers through the bullet-proof glass.

Another service that Murdo would provide was skin-coloured hearing aids which in practical terms were in fact invisible. These were for turning off after the seventh hearing of the same song, such as 'Bheir Mi Ho'. If the hearing aids were visible it would look discourteous to turn them off. So Murdo would advertise for people who would make skin-coloured invisible hearing aids, and sometimes he would even apply for a grant for such people who had to be highly skilled and whose pay was high as they only worked during Mod times.

Another service he provided was special tartans for people from Russia and Japan and other distant countries. His tartan for the Oblomov clan was well thought of. It was a direct and daring perestroika white with a single dove carrying a Mod brochure in its mouth. Sometimes too it might carry a placard 'Welcome to Mod 1992 in Dazzling and Riveting Kilmarnock, home of Gaelic and Engineering Sponsorship'. Indeed his sponsorship from Albania was the high point of his life, and he kept for a long time a transcript of the short interview he had with its president, who at that time was being besieged by 300,000 rebellious people demanding more soap and toilet paper.

Murdo indeed became very animated at the time of the Mod, as if he were emerging out of a long hibernation like the church at Easter. He ran a service well in advance of the Mod for booking Choirs into Bed and Breakfast locations, and he further advertised a service for making rooms soundproof so that pipers could practise their pibrochs, one of which was in fact dedicated to him. It was called *Murdo's Farewell to Harry Lauder*. He invented a device by which a piper could smoke while playing the pipes at the same time. He advertised this by the slogan 'Put that in your pipes and smoke it'.

But I could go on for ever describing Murdo's energy and innovative brilliance at the time of the Mod. It was as if he grew alive again, as if he vibrated with elan.

He was here, there and everywhere, organising dances, selling tickets, raffling salt herring, giving endless votes of thanks, singing songs, defending the Mod in midnight debates, pinpointing the virtues of Mod gold medallists of earlier years and interviewing them in a special geriatric studio which was fitted with bedpans, dressing up as a starving Campbell who needed sponsorship, writing short stories and sending them in under assumed names such as Iain MacRae Hemingway or Hector Maupassant. It was a week of glorious abandon for him, so much so that the rest of the year was an anticlimax, and he could hardly wait until the Mod was to be staged in Gatwick or Henley.

Murdo's closely reasoned paper on why the Mod should be held in Paris was probably his masterpiece. He said first of all that many of the older slightly deafer people might think it was Harris, and before they knew where they were they would be strolling down the Champs Elysees rather than Tarbert. Also there were a number of Gaels in Paris who had been detained there after the last football international as well as some ancient followers of Bonnie Prince Charlie. Furthermore, it was probably from here that the original Celts had come before they had changed from 'P' to 'Q'. Also the word 'église' was very like the Gaelic word 'eaglais' and there was a small French religious sect called L'Eglise Libre to which Pascal had belonged.

So it was that Murdo was busy as a bee when Mod time came, especially with his compilation of Mod medallists into leagues, headed by Morag MacCrimmon (aged 102), and by his selection of raffle prizes headed by his special editions of the Bible with a foreword by Nicholas Fairbairn, and a page three of aged schoolteachers from the Stornoway Gazette.

'I envisage,' he told the press recently, 'that our next Mod will be in East Germany. As a goodwill gesture I have decided that there will be no communists on the committee. I hope to see you all there.'

I should like, but for pressure of time, to detail Murdo's other astonishing achievements, e.g. the year he won the Mod Medal himself by an amazing margin of 90 points, and also his epic poem which won him the Bardic Crown and which was called 'The Church and the Sound of the Sea'. However, I have said enough to demonstrate that Murdo was by far the most interesting President, Secretary, and Treasurer seen at the same time which the Mod is ever likely to have, and his creation of twenty fourth-equals out of a total entry of twenty-one was the most dazzling arithmetical feat ever seen and also the fairest.

His interview in Gaelic with President Mitterand was a sparkling performance when he countered the President's *'Tha e fluich'* with *'C'est la guerre'*.

Sweets to the Sweet

When I went into the shop next door that day, I heard them quarrelling, I mean Diane and her father, Mason, or the Lady, as we called him. Perhaps they hadn't heard the tinkle of the bell or he had forgotten that I often came in at that time.

'And I'm telling you that university is crap. I'm not going and that's the end of it.'

That was beautiful baby-faced Diane with the peroxide, white hair and the heart-shaped ruthless face.

I heard him murmuring and she began again:

'I'm telling you, you can shove these books. And all that stuff about sacrificing yourself for me is a lot of . . . '

At that point I went back to the door, opened it and let it slam as if I had just come in. The voices ceased and the Lady came into the shop.

He looked tired and pale, but his sweet angelic smile was in evidence as usual. I heard a far door slam and judged that it must be his daughter leaving.

'Marzipan?' he said. I agreed. I like sweets and I eat a lot of them.

Mason is the kind of man who was born to serve, and not simply because it is his trade but because his whole nature is servile. I mean, one has seen shopkeepers who are brisk and obliging, but this is something else again, this is obsequiousness, an eagerness to please that is almost unpleasantly oriental. It makes one feel uncomfortable, but it must please a certain type since his shop does a good trade and, in fact, the rumour is that he is thinking of expanding.

I return to his servility. It isn't that he is insincere or any-thing like that. It is as if deep in his soul he has decided that he really is the servant, that you are a different order of being, an aristocrat, and he lower than a peasant. He gives the impression of finding himself in you. If it weren't for you he wouldn't exist. Frankly, if you haven't met that kind of person, it is difficult to explain it. I hope I won't be accused of anti-Semitism if I say that he reminds me of a Jew, and yet he isn't a Jew, he belongs to this small town and was born and bred here. I suppose there is something about that kind of person which brings out the fascist in one, a desire to kick him as if he were a dog, he looks so eager to please, hanging on your every word, on your every order, as if a few ounces of sweets is more important to him than anything else you can conceive of. (Some day, if I have the time, I shall write a paper about the psychology of service. I think it's important, I imagine a shopkeeper who screams at you because you don't buy anything from his shop as if 'you had something against him'.) The Lady will even cross his hands and stare at you like a lover till you decide what you want, and then he will sigh as if an accomplishment had taken place.

I come here fairly often, and I know his daughter reasonably well. He has only the one daughter and no sons, his wife is dead. They say that he treated her badly. I don't know about that, but I'm sure that he loved his jars of sweets more than her. Imagine living among sweets all day: one would have to be sour when one had left them surely. Is that not right? He wants Diane to go to university since somewhere buried beneath that servility is ambition. I know her, and she is a bitch. Anyone with half an eye could see that, but she's sweet in public, dewy-eyed and cool above the mini-skirt. One of these peroxide blondes and the kind of nutty mind that may get her yet into a students' riot in our modern educational system.

He has brought her up himself, of course. I have played chess with him in the local chess club; I always win, naturally. After all, would he want to lose a customer? But sometimes, I have seen him looking at me ... He thinks the world of his daughter. You know the kind of thing; if she's first in Domestic Science, he'll give her a bicycle. As a matter of fact, I know that she goes with this fellow Marsh, who's at least ten years older than her, and he takes her out to the beach at night on his motor-cycle. His father owns a hotel in the town, and he's got quite a reputation with the ladies. You're not going to tell me that they are innocently watching the sea and the stars.

She doesn't like me. I know that for a fact. I can tell when people don't like me. I have antennae. She thinks I'm some kind of queer because I'm fifty and not married, and because I'm always going to the library for books. And because I wear gloves. But why shouldn't one wear gloves? Just because young girls wear mini-skirts up to their waists doesn't mean that all the decencies should be abandoned, that the old elegancies should go. I like wearing gloves and I like carrying an umbrella. Why shouldn't I?

That day – as so often before – I got into conversation with the Lady while he hovered round me, and we came round to education.

'They're doing nothing in those schools these days,' I said, and I know it's the truth. 'Expressionism, that's what they call it. I call it idleness.'

He looked at me with his crucified expression and said,

'Do you really believe that?' He had a great capacity for listening, he would never volunteer anything. Some people are like that, they hoard everything, not only books, not only money, but conversation itself. Still, I don't mind as I like talking.

'In our days we had to work hard,' I continued. 'We had to get our noses to the grindstone. Arithmetic, grammar and Latin. Now they write wee poems and plays. And what use are they? Nothing. How many of them will ever write anything of any value? It's all a con game. Trying to make people believe that Jack is as good as his master. I'm afraid education is going down the drain like everything else. They can't even spell, let alone write.'

Suddenly he burst out – rather unusual for him –

'She doesn't want to go to university.' Then he stopped as if he hadn't meant to say so much, and actually wrung his hands in front of me.

'You mean Diane?' I said eagerly.

'Yes. I'm so . . . confused. I wouldn't have said it only I have to talk to someone. You know that I don't have many friends. I can count on you as my friend, can't I?'

As far as you can count on anyone, I thought. As far as anyone can count on anyone.

'She says to me, "I can't stand the books". That's what she says. What do you think of that? "I can't stand the books," she says. She says a haze comes over her mind when she is asked to study. She says that she has read all the books she wants to read. "What is the good of education anyway?" she asks. "All that's over. We don't need education any more and anyway," she says, "we're not poor". What do you make of that?'

'Oh, that's what it's come to,' I answered. 'There was Mr Logan died the other day. Now he spent all his years teaching in that school. He read and read. You won't find many like him any more. Nobody needs him. Nobody wants him.'

He wasn't listening. All he said was, 'After what I did for her too. I used to go with her to get dresses fitted and her shoes and everything, and I'm not a woman you know.'

There might be two opinions about that, I thought to myself. 'I don't understand it,' he said, wringing his hands. 'What's wrong with them? She wanted a guitar. I gave her a guitar. She used to go to the folk club Thursday nights and play it. Then she grew tired of that. She wanted to go to France for her holidays and I let her do that. Do you think it's a phase?' he asked eagerly, his face shining with innocence and agony, the crucified man.

I thought of the little white-headed bitch and said, 'No, it's not a phase.'

'I was afraid it might not be. I don't know what I'm going to do.' He was almost crying, such a helpless little man that you couldn't help but despise him.

'I think you should beat some sense into her,' I said suddenly. He looked horrified. 'I didn't know you believed in corporal punishment,' he said.

'In extreme cases I do,' I answered, 'and this seems to be an extreme case. If it was my daughter, that's what I'd do.'

I took my umbrella in my hands, sighting along it like a gun, and said, 'She's betrayed you, kicked you in the teeth. But that's the younger generation for you. They're like bonbons, mealy on the outside but hard on the inside.'

He smiled, for I had used a simile which he would understand. Deliberately.

'Do you really think so?' he said at last, almost in tears, his lips trembling. 'But it's true, you give them everything and they throw it back in your teeth. I slaved to make this shop what it is and it was all for her and she doesn't care. She's never served a customer and I, I have to do it all. I've even got books to study so that I can help her with her lessons. I've got the whole Encyclopaedia Britannica. What will I do? She says she's going abroad. I gave her everything and her mother too, for five years when she was dying, I'm tired, so tired.'

Aren't we all, I thought, aren't we all.

Anyway, that was the last glimpse I had of him, his wet tremulous lips, his doglike expression, his low emotional voice.

The next part of this story is rather undignified, but I must tell it just the same, and the more so because it is undignified. I am not the sort of person who hides things just because they are unpleasant. On the contrary, I feel that the unpleasant things must be told. And I must justify myself too, especially in this situation, in this unprecedented situation.

I have lived in this town for many years now and people are always hiding their little pseudo-tragedies in holes and corners when, if they only knew it, their tragedies are comedies to the rest of us, and as clear as glass doors, too. But I know all about them. I could blackmail the lot of them if I wished, even the most important people in our town, though they sit at their dinners and lunches, among their glasses and champagne. Walking about the town – stopping here, stopping there, speaking to one person at one corner and to another at another corner – I hear many things. I am one of the sights of the town with my kid gloves and my hat. They all know me, but they don't know how dangerous I am. After all Socrates told the truth and he was put to death.

However, let me continue, though it should rend me. One night, not long after my talk with the Lady, I was taking my walk out to the bay in the moonlight. I like the evening. Everything is so apparently innocent, the stars are beginning to shine, you can see the boats in the water lying on their own reflections, and you can hear the gentle movement of the sea. All is cool and gentle and without intrigue. Now and again as you pass some trees you may hear a rustle in the undergrowth, a desperate movement and perhaps a squeal, but that's only rarely. The thing about animals is that they don't wear gloves or hats, and they don't gossip about each other.

Sometimes, as I walk along, I think of people and sometimes of books. I doff my hat carefully to people I know and glance equally carefully at people I don't know.

Of course, things are noisier now than they used to be. Cars race past, youths craning their heads out of windows and shouting at the passers-by. And they are crammed full of girls, these sports cars. But I ignore them. I walk past the trees which line the road, and I glance now and again at the sea with its lights. I think of . . . Well, what does one think of?

Anyway, this evening I was walking along slowly, feeling benign and calm, and eventually I came to the bay. The sun was setting in its splendour of gold and red, and I sat down on a seat near the water. What is more beautiful and peaceful than that, watching the purple clouds and the pale moon, and the sun setting in barbaric splendour? The world was calm except for the twittering of birds. All round me was desolate and I was staring out towards the horizon where the sunset was turning the sky into, as they say, technicolour.

What beautiful thoughts we have at such moments! How good and guiltless we appear to ourselves, sitting there as if on thrones, hat on head, gloves on hands, and umbrella in case of a shower! We feel like gods, clean, urbane, without sorrow or guilt.

And as I was sitting there that evening, surrounded by rocks and sand, in the strange music of the sea birds, and confronting a sky of scarlet and purple, who should materialise – and I use the word advisedly – but Diane herself.

How beautiful she was, how young! I cannot describe it. Her face at first looked more peaceful and calm than I had ever seen it.

She spoke.

'You told my father to beat me,' she said, 'didn't you?'

Her voice was musical and low (where did I hear that before?).

Her eyes were green and she wore this mini-skirt of pure gold.

I tried to stand up in confusion, clutching my umbrella.

'No,' she said, 'stay where you are. You look like a king sitting there.' I can swear those were her exact words. But it was like a dream. You must remember the atmosphere: you have to remember that, the colours, the dreams.

Then she leaned down towards my right ear and she said, still in that dreamy voice,

'Beat me then. You can if you want. My father never beats me, that's why I despise him. Don't you do the same? Don't you despise these weaklings, these sellers of goods? Can't you imagine a world beautiful and strong and young? I think that you're young. I was afraid of you at first, but now I realise what you are, what you truly are. You are aloof as if you had a destiny of your own. You watch everyone. Not everyone can do what you do, live in freedom.'

What was I to say? She had a whip in her hand. She handed it to me there in that confusion of red and gold.

And stood there waiting like a little girl.

'I followed you, you know,' she said. 'I know you always take your constitutional and think your great thoughts while you do so. My father told me what you said. I made a great mistake in you. You always looked so mealy-mouthed. But then, when you said that, I knew you were not like my father, that you would not bow and scrape to anyone.'

And all this time, I must have been peeling off my gloves very slowly. I couldn't help myself, I tell you. I was taking the whip into my hands. Was I not right? Had she herself not asked me to?

'You have a shop too,' she said, 'but you don't bother to serve in it. You get others to do that.' (Actually, it is a jeweller's and my sister serves in it. A long time ago I left it. I couldn't bring myself to serve people.)

She kept saying, 'I know now you couldn't do that. Your nature isn't like that, is it? You can't bear to serve, you want to dominate.'

By this time darkness was coming down. She bent over and I raised the whip, and as I did so I knew that this was what I was meant to do, to dominate and not to serve, to impose my will on others, to cleanse the sins of the world. And I knew that volunteers would come to me because they recognised who I really was, the jewel hardness of my will.

She was so beautiful, so submissive. I raised the whip, and as I did so lights flashed all round me, and there was her boy-friend, and she was laughing and giggling and almost rolling on the sand in ecstasy. Naturally, he used a flashlight. And naturally ... But this I won't go over. The devil, that's what she was, the snake with the green eyes. And so beautiful, wriggling like a fish on the sand. If he hadn't taken the whip from my hands, I would have lashed her and lashed her. I had to wipe the blood from my face with the gloves.

Naturally, my sister left the shop and left the town and naturally ... Well, naturally, my bowing friend put in for the shop and got it fairly cheap. Who else would buy? Not that he put a direct bid in himself, he did it through intermediaries. It was next door to his sweet shop.

He never came to see me. I never saw him again.

They tell me she's going to university after all, to study psychology. A soft option, if ever there was one.

It was funny though. That moment was the most intense of my life. I'll never forget it. I keep going over and over it in my mind, that duel in scarlet and red. Who would have believed evil would be so beautiful and young? And him so servile too. No wonder we get fascists in the world, fascists with blue eyes like mine.

They deceive you and then turn nasty.

But these green eyes, these ... sweets.

The Bridge

My wife and I met them in Israel. They were considerably younger than us and newly married. They came from Devon and they had a farm which they often talked about. For some reason they took a fancy to us, and were with us a fair amount of the time, sometimes on coach trips, sometimes at dinner in the evenings. They were called Mark and Elaine.

I didn't like Israel as much as I had expected I would. I read the *Jerusalem Post* regularly, and was disturbed by some of the stories I found there, though the paper itself was liberal enough. There were accounts of the beatings of Palestinians, and pictures of Israeli soldiers who looked like Nazis.

Certainly it was interesting to see Bethlehem, Nazareth, the Garden of Gethsemane, and they reminded me of the security of my childhood: but at the same time seemed physically tatty, and without romance. Also we were often followed, especially in Jerusalem, by Arab schoolchildren who tried to sell us postcards. the schools were in fact shut by official order.

Though this was the first time Mark and Elaine were abroad they were brighter than us with regard to money. Mark had a gift for finding out the best time for exchanging sterling and was, I thought, rather mean. Sometimes we had coffee in a foursome during the day or at night, and he would pull his purse out very carefully and count out the money: he never gave a tip. He was also very careful about buying for us exactly what we had bought for him on a previous occasion. On the other hand he bought his wife fairly expensive rings which she flourished expansively. They walked hand in hand. They were both tall and looked very handsome.

One day the coach took us to the Golan Heights. There were red flowers growing there, and some abandoned tanks were lying in a glade. The guide, who was a Jew originally from Iraq, told us that a few tanks had held off the attacks till the reservists had been called up. 'They can be called up very quickly,' he said. It was very peaceful, looking across the valley to the other side but there were notices about unexploded mines.

Often we met young boys and girls on the buses. They hitched rides from place to place in their olive-green uniforms. They were of the age of schoolboys and schoolgirls. One morning on a bus I heard a girl listening to a pop song on a radio that she carried with her. It seemed very poignant and sad.

I used to talk quite a lot about articles I had read in the *Jerusalem Post*, which was my Bible because it was the only paper written in English. But neither Mark nor Elaine read much, not even the fat blockbusters that passengers on the coach sometimes carried with them. They told us a great deal about their farm, and what hard work it was. Then there was also a lot of paper work, including VAT. They were very fond of each other, and, as I have said, often walked hand in hand. He was very handsome: she was pretty enough in a healthy sort of way.

We were told by the guide a great deal about the history of Israel, about the Assyrians, about the Crusaders, about the Philistines. I especially remember a beautiful little simple Catholic church above Jerusalem. Then in Jerusalem we were shown the Via Dolorosa. At intervals along the route, young Jewish soldiers with guns were posted. 'Here is where Christ's hand rested,' said the guide, pointing to the wall. He himself had emigrated to Israel from Iraq. 'They took everything from us, even our clothes,' he said; 'for years we lived in a tent.' He had served in the paratroopers and was still liable for call-up.

We saw Masada, which was very impressive. Here the Jews had committed suicide *en masse* rather than surrender to the Romans. At one time the Israeli soldiers had been initiated into the army at a ceremony held at Masada, but that had been discontinued because of its passive associations. Thoughts of suicide were not useful against the Arabs.

I found it difficult to talk to the young couple about farming since I didn't know much about it. My wife, however, who had been brought up on a farm, chattered away about sheep, cattle, and hay. For myself I was more interested in the information I was getting from the *Jerusalem Post*. For instance, an American rabbi had said that the reason for the stone-throwing which had started was that the cinemas at Tel Aviv had been opened on a Saturday night.

We often saw Orthodox Jews wearing black hats, and beards. They sometimes read books while they were walking along the street. Also we saw many of them chanting at the Wailing Wall, where the men were separated from the women. My wife wrote a message and left it in the Wall as if it were a secret assignation. There was one comic touch: some of the Orthodox Jews covered their hats with polythene if it was raining, as the hats were very expensive.

I read diligently in the *Jerusalem Post*. Apparently in the past there has been stone-throwing against Jews. This was in mediaeval times and when they were living in Arab countries. But though Jews complained nothing was done about it. It was considered a reasonable sport.

My wife often used to wonder why Mark and Elaine had picked us for friends since they were so much younger. Did we look cosmopolitan, seasoned travellers, or did they simply like us? Sometimes Elaine talked to my wife as if she were talking to her mother. I found it hard to talk to Mark when the women were in the shops. He often spoke about money, I noticed, and was very exact with it. I sometimes thought that it was he who looked like the seasoned traveller, since he was always totally at ease and was excellent with maps.

The two of them didn't take so many coach trips as we did. Often they went away on their own, and we only met them in the evening.

They didn't go to the Holocaust Museum with us the day we went there. The place was very quiet apart from some French schoolchildren who scampered about. My wife hissed at them to be quiet, but they only grinned insolently. There were piles of children's shoes on the floor: these had been worn by victims of the Holocaust. There were many photographs, and a film that ran all the time.

There was also a room which was in complete darkness apart from thousands of candles reflected from a range of mirrors, so that it seemed that we were under a sky of stars. A voice repeated over and over again the names of the children who had been killed. The Jews had suffered terribly, but were now in turn inflicting terror themselves.

We met a woman who had come to Israel from South Africa. She opposed the Jewish attitude to the Palestinians, though she was a Jew herself. She said that mothers everywhere were against the continued war. She herself had driven her son in her own car to the front, not during the Seven Days War but the one after it.

We were in Israel on Independence Day. Jewish planes, streaming blue and white lines of smoke behind them, formed the Jewish flag. It was very impressive and colourful but also rather aggressive.

The coach took us to a kibbutz where we were to stay for two nights. Immediately we arrived, Mark and Elaine found that there were cattle there, and they left us in order to find out about the price of milk, etc.

The kibbutz itself had been raised out of a malarial swamp. Everyone had to work, and the place looked prosperous. It even had a beautiful theatre which the kibbutzers had built themselves. I ordered coffee from an oldish waiter, and when I offered him a tip he wouldn't accept it. I found out that he had been a lieutenant-colonel on Eisenhower's staff.

The kibbutzers, we were told by the guide, had their own problems. Sometimes when the young ones who had been reared in a kibbutz were called up on national service they entered an enviable world which they had not known of, and they left the kibbutz forever. Also some Jews had accepted compensation money from the Germans while others hadn't, and so there was financial inequality. Thus some could afford to take holidays while others couldn't. This introduced envy into the kibbutz.

Mark and Elaine were pleased with the cattle they had seen

and full of praise. Mark had brought a notebook with him and had jotted down numbers of cattle, type of feeding stuff, etc. They had been given a tour of the farm with which they had been very happy.

One night they had told us that they recently had been in a place in England, it might have been Dorset, and they had come to a little bridge. There was a notice on the bridge that according to legend a couple who walked across the bridge hand in hand would be together forever. They smiled tenderly as they told us the story. In fact they had been on a coach trip at the time, and the passengers on the coach had clapped as the two of them volunteered to walk across the bridge. I thought it was a touching little story and I could imagine the scene; on the other hand I am not superstitious. 'How lovely,' said my wife.

My wife and I had been to Devon once. One day quite by accident we arrived at a house which was said to be haunted, and which had been turned into a restaurant. The owner of the restaurant, who made full use of the legend for commercial purposes, told us that many years before, there used to be criminals who used lanterns to direct ships onto the rocks. One man had done this only to find that one of the passengers on the wrecked ship had been his own daughter coming home from America. He had locked the body up in a room in his house. Many years afterwards the farmer who now owned the house noticed a mark on the wall which suggested the existence of an extra room. He knocked the wall down and found a skeleton there. An American tourist had said that she had seen the ghost of the young girl in broad daylight, and so had been born the legend of the Haunted House. So romance and death fed money and tourism.

We told Mark and Elaine the story, which they hadn't heard before. Suddenly there was a chill in the day as I imagined the father bending down to tear the jewellery from a woman's neck and finding that it was his own daughter.

'Should you like a coffee?' I said. I saw Mark fumbling with his purse. I thought of the Samaritan Inn which had been built at the presumed point where the Good Samaritan had helped his enemy. And indeed in Israel much of the biblical story had been converted into money.

Nevertheless I couldn't love Israel. There was too much evidence of Arab poverty. The dead bodies of Palestinian children were mixed up in my mind with the dead bodies of Jewish children. The mound of worn shoes climbed higher and higher.

On the last night of the tour we exchanged addresses. Mark and Elaine said they would write and my wife and I said we would do the same. And in fact we did do that for a while.

Today, this morning in fact, my wife received a letter from Elaine saying that she and Mark had split up. She said little, but reading between the lines we gathered that he had met a richer woman who was able to invest money in his farm.

We looked at each other for a long time, thinking of the young radiant couple who had walked hand in hand across the bridge.

Finally my wife said, 'At least they didn't have children. It would have been much worse if they had children.'

The Long Happy Life of Murdina the Maid

And now we arrive at the island of Raws, well known in legend and in song. To this island, rich in peat and some deposits of iron, there came St Murriman, clad in monk's habit and hair-shirt. A great man, he is said to have baptised in his old age a number of seals which he thought to be children as they rolled by the shore in their innocent gambols. (And indeed seals do have a peculiar childlike appearance if you scrutinise them carefully enough.) This island too is famous for the story of the Two Bodachs, one of these stories in which our history is perennially rich. But perhaps the most famous story of all is that of Murdina the Maid. (I speak under correction but I believe that a monograph has been written on this story and that a paper was once delivered on it at a Celtic Congress.)

Murdina the Maid was born of good-living parents, the father a blacksmith and the mother a herdsgirl. They lived together in harmony for many years till the mother, whose name was Marian (a relation it is said on the distaff side to the MacLennans of Cule), delivered a fine girl. She grew up, as Wordsworth says, in 'sun and in shower' till she attained the age of seventeen years. We may think of her as apple-cheeked, dewy-eyed, with sloe-black eyes and a skin as white as the bogcotton. However, matters were not allowed to remain like that.

This poor innocent girl one night was attending what we call in the vernacular a dance (though different indeed were the dances of those days from the dances of our degenerate time) and there she met a man, let us call him a man for want of a better name, though he was more like a beast in human form. He was a Southron man, and he was addicted to the music of the melodeon, an instrument which in those days provided our people with much innocent amusement.

We have no record of their dalliance and of his wicked wiles but sufficient to say that he persuaded her to run away with him to Glassgreen, the great metropolis, albeit she went home for her wardrobe (poor as it was) first. One may imagine what such a wardrobe would consist of, two long skirts, a coiffed headdress, two pairs of stockings woven at home, one pair of shoes and one pair of tackety boots, with, of course, some underclothes of the colour pink.

Compare with this the wardrobe of her seducer which would contain brightly painted ties (all bought in a shop), trousers of an alien style, shirts of a sordid cut, and shoes of a hitherto unseen mode. The man's name was Horace.

Thus it was that playing his melodeon and providing her with deceitful music he led her like the Pied Piper to Glassgreen.

Imagine, however, the consternation of the blacksmith and his spouse. Day after day he would lift his hammer and not even hit the anvil with it. Sunk into depression, his stalwart arms rapidly losing their strength, he sank into an early grave and his wife did not outlive him long. O Murdina, how hapless your expedition to the metropolis! Hapless indeed our lives unless we obey our parents. Where she expected a mansion she was led at last into a small room which contained one bed, a gas cooker, a cupboard and not much more. But the tears she shed that evening were more than compensated for by the dallyings of her lover, whose moustache brushed her mouth as he yawned copiously through the long night.

So she began to visit dens of iniquity. Psychedelic were her days and drugged her evenings. The water of the earth did not suffice her but she must be stayed by beverages unknown to her parents. Ravaged by music which stole her soul away she would sing in these same dens of iniquity intertwined with her lover. But sorrowful too were her thoughts for her lover had not as much money as would sustain her wicked delights, such as splendid clothes and furniture of a rare ilk. Thus one night when he was sleeping the sleep of the sinful, she stole from his small den taking with her his pocket book, a number of his ties

(which she hoped to sell) and a diamond necklace which he
said he had got from his mother, long under the sod in his
native Donegal.

With these, she found herself another protector who was in
the habit of giving room to a number of girls who had nowhere
else to go. Laudable and charitable as this was, we must however acknowledge that his mode of living was not what one
would require from a godly man, for he was not above sending
these girls out into the cold to hold converse with strangers
such as seamen, foreigners, and persons of diverse vices.

Thus passed her nights and her days, yearning as she said for
the innocent pleasures of Raws, with its limpid streams, and its
snow-covered bens.

One night the island came to her as in a vision. She saw it,
as it were, clearly delineated on the walls of her luxurious
room, and she heard in her ears the sound of its innumerable
waves. In the morning she arose, put on her new-bought furs,
and set off to find the mode of transport which would take
her to her home. In the carriage were many young men who
(on hearing of her adventures) were desirous to approach
with many friendly overtures and those she was not loathe to
deny, only saying that she would bring them to her house.
She handed out to them with much magniloquence cards
which showed both her own and the name of her house.

Arrived in Raws, she was welcomed with open arms by those
who saw in her the penitent returned with her spiritual gains.
This gave no small encouragement to the indigenous folk for
it showed them that they themselves might do what she had
done. She set up house in Raws and many were the guests who
came to her house. Indeed it can safely be said that hers was
the most popular house in the island, and not until the early
hours of the morning did her visitors depart, fortified by her
conversation and her kindly dalliance.

Often with tears she would lay a wreath of orchids on the
graves of her parents and caused a marble monument to be
built to them on which she had carved these words: 'Gone
Before, But not much Before.'

So she lived to a good old age, providing pleasure and benefit to all and had no cause to regret the day she had left Glass-green for as she herself once remarked in one of her more serious moments, 'The competition here is not so fierce as in the wicked world of the south.'

Thus, therefore, is told the legend of Murdina who from being an apple-cheeked girl became a dowager of the neigh-bourhood, contributing much tablet to the local sale of work as well as many cast-off dresses some of which are to be seen to this day in colours like purple and pink.

It is easy to see therefore that those who leave these beautiful islands with their lovely airs and golden sands always have the urge to return as she did, happy in that they have abandoned the snares and competition of the metropolis.

The Wedding

It was a fine, blowy, sunshiny day as I stood outside the church on the fringe of the small groups who were waiting for the bride to arrive. I didn't know anybody there, I was just a very distant relative, and I didn't feel very comfortable in my dark suit, the trousers of which were rather short. There were a lot of young girls from the Highlands (though the wedding was taking place in the city) all dressed in bright summery clothes and many of them wearing corsages of red flowers. Some wore white hats which cast intricate shadows on their faces. They all looked very much at ease in the city and perhaps most of them were working there, in hotels and offices. I heard one of them saying something about a Cortina and another one saying it had been a Ford. They all seemed to know each other and one of them said in her slow soft Highland voice, 'Do you think Murdina will be wearing her beads today?' They all laughed. I wondered if some of them were university students.

The minister who was wearing dark clothes but no gown stood in the doorway chatting to the photographer who was carrying an old-fashioned black camera. They seemed to be savouring the sun as if neither of them was used to it. The doors had been open for some time as I well knew since I had turned up rather early. A number of sightseers were standing outside the railings taking photographs and admiring the young girls who looked fresh and gay in their creamy dresses.

I looked at the big clock which I could see beyond the church. The bride was late though the groom had already arrived and was talking to his brother. He didn't look at all nervous. I had an idea that he was an electrician somewhere and his suit didn't seem to fit him very well. He was a small person with a happy, rather uninteresting face, his black hair combed back sleekly and plastered with what was, I imagined, fairly cheap oil.

After a while the minister told us we could go in if we wanted to, and we entered. There were two young men, one in a lightish suit and another in a dark suit, waiting to direct us to our seats. We were asked which of the two we were related to, the bride or the groom, and seated accordingly, either on the left or the right of the aisle facing the minister. There seemed to be more of the groom's relatives than there were of the bride's and I wondered idly whether the whole thing was an exercise in psychological warfare, a primitive pre-marital battle. I sat in my seat and picked up a copy of a church magazine which I leafed through while I waited: it included an attack on Prince Philip for encouraging Sunday sport. In front of me a young girl who appeared to be a foreigner was talking to an older companion in broken English.

The groom and the best man stood beside each other at the front facing the minister. After a while the bride came in with her bridesmaids, all dressed in blue, and they took their positions to the left of the groom. The bride was wearing a long white dress and looked pale and nervous and almost somnambulant under the white headdress. We all stood up and sang a psalm. Then the minister said that if there was anyone in the church who knew of any impediment to the marriage they should speak out now or forever hold their peace. No one said anything (one wondered if anyone ever stood up and accused either the bride or groom of some terrible crime): and he then spoke the marriage vows, asking the usual questions which were answered inaudibly. He told them to clasp each other by the right hand and murmured something about one flesh. The groom slipped the ring onto the bride's finger and there was silence in the church for a long time because the event seemed to last interminably. At last the ring was safely fixed and we sang another hymn and the minister read passages appropriate to the occasion, mostly from St Paul. When it was all over we went outside and watched the photographs being taken.

Now and again the bride's dress would sway in the breeze

and a woman dressed in red would run forward to arrange it properly, or at least to her own satisfaction. The bride stood gazing at the camera with a fixed smile. A little boy in a grey suit was pushed forward to hand the bride a horseshoe after which he ran back to his mother, looking as if he was about to cry. The bride and groom stood beside each other facing into the sun. One couldn't tell what they were thinking of or if they were thinking of anything. I suddenly thought that this must be the greatest day in the bride's life and that never again would a thing so public, so marvellous, so hallowed, happen to her. She smiled all the time but didn't speak. Perhaps she was lost in a pure joy of her own. Her mother took her side, and her father. Her mother was a calm, stout, smiling woman who looked at the ground most of the time. Her father twisted his neck about as if he were being chafed by his collar and shifted his feet now and again. His strawy dry hair receded from his lined forehead and his large reddish hands stuck out of his white cuffs.

Eventually the whole affair was over and people piled into the taxis which would take them to the reception. I didn't know what to make of it all. It had not quite had that solemnity which I had expected and I felt that I was missing or had missed something important considering that a woman to the right of me in church had been dabbing her eyes with a small flowered handkerchief all through the ceremony. Both bride and groom seemed very ordinary and had not been transfigured in any way. It was like any other wedding one might see in the city, there didn't seem to be anything Highland about it at all. And the bits of conversation that I had overheard might have been spoken by city people. I heard no Gaelic.

For some reason I kept thinking of the father, perhaps because he had seemed to be the most uncomfortable of the lot. Everyone else looked so assured as if they had always been doing this or something like this and none of it came as a surprise to them. I got into a taxi with some people and without being spoken to arrived at the hotel which was a very good one, large and roomy, and charging, as I could see from a ticket at the desk, very high prices.

We picked up either a sherry or whisky as we went in the door and I stood about again. A girl in a white blouse was saying to her friend dressed in creamy jacket and suit, 'It was in Luigi's you see and this chap said to me out of the blue, "I like you but I don't know if I could afford you".' She giggled and repeated the story a few times. Her friend said: 'You meet queer people in Italian restaurants. I was in an Indian restaurant last week with Colin. It doesn't shut till midnight you know . . . ' I moved away to where another group of girls was talking and one of them saying: 'Did you hear the story about the aspirin?' They gathered closely together and when the story was finished there was much laughter.

After a while we sat down at the table and watched the wedding party coming in and sitting down. We ate our food and the girl on my left spoke to another girl on her left and to a boy sitting opposite her. She said: 'This chap came into the hotel one night very angry. He had been walking down the street and there was this girl in a blue cap dishing out Barclay cards or something. Well, she never approached him at all though she picked out other people younger than him. He was furious about it, absolutely furious. Couldn't she see that he was a business man, he kept saying. He was actually working in insurance and when we offered him a room with a shower he wouldn't take it because it was too expensive.'

The other girl, younger and round-faced, said: 'There was an old woman caught in the lift the other day. You should have heard the screaming . . . ' I turned away and watched the bride who was sitting at the table with a fixed smile on her face. Her father, twisting his neck about, was drinking whisky rapidly as if he was running out of time. Her mother smiled complacently but wasn't speaking to anyone. The minister sat at the head of the table eating his chicken with grave deliberation.

'Did you hear that Lindy has a girl?' said the boy in front of me to the girls. 'And she's thinking of going back home.'

They all laughed. 'I wouldn't go back home now. They'll be at the peats,' said the girl on my left.

'Well,' said the boy, 'I don't know about that. There was a student from America up there and he wanted to work at the peats to see what it was like. He's learned to speak Gaelic too.'

'How did he like it?' said the girl at my left.

'He enjoyed it,' said the boy. 'He said he'd never enjoyed anything so much. He said they'd nothing like that in America.'

'I'm sure,' said the small girl and they laughed again.

'Wouldn't go back for anything anyway,' said the girl to my left. 'They're all so square up there.'

When we had all finished eating, the Master of Ceremonies said that the groom would make a speech which he did very rapidly and incoherently. He was followed by the best man who also spoke very briefly and with incomprehensible references to one of the bridesmaids who blushed deeply as he spoke. There were cheers whenever an opportunity arose such as, for instance, when the groom referred for the first time to his wife and when there was a reference to someone called Tommy.

After that the telegrams were read out. Most of them were quite short and almost formal, 'Congratulations and much happiness' and so on. A number, however, were rather bawdy, such as, for instance, one which mentioned a chimney and a fire and another which suggested that both the bride and groom should watch the honey on their honeymoon. While the telegrams were being read some of the audience whispered to each other, 'That will be Lachy', and 'That will be Mary Anne'. I thought of those telegrams coming from the Highlands to this hotel where waitresses went round the tables with drinks and there were modernistic pictures, swirls of blue and red paint, on the walls. One or two of the telegrams were in Gaelic and in some strange way they made the wedding both more authentic and false. I didn't know what the bride thought as she sat there, as if entranced and distant. Everything seemed so formal, so fixed and monotonous, as if the participants were trying to avoid errors, which the sharp-witted city-bred waitresses might pick up.

Eventually the telegrams had all been read and the father got up to speak about the bride. I didn't know what I expected but he certainly began with an air of businesslike trepidation. 'Ladies and gentlemen,' he said, 'I am here today to make a speech which as you will know is not my speciality.' He twisted his neck about inside the imprisoning collar and continued. 'I can tell you that the crossing was good and the skipper told me that the *Corona* is a good boat though a bit topheavy.' He beamed nervously and then said, 'But to my daughter. I can tell you that she has been a good daughter to me. I am not going to say that she is good at the peats for she is never at home for the peats and she never went to the fishing as girls of her age used to do in the past.' By this time people were beginning to look at each other or down at their plates and even the waitresses were smiling. 'I'll tell you something about the old days. We turned out good men and women in those days, good sailors who fought for their country. Nowadays I don't know about that. I was never in the city myself and I never wore a collar except to the church. Anyway I was too busy. There were the calves to be looked after and the land as you all know. But I can tell you that my daughter here has never been a burden to us. She has always been working on the mainland. Ever since she was a child she has been a good girl with no nonsense and a help to her mother, and many's the time I've seen her working at the hay and in the byre. But things is changed now. Nowadays, it's the tractors and not the horses. In the old days too we had the gig but now it's the train and the plane.' The bride was turning a deadly white and staring down at the table. The girls on my left were transfixed. Someone dropped a fork or a spoon or a knife and the sound it made could be heard quite clearly. But the father continued remorselessly: 'In my own place I would have spoken in the Gaelic but even the Gaelic is dying out now as anyone can read in the papers every week. In the old days too we would have a wedding which would last for three days. When Johnny Murdo married, I can remember it very well, the wedding went on for four days. And he married when he was quite old. But as for my daughter here I am very happy that she is getting married though the city is not the place for me and I can tell you I'll be very glad to get back to the dear old home again. And that is all I have to say. Good luck to them both.'

When he sat down there was a murmur of conversation which rose in volume as if to drown the memory of the speech.

The girls beside me talked in a more hectic way than ever about their hotels and made disparaging remarks about the islands and how they would never go back. Everyone avoided the bride who sat fixed and miserable at the table as if her wedding dress had been turned into a shroud.

I don't know exactly what I felt. It might have been shame that the waitresses had been laughing. Or it might have been gladness that someone had spoken naturally and authentically about his own life. I remember I picked up my whisky and laid it down again without drinking it and felt that this was in some way a meaningful action.

Shortly afterwards the dancing began in an adjoining room. During the course of it (at the beginning they played the latest pop tunes) I went over and stood beside the father who was standing by himself in a corner looking miserable as the couples expressed themselves (rather than danced) in tune to the music, twisting their bodies, thrusting out their bellies and swaying hypnotically with their eyes half shut.

'It's not like the eightsome reel,' I said.

'I don't know what it is like,' he said. 'I have never seen anything like it.'

'It is rather noisy,' I agreed. 'And how are the crops this year?' I said to him in Gaelic.

He took his dazed eyes off a couple who were snapping their fingers at each other just in front of him, and said: 'Well, it's been very dry so far and we don't know what we're going to do.' He had to shout the words against the music and the general noise. 'I have a good few acres you know though a good many years ago I didn't have any and I worked for another man. I have four cows and I sell the milk. To tell you the honest truth I didn't want to come here at all but I felt I couldn't let her down. It wasn't an easy thing for me. I haven't left the island before. Do you think this is a posh hotel?'

I said that I thought it was. He said, 'I tell you I've never been in a hotel before now. They've got a lot of carpets, haven't they? And mirrors, I've never seen so many mirrors.'

'Come on,' I shouted, 'let's go into the bar.' We did so and I ordered two beers.

'The people in there aren't like human beings at all,' he said. 'They're like Africans.'

After a while he said, 'It was the truth I said about her, she's never at home. She's always been working in hotels. I'll tell you something, she's never carried a creel on her back though that's not a good thing either. She was always eating buns and she would never eat any porridge. What do you think of her husband, eh? He was talking away about cars. And he's got a good suit, I'll give him that. He gave the waiter a pound, I saw it with my own eyes. Oh, he knows his way around hotels, I'll be bound. But where does he come from? I don't know. He's never ploughed any ground, I think.'

I thought at that moment that he wouldn't see his daughter very often in the future. Perhaps he really was without knowing it giving her away to a stranger in a hired cutprice suit.

After a while we thought it politic to go back. By this time there was a lull in the dancing and the boy in the lightish suit had started a Gaelic song but he didn't know all the words of it, only the chorus. People looked round for assistance while red-faced and embarrassed he kept asking if anyone knew the words because he himself had lost them. Suddenly the father pushed forward with authority and standing with his glass in his hand began to sing – verse after verse in the traditional manner. They all gathered round him and even the waitresses listened, there was so much depth and intensity in his singing. After he had finished there was much applause and requests for other songs for he seemed to know the words of all of them. The young girls and the boys gathered round him and sat on the floor in a circle looking up at him. He blossomed in the company and I thought that I could now leave, for he seemed to be wholly at home and more so than his audience were.

The Hermit

We were on a touring bus one morning and it stopped at a
shed by the side of the road. A hermit lived there. The shed
was made of tin and had a long chimney sticking out of it. The
bus driver, very upright behind the wheel, tooted the horn a
few times and then stopped. We were looking out the window
at the hut. After the driver had stopped tooting a man came
out. He was very thin, and white, bristly hair was seen not only
on his head but on his cheeks as well. His trousers were held
up by braces. He was carrying a chanter. He scratched his
head and then came over to the bus. He stood on the step and
said, 'Good morning, ladies and gentlemen, I'm afraid I was
late getting up.' He spoke in a sort of educated voice.

He looked down at the ground and then up again and,
laughing a little, said, 'Would you like if I played you some
tunes to speed you on your way?'

He took out his chanter and blew through it. Then he took
out a dirty white handkerchief and wiped it. He played 'Loch
Lomond' very badly, and put the chanter on a case beside him,
a case belonging to one of the passengers.

'This is the day I go for my pension,' he said, and someone
laughed.

'I go down the road there to the Post Office.' He pointed
into the slight mist ahead of us.

The driver said, 'He's been on TV, haven't you?'

The hermit scratched his head again, looking down at the
floor, and then, looking up again with an alert bright look on
his unshaven ravaged face,

'Yes, I was on TV,' he said.

'What programme were you on?' someone shouted from
the back, greatly daring. It was a woman's voice.

'It was called "Interesting People". I was interviewed, I played the chanter.'

'Will you be on again?' someone asked.

'I don't know. I may be. Depends if they like me.'

Everyone laughed, and he grinned impudently.

'I was late getting up,' he said to the driver.' I was washing my clothes last night.'

'You should get married,' another woman shouted out.

'It's too late now,' he said perkily. 'Would you like to hear another tune? I must play for my money.'

This time he played 'Scotland the Brave'. He put the chanter down and said – 'It's too early to play.' He had played it very badly. In fact, his playing was so bad it was embarrassing.

He handed his cap round. When it came to my turn I debated whether to put threepence or sixpence in. After all, even though he was a hermit, he did play very badly.

As the cap was being handed round he stood on the steps and said – 'No, I don't have a gun. Anyway, there's nothing here to kill, madam. I get my cheese and bread from down the road, and that's all I need.'

When the cap was handed back to him he took out his chanter again and said – 'I hope it'll behave better this time. I'll play you one for the road if my chanter behaves.' He played 'I'm no' awa' tae bide awa'. 'I'm afraid my chanter is playing up on me today,' he said, laughing. He got down from the step on to the road. The driver let in the clutch just as the hermit was saying, 'I hope you have a pleasant day.' The bus picked up speed. I saw him turning away and going into his hut. He didn't wave or even look back, though some people in the bus were waving.

I didn't know whether I hoped he got on TV or not. Playing like that he didn't deserve to.

I heard a woman behind me saying: 'Such an educated voice.'

And another one: 'Perhaps he's got a tragedy in his life. He sounded an intelligent sort of man.'

If I'd had the courage I would have spat on them. Who was he, anyway, making money from us just because he was a hermit? Anyone could be a hermit. It didn't take courage to be a hermit. It only took despair. Anyway, he was one of the worst instrumentalists I had ever heard. I'd have given the money to Bob Dylan if he'd stood there singing 'Don't Think Twice, It's All Right', but not to that faker.

The Exiles

She had left the Highlands many years before and was now
living in a council flat (in a butterscotch-coloured block) in
the Lowlands. Originally, when she had first moved, she had
come to a tenement in the noisy warm centre of the town, not
much better than a slum in fact, but the tenement had been
pulled down in a general drive to modernise the whole area.
The council scheme was itself supposed to be very modern
with its nice bright colour, its little handkerchiefs of lawns, its
wide windows. The block swarmed with children of all shapes
and sizes, all ages and colours of clothes. There were prams in
practically all the hallways, and men in dungarees streamed
home at five. Then they would all watch TV (she could see
the blue light behind the curtains like the sky of a strange
planet), drink beer, or shake the flimsy walls with music from
their radiograms. On Saturdays they would go to the football
matches – the team was a Second Division one – or they
would mow the lawn in their shirtsleeves. The gardens were
well kept on the whole, with roses growing here and there; in
general, though, it was easier to lay down grass, and one would
see, lying on the grass, an occasional abandoned tricycle.

The walls of the council houses were scribbled over by the
children who ran in and out of the closes playing and shouting
and quarrelling. Apart from the graffiti, the council houses
would have been all right, she thought, but the children
wouldn't leave anything alone, and they were never looked
after by their mothers who stood talking endlessly at bus
stops, bought sweets for the family when they ought to buy
sustaining food, and went about with scarves on their heads.

She herself was seventy years old. She didn't go out much
now. For one thing, there was the stair which was steep and

narrow and not meant for an old person at all. For another, there weren't many places she could go to. Of course, for a young person there were plenty of places, the cinema, the dance-hall, the skating rink and so on. But not for her. She did sometimes attend the church though she disapproved of it: the minister was a bit too radical, leaving too many things in the hands of women, and there was too much of this catering for young people with societies and groups. That wasn't the job of the church. In any case, it should be left in the hands of the men.

She didn't go to church very often in the winter. The fact was that it would be lonely coming home at night up that road with all these hooligans about. They would stab you as soon as look at you. You could see them hanging about at windows waiting to burgle the shops: a lot of that went on. She herself often put a chain on the door and wouldn't open it till she found out who was behind it. Not that very many people called except the rent man, the insurance man (she was paying an insurance of two shillings a week, which would bury her when she passed on), the milkman, and, occasionally, the postman. She would get an airmail letter now and again from her sister in Canada telling her all about her daughters who were being married off one after the other. There were six, including Marian the eldest. Her sister would send her photographs of the weddings showing coarse-looking, winking Americans sitting around a table with a white cloth and loaded with drinks of all kinds, the bride standing there with the knife in her hand as she prepared to cut the multi-storey cake. The men looked like boxers and were always laughing.

In any case, it wasn't easy for her to get down the stair now. Perhaps it would have been better if she had never come to the Lowlands, but then it was her son who had taken her out, and the house had been sold, and then he had got married and she was left alone. And it was pretty grim. Not that she idealised the Highlands either, don't think that. People there would talk behind your back and let you down in all sorts of ways, and you couldn't tell what they were thinking half the time.

Out here they left you alone, perhaps too much alone. So far she hadn't had any serious illness, which was lucky as she didn't get on well with the neighbours who were young women of about thirty, all with platoons of children who looked like pieces of dirt, with thumbs in their mouths.

Most days she sat at the wide window watching the street below her. Off to the right, she could see the main road down which the great red buses careered at such terrifying speed, rocking from side to side. They would hardly stop for you. One of those days she would fall as she was boarding one. The conductors pressed the bell before you were hardly on, and the conductresses were even worse, very impudent if you said anything to them.

Down below on the road she could see the children playing. She couldn't say that she was very fond of children after what had happened with her son: leaving her like that after what she had done for him. Not that some of the children weren't nice. They would come to the door in their stiff staring masks at Hallowe'en, and she would give pennies to the politest amongst them. They were much more forward than the children at home and they had no nervousness. They would stand there and sing their songs, take their pennies and run downstairs again. Late at night, in summer, the boys and girls would be going past the houses singing and shouting; half drunk, she shouldn't wonder. And their language. You could hear every word as plain as could be. And there were no policemen where they were. Not that the housing scheme she was in was the worst. There was another one where none of the tenants could do anything to their gardens because the others would tear them all up. You got some people these days!

Really, sometimes she thought that if she had enough money she would go back to the Highlands: but she didn't have enough money, she had only the pension, and the fares were going up all the time. In any event, she wouldn't recognise the Highlands now. She had heard that the people had changed and were just as bad as the Lowlanders. You even had to lock the door now, an unheard-of thing in the past. Why, in the past, you could go away anywhere you liked for weeks, leaving the door unlocked, and, when you came back, the house would be exactly as you had left it, apart from the dust, of course.

It was hard just the same, being on your own all the time. All you got nowadays was closed curtains and the blue light of TV. It was just like a desert. Sitting there at the window all day was not a life for anyone. But what could she do about it? She must put up with it. She had been the fool and now she must put up with it. No use crying.

So she rose late in the morning, for time was her enemy, and took in the milk and made the breakfast (she always had porridge) and then went down to the shop in the council house scheme, for bread, meat and vegetables. In the adjacent newspaper shop she bought the Daily Express. When she had had her dinner she sat at the window until it was time for tea. After that she sat at the window again unless it was a Wednesday or a Sunday for on these evenings she went to church. She used the light sparingly in order to save electricity, and sometimes she would walk about in the dark; she was afraid that the lights would fuse and she would be unable to repair them. Her son had left her a small radio to which she listened now and again. What she listened to was the news and the Gaelic programmes and the sermons. The sermons were becoming very strange nowadays: sometimes, instead of a sermon, they had inexplicable discussions about all sorts of abstruse things. Trying to get down to the juvenile delinquents, that's all they were doing. Another programme she sometimes listened to was called *The Silver Lining*. She only used the one station, the Home: she never turned to the Light at all. She was frightened if she moved the hand that she would never get back to the Home again.

But the worst was the lack of visitors. Once or twice the Matron would come in, the minister now and again, and apart from that, no one except the rent man, the milkman and the electric man. But the only thing the last three came for was money. No one ever came to talk to her as a human being. And so the days passed. Endlessly. But it was surprising how quickly they passed just the same.

*

It was a Tuesday afternoon, on a fine summer's day (that morning she had been to the Post Office to collect her pension as she always did on a Tuesday). She was sitting by the window knitting: she had got into the habit of knitting many years ago and she couldn't stop even though she had no one to knit for. The sideboard was full of socks – all different colours of wool – and jerseys. Everyone said that she was good at knitting and that she should go in for prizes, but who wanted to do that? It was really a bright hot day, with the sun reflected back in a glitter from the windows of the houses opposite. Most of them were open to let in the air, and you could see the curtains drifting a little and bulging.

Looking downwards like a raven from its perch, she saw him trudging from house to house. He was pressing the bell of the door opposite, his old case laid down beside him, dilapidated and brown, with a strap across it. She saw him take a big red handkerchief out of his trouser pocket and wipe his face with it. The turban wound round his head, he stood at the door leaning a little against the stone beside it, waiting. He seemed to have been carrying the case for ever, pressing doorbells and waiting, with an immense patience. The windows of the house opposite were open and she could see Mrs whatever-her-name-was moving about in the living room, but she didn't come to the door: probably she had seen him coming and didn't want to let him in. After a while he turned away.

As he did so he happened to glance up, and saw her sitting at the window. It was just pure chance that he saw her, but he would probably have come anyway since he would go to all the houses. On the other hand, on such a hot day, he might not be willing to face the high stair. He bent down, picked up the case and crossed the road, a slim man. She was looking down directly on to the turban. Strange people these, they had a religion of their own.

She listened for his foot on the stairs as she often listened for the step of the postman, who reached her house about eight o'clock in the morning when she was still lying in bed. Most of the time he would have nothing but bills, and she would hear him ring the bell next door, and then his steps retreating down the stair again. Sometimes she would even get up and watch the letter box with bated breath waiting for a letter to drop through on to the mat below.

In a similar manner, she waited this afternoon. Would he come up to the top or wouldn't he? There was the sound of steps and then they faded. That must be someone going into the house on the middle floor, perhaps the woman coming in from her shopping. Then silence descended again. It must have been another five minutes before the ring came at the door. She hurried along the passageway trying to keep calm and when she opened the door on its chain, there he was, his dark face shining with sweat, his red bandana handkerchief in his hand. His case was laid down on the mat outside the door.

'Afternoon, missus,' he said in a deep guttural voice. 'Wish to see dresses?' He seemed young though you couldn't tell with them. He smiled at her; you couldn't tell about the smile either. It seemed warm enough; on the other hand, to him she was just business. She led him along the passageway to the living room which was at the far end of the house, and he sat down in a deep armchair and began to open the case as soon as he had sat down. He gave the room a quick, appraising look, noting the polished side-board full of glasses of all kinds, the copper-coloured carpet, the table in the centre with the paper flowers in the glass.

The case looked very cheap and cracked and was stuffed to the brim. It amazed her to see how much they could cram into their cases and how neat and tidy they were.

'Fine day, missus,' he said, looking up and flashing his white teeth.

'Would you like a glass of milk?' she asked.

'Thank you very much, missus.' He pronounced his consonants in a very strange manner: of course, they didn't know English well, goodness knew where they came from. She handed him a tall cold tumbler of milk and watched as he took it delicately in his dark hand, the blackness contrasting very strongly with the white of the milk. He drank it very quickly and handed it back to her, then began to put stuff on the floor.

'Silk scarf. Blue,' he said. 'Very nice.' He held it up against the light in which the silk looked cold.

'It is very nice,' she said in her precise English.

He stopped.

'You no from here?' – as if he had heard some tone of strangeness in her voice.

'No. No from here,' she half-imitated him.

'I am from Pakistan,' he said, bending down again so that she could only see the bluish turban. 'I am a student,' he added.

She could hardly make out what he was saying, he spoke in such a guttural way.

'Are you a student?' she said at last.

'Student in law,' he said as if that made everything plain. He took out a yellow pullover and left it on the floor for her to look at. She shook her head: it was very nice wool, she thought, picking it up and letting her hands caress it, but she had no use for it. She supposed that Pakistan must be very warm and yet he appeared hot as if the weather didn't agree with him. What must it be like for him in the winter?

'Where you come from then?' he asked, looking up and smiling with his warm, quick, dark eyes.

'I come from the north,' she said slowly.

'North?'

'From the Highlands,' she said.

'Ah,' he said, as if he did not fully understand.

'Do you like here?' he asked innocently.

'Do you like here yourself?' she countered.

He stopped with a scarf in his hand.

'Not,' he said and nodded his head. 'Not. Too cold.' His eyes brightened. 'Going back to Pakistan after law. Parents got shop. Big shop in big town.' He made a motion with his hands which she presumed indicated the size of the shop.

'Do you come here often?' she asked. 'I haven't seen you before.' Nor tinkers. She never saw any tinkers. Up in the Highlands the tinkers would come to the door quite often, but not here. Drummond their name was, it was a family name.

'Not often. I'm on vacation, see? Sometimes Saturdays I come. I work in shop in Glasgow to make money for law. For education. This vacation with me.'

She nodded, half understanding, looking down at the clothes. She wondered what the women wore in Pakistan, what they did. She had seen some women with long dresses and pigtails. But was that India or China?

The stuff he was selling was pretty cheap. 'Men's hand-kerchiefs.' He held up a bundle of them. She shook her head. 'Men's ties,' he said, holding up a bundle of them, garish and painted. He looked quickly round the living room, noting the glass, the flowers . . .

'You live alone, missus?' he said. She said yes without thinking, wondering why he had asked. Perhaps he would come back later and rob her: you couldn't tell with anyone these days.

'Ah,' he said, again mopping his brow.

'City no good,' he said. 'Too hot. Too great traffic.' He smiled warmly, studying her and showing his white teeth. 'Parents go to mountains in summer in Pakistan.'

He placed a nightgown on top of the pile: it had a blue ground with small pink flowers woven into it.

'Nice nightgown,' he said, holding it up. 'Cheap. Very cheap. Bargain. For you, missus.'

She held it in her hands and studied it. 'Too small,' she said finally. She had one nightgown already she had received from her sister in Canada; it had frills as well, but she never wore it.

'Dressing gown then,' he pursued. 'Two pound. Good bargain. Nice quality.' It was far too expensive.

'Would you like a cup of tea?' she said at last.

'No today, missus. Perhaps next time if I come.'

If he came! That meant he might not come again. Of course if he didn't sell much he wouldn't come, why should he? And it didn't look as if he had sold much, what with the case crammed to the top, the children's stuff still there, panties, jerseys, little twin sets. They were all intact. The young wives had been avoiding him, that was clear. But they would buy sweets and cakes all right though they wouldn't buy clothes for their children. It was scandalous.

'Knickers,' he said. 'Silk knickers.' He held them, very cool, very silky, letting them run through his fingers, his black fingers.

There was hardly anything else there that she could buy, except for the ladies' handkerchiefs but she had plenty of these already, some even from the best Irish linen. One always gathered handkerchiefs, though one hardly ever used them, not these delicate ones anyway.

'Do you ever go home to Pakistan?' she asked.

'Not to Pakistan since I came to this place two years ago. No money.' He smiled winningly, preparing to return everything to the case. 'Some day, perhaps. Two year from this time.' He held up two fingers. 'When law finished.'

She watched his black hands busy against the whites and reds and greens. She noticed for the first time that his own clothes were quite cheap; a painted tie, a dirty looking collar, a dark suit and scuffed shoes, shoes so dusty that it looked as if he had been walking for ever. She was standing by the window, and as she watched him she could see a big red bus flashing and glittering down the road.

He was really quite young when you studied him. For some reason she thought of the time that Norman had come home drunk at two in the morning after the dance, the sickness in the bathroom under the hard early-morning light of the bulb, his refusal to get up the following morning for work . . . She wondered if this young man drank. Probably not. There would be some law against it in their religion. They had a very funny religion, but they were clean-living people, she had heard. They didn't have churches over there as we had. It was more like temples or things like that.

As he was putting all the clothes back in the case, she put out her hand and picked up the silk knickers, studying them again. She stood at the window looking at them. Lord, how flimsy they were! Who would wear such things? What delicate airy beings, what sluts, would put these next to their skin? She wouldn't be seen dead buying that stuff. It wouldn't even keep out the winter cold. Yet they were so cool in your hands, so silky, like water running, like a cool stream in the north.

'How much?' she said.

'Fifteen shillings,' he said looking at her devotedly, his hands resting lightly on the case.

She put them down again.

'Have you any gents' socks?' she asked.

He nodded.

'How much are they?'

'Five shilling,' he said. 'Light socks. Good bargain. Nice.' He handed over two pairs, one grey, the other brown. As she held them in her hands, stroking them gently, she realised how inferior they were to her own, she knew that no love had gone into their making. She had never bought a pair of shop socks in her life: she had always knitted Norman's socks herself. Why, people used to stop him in the street and admire them, they were so beautiful, so much care had gone into them! And she knew so many patterns too, all those that her mother had taught her so long ago and so far away. In another country, in another time, in another age.

'Five shillings,' she repeated dully. Still, that was about the cheapest thing he had. She said decisively, 'I'll take them,' though her heart was rent at their cheapness.

She went into the bedroom and took the five shillings out of the shiny black bag, shutting the door in case he might follow her. That left her with three pounds five for the week. Still, in summer it wasn't too bad, she didn't have to use so much electricity and she could save on the coal.

She counted the two silver half-crowns coldly into his warm black hand, and he gave her the socks.

'Thank you, missus,' he said. Could she detect just a trace of Glasgow accent behind the words? That displeased her for some reason. He bent down, strapping the case tight, and, when he was ready to go, he smiled at her radiantly.

'Will you be coming again?' she asked, thinking how quickly the hour had passed.

'Every Tuesday while vacation is on,' he said, looking out of the window at the traffic and the children playing.

She followed him down the lobby.

'You sit at window much?' he said, and she didn't like that, but she said, 'Sometimes.'

'See you Tuesday then,' he said. 'Maybe have something else. Something nice.'

She closed the door behind him and heard his steps going downstairs, and it was almost as if she was listening to Norman leaving. She went back to the window, looking down, but she couldn't see him: he must be keeping to this side of the street. Later on, however, she saw him crossing the road. He stopped and laid the case down and waved up at her, but she couldn't make out the expression on his face. Then he continued and she couldn't see him at all.

She got up slowly and put the socks in with the pile of the ones she had knitted herself, the loved ones, as if she were making an offering to the absent, as if she were asking for forgiveness. She hoped that next week he would have something cheap. She continued knitting the socks.

The Maze

It was early morning when he entered the maze and there were still tiny globes of dew on the grass across which he walked, leaving ghostly footprints. The old man at the gate, who was reading a newspaper, briefly raised his head and then gave him his ticket. He was quite easy and confident when he entered: the white handkerchief at his breast flickered like a miniature flag. It was going to be an adventure, fresh and uncomplicated really. Though he had heard from somewhere that the maze was a difficult one he hadn't really believed it: it might be hard for others but not for him. After all wasn't he quite good at puzzles? It would be like any puzzle, soluble, open to the logical mind.

The maze was in a big green park in which there was also a café, which hadn't as yet opened, and on the edge of it there was a cemetery with big steel gates, and beyond the cemetery a river in which he had seen a man in black waterproofs fishing. The river was as yet grey with only a little sparkle of sun here and there.

At first as he walked along the path he was relaxed and, as it were, lounging: he hadn't brought the power of his mind to bear on the maze. He was quite happy and confident too of the outcome. But soon he saw, below him on the stone, evidence of former passage, for there were empty cigarette packets, spent matches, empty cartons of orangeade, bits of paper. It almost irritated him to see them there as if he wished the maze to be clean and pure like a mathematical problem. It was a cool fresh morning and his shirt shone below his jacket, white and sparkling. He felt nice and new as if he had just been unpacked from a box.

When he arrived at the first dead-end he wasn't at all perturbed. There was plenty of time, he had the whole morning in front of him. So it was with an easy mind that he made his way back to try another path. This was only a temporary setback to be dismissed from his thoughts. Obviously those who had designed the maze wouldn't make it too easy, if it had been a group of people. Of course it might only have been one person. He let his mind play idly round the origin of the maze: it was more likely to have been designed by one person, someone who in the evening of his days had toyed idly with a puzzle of this nature: an engineer perhaps or a setter of crosswords. Nothing about the designer could be deduced from the maze: it was a purely objective puzzle without pathos.

The second path too was a dead-end. And this time he became slightly irritated for from somewhere in the maze he heard laughter. When had the people who were laughing come in? He hadn't noticed them. And then again their laughter was a sign of confidence. One wouldn't laugh if one were unable to solve the puzzle. The clear happy laughter belonged surely to the solvers. For some reason he didn't like them; he imagined them as haughty and imperious, negligent, graceful people who had the secret of the maze imprinted on their brains.

He walked on. As he did so he met two of the inhabitants of the maze for the first time. It was a father and son, at least he assumed that was what they were. They looked weary, and the son was walking a little apart from the father as if he was angry. Before he actually caught sight of them he thought he heard the son say, 'But you said it wouldn't take long.' The father looked guilty and hangdog as if he had failed his son in some way. He winked at the father and son as he passed them as if implying, 'We are all involved in the same puzzle.' But at the same time he didn't feel as if he belonged to the same world as they did. For one thing he was unmarried. For another the father looked unpleasantly flustered and the son discontented. Inside the atmosphere of his own coolness he felt superior to them. There was something inescapably dingy about them, especially about the father. On the other hand they would probably not meet again and he might as well salute them as if they were 'ships of the night'. It seemed to him that the father was grey and tired, like a little weary mouse redolent of failure.

He continued on his way. This too was a dead-end. There was nothing to do but retrace his steps. He took his handkerchief out of his pocket, for he was beginning to sweat. He hadn't noticed that the sun was so high in the sky, that he had taken so long already. He wiped his face and put his handkerchief back in his pocket. There was more litter here, a fragment of a doll, a torn pair of stockings. What went on in this maze? Did people use it for sexual performance? The idea disgusted him and yet at the same time it argued a casual mastery which bothered him. That people should come into a maze of all places and carry out their practices there! How obscene, how vile, how disrespectful of the mind that had created it! For the first time he began to feel really irritated with the maze as if it had a life of its own, as if it would allow sordid things to happen. Calm down, he told himself, this is ridiculous, it is not worth this harassment.

He found himself standing at the edge of the maze, and over the hedge he could see the cemetery which bordered the park. The sun was flashing from its stones and in places he could see bibles of open marble. In others the tombstones were old and covered with lichen. Beyond the cemetery he could see the fisherman still angling in his black shiny waterproofs. The rod flashed back from his shoulder like a snake, but the cord itself was subsumed in bright sunlight.

And then to his chagrin he saw that there was a group of young people outside the maze and quite near him. It was they who had been the source of the laughter. One of them was saying that he had done the maze five times, and that it was a piece of cake, nothing to it. The others agreed with him. They looked very ordinary young people, not even students, just boys from the town, perhaps six or seven years younger than himself. He couldn't understand how they had found the maze easy when he himself didn't and yet he had a better mind, he was sure of that. He felt not exactly envy of them in their assured freedom but rather anger with himself for being so unaccountably stupid. It sounded to him as if they could enter and leave the maze without even thinking about it. They were eating chips from brown paper, and he saw that the café had opened.

But the café didn't usually open till twelve o'clock, and he had entered the maze at half past nine. He glanced at his watch and saw that it was quarter past twelve. And then he noticed something else, that the veins on his wrists seemed to stand out more, seemed to glare more, than he had remembered them doing. He studied both wrists carefully. No, no question about it, his eyes had not deceived him. So, in fact, the maze was getting at him. He was more worried than he had thought.

He turned back down the path. This time something new had happened. He was beginning to feel the pressure of the maze, that was the only way that he could describe it. It was almost as if the maze were exerting a force over him. He stopped again and considered. In the beginning, when he had entered the maze in his white shirt, which now for some reason looked soiled, he had felt both in control of himself and the maze. It would be he who would decide what direction he would take, it would be he who would remain detached from the maze, much as one would remain detached from a crossword puzzle while solving it in front of the fire in the evening. But there had been a profound change which he only now recognised. The maze was in fact compelling him to choose, pushing him, making demands on him. It wasn't simply an arrangement of paths and hedges. It was as if the maze had a will of its own.

Now he began to walk more quickly as if feeling that he didn't have much time left. In fact he had an appointment with Diana at three o'clock and he mustn't break it. It would be ridiculous if he arrived late and said, 'I couldn't come because I was powerless to do so. I was a prisoner.' She was sure to think such an explanation odd, not to say astonishing. And in any case if he arrived late she wouldn't be there. Not that deep down he was all that worried, except that his non-appearance would be bad manners. If he was going to give her a pretext for leaving him, then it must be a more considered pretext than that.

He noticed now that his legs were becoming tired and heavy. He supposed that this was quite logical, as the stone would be absorbing some of the energy that he was losing. But what bothered him more than anything was the feeling that it would be a long time before he would get out of the maze, that he was going round in circles. Indeed he recognised some of the empty cigarette packets that he was passing. They were mostly Players and he was sure that he had seen them before. In fact he bent down and marked some of them with a pen to make sure of later identification. This was the sort of thing that he had read of in books, people going round and round deserts in circles. And yet he thought that he was taking a different path each time. He wiped his face again and felt that he was losing control of himself. He must be if he was going round and round in helpless circles all the time. Maybe if he had a thread or something like that he would be able to strike out on fresh paths. But he didn't have a thread and some remnant of pride determined that he would not use it, rather like his resolve not to use a dictionary except as a last resort when he was doing a crossword puzzle. He must keep calm. After all, the café and the cemetery were quite visible. It wasn't as if he was in a prison and couldn't shout for help if the worst came to the worst. It wasn't as if he was stranded on a desert island. And yet he knew that he wouldn't shout for help: he would rather die.

He didn't see the father and son again but he saw other people. Once he passed a big heavy man with large black-rimmed spectacles who had a briefcase in his hand, which he thought rather odd. The man, who seemed to be in a hurry, seemed to know exactly where he was going. When they passed each other the man didn't even glance at him, and didn't smile. Perhaps he looked contemptible to him. It was exactly as if the man was going to his office and the path of the maze was an ordinary high road.

Then again he saw a tall ghostly-looking man passing, and he turned and stared after him. The man was quite tall, not at all squat like the previous one. He looked scholarly, abstracted and grave. He seemed to drift along, inside an atmosphere of his own, and he himself knew as if by instinct that the first man would have no difficulty in solving the riddle of the maze but that the second would. He didn't know how he knew this, but he was convinced just the same. The maze he now realised was infested with people, men, women and children, young people, old people, middle-aged people. Confident people and ghostly people. It was like a warren and he felt his bones shiver as the thought came to him. How easy it had been to think at the beginning that there was only himself: and now there were so many other people. People who looked straight ahead of them and others who looked down at the ground.

One in particular, with the same brisk air as the black-spectacled man, he had an irresistible desire to follow. The man was grey-haired and soldierly. He, like the first one, didn't look at him or even nod to him as he passed, and he knew that this was another one who would succeed and that he should follow him. But at the same time it came to him that this would be a failure of pride in himself, that he didn't want to be like a dog following its master as if he were on a string. The analogy disgusted him. He must not lose control of his will, he must not surrender it to someone else. That would be nauseating and revolting.

He noticed that he was no longer sweating and this bothered him too. He should be sweating, he should be more frightened. Then to his amazement he saw that the sun had sunk quite far in the direction of the west. He came to a dead halt almost in shock. Why was time passing so rapidly? It must be four o'clock at least and when he glanced at his watch he saw that it was actually half past four. And therefore he had missed Diana. What a ludicrous thing. This maze, inert and yet malevolent, was preventing him from doing what he ought to have done and forcing him to do other things instead. Probably he would never see Diana again. And then the thought came to him, threatening in its bareness, what if he had chosen to walk into this maze in order to avoid her? No, that was idiotic. Such an idea had never come into his head. Not for one moment.

He looked down at his shoes and saw that they were white with dust. His trousers were stained. He felt smelly and dirty.

And what was even more odd when he happened to see the backs of his hands he noticed that the hair on them was grey. That surely couldn't be. But it was true, the backs of his hands had grey hair on them. Again he stood stock-still trying to take account of what had happened. But then he found that he couldn't even stand still. It was as if the maze had accelerated. It was as if it could no longer permit him to think objectively and apart from himself. Whenever a thought came into his head it was immediately followed by another thought which devoured it. He had the most extraordinary vision which hit him with stunning force. It was as if the pathways in his brain duplicated the pathways of the maze. It was as if he was walking through his own brain. He couldn't get out of the maze any more than he could get out of his own head. He couldn't quite focus on what he sensed, but he knew that what he sensed or thought was the truth. Even as he looked he could see young people outside the café. They seemed amazingly young, much younger than he had expected. They were not the same ones as the early laughers, they were different altogether, they were young children. Even their clothes were different. Some of them were sitting eating ice-cream at a table which stood outside the café and had an awning over it. He couldn't remember that awning at all. Nor even the table. The fisherman had disappeared from the stream. The cemetery seemed to have spawned more tombstones.

His mind felt slow and dull and he didn't know where to go next. It came to him that he should sit down where he was and make no more effort. It was ludicrous that he should be so stupid as not to get out of the maze which others had negotiated so easily. So he couldn't be as intelligent as he thought he was. But it was surely the maze that was to blame, not himself. It quite simply set unfair problems, and those who had solved them had done so by instinct like animals. He remembered someone who had been cool and young and audacious and who had had a white handkerchief in his pocket like a flag. But the memory was vaguer than he had expected, and when he found the handkerchief it was only a small crumpled ball which was now in his trouser pocket. He turned and looked at the flag which marked the centre of the maze. It seemed that he would never reach it.

He felt so sorry for himself that he began to cry a little and he couldn't stop. Water drooled from his eyes, and he wiped it away with his dirty handkerchief. There didn't seem to be so many people in the maze now. It was a stony wilderness. If there was one he could recognise as successful he would follow him like a dog. He would have no arrogance now. His brow puckered. There was someone he remembered as existing outside the maze, someone important, someone gracious, elegant, a magnet which he had somehow lost. She was . . . but he couldn't remember who she was. And in any case had she been outside the maze? Had she not always been inside it, perhaps as lost as he was himself?

Slowly and stubbornly he plodded on, no longer imagining that he would leave the maze, walking for the sake of walking. The twilight was now falling, and the café was shut. He could hear no sounds around him, no infestation of the maze, and yet strangely enough he sensed that there were beings there. If he could no longer escape from the maze then he might at least reach the centre and see what was there. Perhaps some compensating emblem, some sign, some pointer to the enigma. Perhaps even the designer of the maze sitting there in a stony chair. He set his teeth, he must not give in. He must not allow the thought to control him that he had no power over the maze, that in fact the power was all the other way. That would be the worst of all, not only for him but for everybody else.

And then quite ironically, as if the seeing of it depended on his thought, there was the centre, barer than he had expected, no emblem, no sign, no designer.

All that was there was a space, and a clock and a flag. The clock pointed to eleven. The sun was setting, red and near in the sky. It was a big ball that he might even clutch. The twilight was deepening. For a moment there, it was as if in the centre of the maze he had seen a tomb, but that couldn't be true. That must have come from his brooding on the cemetery. On the other hand it might be a cradle. And yet it wasn't that either. There was nothing there at all, nothing but the space on which the paths converged.

He looked at the space for a long time, as if willing something to fill it. And then very slowly from the three other paths he saw three men coming. They seemed superficially to be different, but he knew that they were all the same. That is to say, there hovered about the faces of each of them a common idea, a common resemblance, though one was dressed in a grey suit, one in a gown, and one in jacket and flannels. They all stood there quite passively and waited for him to join them. They were all old. One of them to his astonishment held a child by the hand. He stood there with them. Slowly the sun disappeared over the horizon and darkness fell and he felt the pressure of the maze relaxing, as if in a dream of happiness he understood that the roads were infinite, always fresh, always new, and that the ones who stood beside him were deeper than friends, they were bone of his bone, they were flesh of his disappearing flesh.

In the Silence

The stooks of corn glimmered in the moonlight and boys' voices could be heard as they played hide and seek among them. How calm the night was, how stubbly the field! Iain crouched behind one of the stooks listening, watching for deepening shadows, his face and hands sweaty, his knees trembling with excitement. Then quite suddenly he heard the voices fading away from him, as if the boys had tired of their game and gone home, leaving him undetected. Their voices were like bells in the distance, each answering the other and then falling silent. He was alone.

The moonlight shimmered among the stooks so that they looked like men, or women, who had fallen asleep upright. The silence gathered around him, except that now and again he could hear the bark of a dog and the noise of the sea. He touched the stubble with his finger and felt it sharp and thorny as if it might draw blood. From where he was he could see the lights of the houses but there was no human shape to be seen anywhere. The moon made a white road across the distant sea.

He moved quietly about the field, amazed at the silence. No whisper of wind, no rustle of creature – rat or mouse – moving about. He was a scout on advance patrol, he was a pirate among his strawy treasure chests. If he thrust his hand into one, he might however find not gold but some small nocturnal animal. Very faintly he heard the soft throaty call of an owl. He was on a battlefield among the dead.

He began to count the stooks and made them twelve in all. It was a struggle for him for he was continually distracted by shadows and also not at all good at arithmetic, being only seven years old and more imaginative than mathematical. Twelve stooks set at a certain glimmering distance from each other. Twelve treasure chests. Twelve men of straw. He counted them again, and again he got twelve so he had been right the first time.

A cat slanted along in front of him, a mouse in its jaws, its eyes cold and green. The mouse's tail was dangling from its mouth like a shoelace. He put out his hand, but the cat quickly ran away from him towards its busy house, carrying its prey. Its green eyes were solid and beautiful like jewels.

He took a handkerchief from his pocket and began to dry his face. In the darkness he couldn't see the handkerchief clearly, it appeared as a vague ghostly shape, and though it had red spots on it he couldn't make them out. This was the quietest he had ever heard the world before. Even the cat had made no noise when it passed him. During the daytime there was always sound, but now even the dog had stopped barking. He could hear no sound of water, not any noise at all. He put his hand out in front of him and could see it only as a faint shape, as if it were separate from the rest of his body.

He looked up at the moon which was quite cold in the sky. He could see the dark spots on it and it seemed to move backwards into the sky as he looked. What an extraordinary calm was everywhere. It was as if he had been left in charge of the night, as if he was the only person alive, as if he must take responsibility for the whole world. No sound of footsteps could be heard from the road that lay between the wall and the houses.

The silence lasted so long that he was afraid to move. He formed his lips as if to speak but he didn't have the courage. It was as if the night didn't want him to speak, were forbidding him to do so, as if it were saying to him, This is my kingdom, you are not to do anything I don't wish you to do. He could no longer hear the noise of the sea, as if it too had been commanded to be quiet. It was like a yellow shield in the distance, flat and made of hammered gold.

For the first time in his life he heard the beating of his own heart. Pitter patter it went, then it picked up power and became stronger, heavier. It was like a big clock in the middle of his chest. Then as quickly as it had started, it settled down again and he held his breath. The laden enchanted night, the strangeness of it. He would not have been surprised to see the stooks beginning to dance, a strawy dance, one which they were too serious to do in the daytime, when everyone was watching. He felt daring as well as frightened, that he should be the only one to stay behind, that he should be the dweller among the stooks. How brave he was and yet how unreal and ghostly he felt. It was as if the boys had left him and gone to another country, pulling the roofs over their heads and putting off the switch beside the bed.

This was the latest he had ever been out, even counting Hallowe'en last year. But tonight he could feel there were no witches, the night was too still for that. It wasn't frightening in that way, not with broomsticks and masked heads, animal faces. Not even Stork would be out as late as this, his two sticks pointed at the boys like guns, as he seemed to fly from the wall which ran alongside the road. No, it wasn't that kind of fear. It was as if he didn't . . . as if he wasn't . . . as if the night had gone right through him, as if he wasn't actually there, in that field, with cold knees and ghostly hands.

He imagined himself staying out there all night and the boys appearing to him in the morning, their faces red with the sun, shouting and screaming, like Red Indians. The sun was on their faces like war paint. They came out of their boxes pushing the lids up, and suddenly there they were among the stubble with their red knees and their red hands.

The stooks weren't all at the same angle to the earth. As he listened in the quietness he seemed to hear them talking in strawy voices, speaking in a sort of sharp, strawy language. They were whispering to each other, deep and rough and sharp. Their language sounded very odd, not at all liquid and running, but like the voice of stones, thorns. The field was alive with their conversation. Perhaps they were discussing the scythe that had cut them down, the boys that played hide and seek among them. They were busy and hissing as if they had to speak as much as possible before the light strengthened around them.

Then they came closer together, and the boys seemed

suddenly very far away. The stooks were pressed against each other, composing a thorny spiky wall. He screamed suddenly and stopped, for at the sound the stooks had resumed their original positions. They were like pieces on a board. He began to count them again, his heart beating irregularly. Thirteen, where there had been twelve before. Where had the thirteenth come from?

He couldn't make out which was the alien one, and then counted them again and again. Then he saw it, the thirteenth. It was moving towards him, it had sharp teeth, it had thorny fingers. It was sighing inarticulately like an old woman, or an old man, its sigh was despairing and deep. Far beyond on the road he could sense that the boys were all gathered together, having got out of their boxes. They were sighing, everyone was sighing like the wind. Straw was peeling away from them as if on an invisible gale. And finally they were no longer there, but had returned to their boxes again and pulled the roofs over their heads.

He didn't notice the lights of the house go out as he walked towards the thirteenth stook, laid his head on its breast and fell asleep among the thorns.